P9-DWD-802

Also by ReShonda Tate Billingsley

ReSHONDA TATE BILLINGSLEY

Her bestselling novels of family and faith have been hailed as

"Emotionally charged . . . not easily forgotten."

—*Romantic Times*

"Steamy, sassy, sexy."

—*Ebony*

"Compelling, heartfelt."

—*Booklist*

"Full of palpable joy, grief, and soulful characters."

—*The Jacksonville Free Press*

"Poignant and captivating, humorous and heart-wrenching."

—*The Mississippi Link*

Don't miss these wonderful novels
WHAT'S DONE IN THE DARK

"An entertaining book with suspense, drama, and a little humor. . . . The twists and turns will have readers rushing to turn the pages."

—*Authors & Readers Book Corner*

THE SECRET SHE KEPT

"Entertaining and riveting. . . . Heartfelt and realistic. . . . A must-read."

—AAM Book Club

SAY AMEN, AGAIN

Winner of the NAACP Image Award for Outstanding Literary Work

"Heartfelt. . . . A fast-paced story filled with vivid characters."

—*Publishers Weekly*

And check out ReShonda's Young Adult titles

Drama Queens

Caught Up in the Drama

Friends 'Til the End

Fair-Weather Friends

Getting Even

With Friends Like These

Blessings in Disguise

Nothing but Drama

MAMA'S BOY

ReShonda Tate Billingsley

Gallery Books

New York   London   Toronto   Sydney   New Delhi

G

Gallery Books
An Imprint of Simon & Schuster, Inc.
1230 Avenue of the Americas
New York, NY 10020

First Gallery Books trade paperback edition July 2015

GALLERY BOOKS and colophon are registered trademarks of Simon & Schuster, Inc.

For information about special discounts for bulk purchases, please contact Simon & Schuster Special Sales at 1-866-506-1949 or business@simonandschuster.com.

The Simon & Schuster Speakers Bureau can bring authors to your live event. For more information or to book an event, contact the Simon & Schuster Speakers Bureau at 1-866-248-3049 or visit our website at www.simonspeakers.com.

Manufactured in the United States of America

10 9 8 7 6 5 4 3 2 1

Library of Congress Cataloging-in-Publication Data is on file.

ISBN 978-1-4767-1495-0
ISBN 978-1-4767-1503-2 (ebook)

A Note from the Author

As a journalist, I have come across an array of stories in my twenty-five-plus years in the industry. Some of them have provided fodder for just plain ol' good drama. Many of them—no, most of them—have sparked that little "What if?" lightbulb in my head. This book was born from one of those "What ifs?"

I'm always posing questions to my readers on social media and as I travel: What if you won the lottery and your ex-husband came back and said your divorce was never finalized and he and the woman he left you for want half? (*The Devil Is a Lie*); What if you have a one-night stand with your best friend's husband and he dies in the hotel room? (*What's Done in the Dark*); What if your son commits a crime, can you turn him in? I'd like to think that as a law-abiding citizen, that answer would be a resounding yes. But as a mother, that answer isn't so black and white, especially if you throw in something that has been dominating the news: race and law enforcement. I don't know about you, but for me, that changes the dynamics. And that's where *Mama's Boy* was born.

I hope you will enjoy the story, even if you don't agree with all the characters' decisions (hey, what kind of writer would I be if you liked everything?).

Now, on to the acknowledgments.

Of course, I give all thanks to God, who blessed me with this gift of writing and is allowing me to live my dreams.

I wouldn't have been able to do this book (like all the others) without a phenomenal support system. These are people who pushed me, who motivated me, inspired me, and cheered from the sidelines. So as redundant as this may sound, I must do it again . . . My husband, Dr. Miron Billingsley, who has been my biggest cheerleader and continues to give me advice, even though he swears I never listen to any of it. My children, who just aren't that impressed with what I do (until, of course, their friends talk about how cool it is). Thank you for your love, patience, and understanding. A special thanks to my middle child, Morgan, who has become my personal literary assistant (not to mention an author in her own right). Mya and Myles, you know I love you to the moon and back . . . but when there's work to be done, y'all know you disappear.

Big ups to my sister, who gave up her personal assistant job on book number three, something about "not working for free" and "needing compensation," yada, yada. But thank you for your ongoing support and for stepping up to the plate to care for Mama and carrying the load alone when I'm on the road.

To my business partner, writing twin, and just all around great friend, Victoria Christopher Murray. You are the ying to my yang and I could fill the pages thanking you for all you do—especially on this book. I'm grateful to have you as a friend.

To my ride-or-die, Pat Tucker, thank you for your years of

friendship and for navigating these literary waters with me. To my other literary friends: Nina Foxx, Eric Jerome Dickey, Kimberla Lawson Roby, Lolita Files, Tiffany Warren, Rhonda McKnight, Booker T. Mattison, Brian Egeston, JE Jones, Tamika Newhouse, Renee Flagler, and Lutishia Lovely . . . thanks for your words of encouragement, support, and for just putting a smile on my face.

To my BGB admin family: Jason, Princess, Pam, Jessica, Kimyatta, Lasheera, Yolanda, Sheretta, and Raine . . . thank you so much for all that you do. To our amazing author partners: I'm so honored to be affiliated with you! We're truly changing the game!

I must give lots of love to my girls, who keep me grounded, who support me, and have my back no matter what: Jaimi, Raquelle, Clemelia, and Kim, love you for life. Special thanks to my Delta Xi sorors who love me from afar.

Huge bouquet of thanks to my agent from the very beginning, Sara Camilli, my awesome workaholic editor, Brigitte Smith, my publicist, Melissa Gramstad ("amazing" is an understatement to describe you), and the rest of my family at Gallery, thank you for believing in me!

To my right hand, my assistant, Sheretta, you have no idea how much better you've made my professional life. Thank you! To assistant extraordinaire, Yolanda Gore, you know how awesome you are, but please allow me to tell you once again! Gina Johnson, thanks for your assistance in bringing this book to fruition.

My journey to bring *Let the Church Say Amen* to the screen has been a verrrrryyyy long (and often frustrating) one. Thank you so much to Regina King and Reina King for never giving up. To Queen Latifah's Flava Unit, BET, Bobcat Films, and all the talented actors and crew, thank you for helping this li'l author realize a big dream.

I'm always skeptical about this next part as I know there are so many book clubs that support me and I hate leaving folks out. But again, it's just too hard not to take a moment and say thanks. This time around, thanks goes to Sistahs in Conversation and Sistahs in Harmony, Arnesha SoFly Foucha, Cover 2 Cover, Savvy, Nubian Pageturners, Cush City, Black Pearls Keepin It Real, Mahogany, Women of Substance, My Sisters & Me, Pages Between Sistahs, Shared Thoughts, Brag about Books, Mocha Readers, Characters, Christian Fiction Café, Sisters Who Like to Read, Readers of Delight, Tabahani Book Circle, FB Page Turners, African-American Women's Book Club, Women of Color, Zion M.B.C. Women's Book Club, Jus'Us, Go On Girl Texas 1, Book Club Etc., Pearls of Wisdom, Alpha Kappa Omega Book Club, Lady Lotus, Soulful Readers of Detroit, Brownstone, and First Baptist Church—Agape Book Ministry (please know that if you're not here, it doesn't diminish my gratitude).

Thank you to all the wonderful libraries that have supported my books, introduced me to readers, and fought to get my books on the shelves. Thank you also to Yasmin Coleman, Orsayor Simmons, Ed Jones, Hiawatha Henry, King Brooks, Curtis Bunn, Troy Johnson, and Gwen Richardson.

To all my wonderful Social Media Friends, especially the ones who help me spread the word about my work and comment regularly . . . Tonia, Heather, Gloria, Pam, Tracy, Nelvia, Phyllis, Erika, Leslie, Ashara, Nita, Jetola, Cassandra, Renee, Michelle, Kathy, Jackie, Lisa, Carla, Kendria, Denise, Ina, Sharon, Neuropath, Monique, Chevonne, Dasaya, Lilo, Gina, Raquel, Felicia, Crystal,

Makasha, Loureva, Victoria, Jewel, Folake, Maleika, Cebrina, Lolita, Tyra, Cindy, Joanna, Maurice, Cecelia, Deborah, Lachelle, Vonda, Paula, Tamara, Martha, and Sophie (yes, I could go on . . . but I guess I should wrap it up). Just know that I'm grateful to all of you who have supported and sent encouraging words.

Lots of love and gratitude to my sorors of Alpha Kappa Alpha Sorority, Inc. (including my own chapter, Mu Kappa Omega), my sisters in Greekdom, Delta Sigma Theta Sorority, Inc., who CONSTANTLY show me love . . . and my fellow mothers in Jack and Jill of America (particularly, the Missouri City/Sugar Land chapter).

And finally, thanks to you . . . my beloved readers. If it's your first time picking up one of my books, I truly hope you enjoy. If you're coming back, words cannot even begin to express how eternally grateful I am for your support. Thank you. I will continue saying it . . . I am where I am because of you.

Much love,
ReShonda

1
―――
――

This had to be what death felt like. What it meant to have the Grim Reaper sneak up on you, wrap his claws around your heart, and squeeze. That's what Gloria Jones felt right now. Her heart tightened, her breath slowed, and Gloria wondered how it was that she hadn't passed out. All because of the story that she'd just seen on the news.

"Again, we want to warn you that this video is disturbing," the red-haired female anchor from Channel 12 News said. "Police have released this footage in hopes that someone can identify the suspect or the other two boys in the video."

The video that had initially stopped Gloria in her tracks during the news introduction began playing again.

"Are you recording me?" the police officer in the video yelled.

"Yep. I know my rights. I'm not violating any laws. I have a right to film. As long as I'm not interfering in your arrest, I have a legal right to film," the young boy replied as he turned the camera on himself. It was dark and the picture was grainy, but he was clearly recognizable. And even if he wasn't, the tiny cross tattoo on his neck was a dead giveaway. "You see how they treat us? If you're young and black in America, you're guilty until proven innocent."

The boy turned the camera lens back on the officer, who was stomping toward him. The officer's hand went up to block the camera shot.

"I said, get that camera off me."

Before Jamal could respond the officer raced over and knocked the phone out of his hand. The phone tumbled into the grass.

It looked like the boy was pushed, because the camera toppled to the ground and the screen went to black, though the sound remained on. There was a ruffling noise, then an unintelligible exchange of words, then more yelling.

"Shoot that racist pig!"

"You gon' die tonight, cop!"

More scuffling.

And then, a single gunshot pierced the night air.

The video grew momentarily silent, then one of the boys yelled, "Let's get out of here!" followed by the sound of footsteps running away.

Gloria stood in petrified silence as the scuffling continued, until finally, the anchor came back on.

"Police in the entire Golden Triangle have joined forces in search of the suspects. Anyone with information is asked to call authorities." The anchor's disdain was evident. Whatever happened to objectivity in news?

"I have a right to film!"

Even if Gloria didn't recognize the grainy image, or the cross tattoo that had sent Elton through the roof, there was no denying the voice. The suspect who was now the subject of a massive tri-city manhunt was her only son, Jamal.

"What in blue blazes is going on here?"

Gloria jumped and then turned as her husband, Elton, made his way into the den of their modest ranch-style home. She quickly slammed the television off, and then looked down at the shattered vase at her feet.

"Did you cut yourself?" Elton said, looking at a trickle of blood oozing out of the top of her foot.

Gloria hadn't even realized that a piece of glass had pierced her foot. When she'd seen that video, everything else became a blur.

"What's going on?" Elton repeated, studying her. "Are you okay?"

"Yeah, yeah. I'm fine. Just dropped a vase." Gloria knelt down and began picking up the shattered pieces.

Elton eyed her suspiciously. "You were standing there, just staring at the TV. What were you looking at?"

She would have tried to force a smile, but no amount of acting could make that happen. "Oh no, I was just catching something on the Home Shopping Network when the vase slipped out of my hand." She turned her back to her husband because if he saw her eyes—and her absolute fear—he'd know that she was lying.

"Woman, I done told you about being so clumsy." He walked over, knelt down next to her, then kissed her on the cheek. "But I love you, clumsy self and all. I gotta get over to the church. Got a board meeting and you know Deacon Wade will throw a fit if I'm not there on time."

Gloria knew that she should tell her husband what she'd just seen. She knew that he didn't need to be blindsided at church. But Elton hadn't wanted Jamal to go out last night. He hated Jamal's friends. He despised his son's rebel-with-a-cause attitude and they fought all the time. But Jamal was sixteen and Gloria was scared Elton's strict ways would push their son away. So she'd convinced her husband to let Jamal go hang out with his friends. She'd told Elton that they had to loosen the reins on their only child. Elton had finally given in. And now look at the price they were paying.

She stopped him just as he got to the front door. "Ah, Elton . . ." He paused, but she couldn't find her words. She needed to tell her husband that police were hunting their son. A massive manhunt at that. She had to let Elton know. But when he turned to face her, no words would come out of her mouth.

"What is it?" he asked.

"Nothing. Just wanted to say, um, have a good day. I'll see you later," Gloria said instead.

Elton studied her for a moment. "Are you sure you're all right?"

"Yeah, yeah," she said, finally forcing a smile. She ran her fingers through her shoulder-length tresses, a nervous habit that she hoped he didn't notice. "I'm fine."

"You don't look fine." He pushed a strand of her graying hair out of her face. After twenty-eight years of marriage, he could tell when something was wrong with her.

"Oh, I'm just tired. I was out in the garden this morning and you know this August heat." She fanned herself, hoping to seem more convincing.

He stared at her a moment, and then, as if he finally believed her, simply nodded. "Well, get some rest today. Where's Jamal? Don't tell me he's still asleep." Elton looked down the hall toward

Jamal's room. It was Saturday and Jamal usually slept in until they came in and made him get up.

Gloria couldn't tell her husband that Jamal hadn't come home last night. She was praying that he returned before Elton noticed that he wasn't home.

Gloria hated lying to her husband but ever since Jamal had turned thirteen, his already strained relationship with his father had gone to a whole other level of contention. Jamal wasn't a disrespectful child but lately it was as if an independent streak had kicked in. He started hanging out with the wrong people, cutting school, and getting fed up with Elton's strict ways. He'd even started talking about feeling like Elton wished he'd never been born. Gloria had tried to convince her son that wasn't the case, but it didn't help that Elton sometimes did act that way.

And then there was that tattoo. That had been the latest act of rebellion. When Jamal told his dad he'd "gotten a cross in honor of the good reverend," Elton had gone utterly ballistic.

Gloria turned to go get the dustpan so that she didn't have to look her husband in the eye.

"Oh, Jamal left early this morning to, uh, to go meet up with Brian to catch up on some schoolwork." The lies were piling up.

Lord, forgive me, Gloria thought.

"Well, you tell him that I said to make sure he cleans those gutters today. They'd better be done by the time I get home."

"Yes, sweetheart," she managed to say as he headed out the front door.

Gloria tried to still her trembling hands as she got the last of the glass cleaned up. It took everything in her power to keep from spilling the glass out of the dustpan.

Police were looking for her son. Her son, who despite his recent change in attitude had never been in any real trouble. He'd been suspended once for skipping school, but other than that, nothing.

Gloria dumped the glass in the trash can, then, as soon as she saw Elton pull out of the driveway, she raced over to the cordless phone and snatched up the receiver. She dialed Jamal's cell phone number and again it went straight to voice mail. She'd been calling all morning, praying that he'd just fallen asleep over at Brian's house or something. She'd been praying that this all could be explained away.

"Jamal, this is Mama. Oh, my God, son, what's going on? Where are you? Please call me. I'm going crazy with worry."

She ended the call, then fell back against the wall and said a silent prayer. Not only that this was all some big misunderstanding but that she'd find her son before the police did. He was wanted for killing a cop in Jasper, Texas, a small town rocked by racism after the 1996 dragging death of James Byrd. Even though that was almost two decades ago, Jasper was still plagued by racial discord. A young black boy shooting a white cop? The racial unrest was about to go to a whole different level.

Yes, Gloria had to find her son first, because if she didn't, Jasper police would sure enough kill him.

2

The beaming rays of the August sun tickled Kay Christiansen out of her sleep. She snuggled deeper into the Egyptian down comforter. Kay didn't want to get up, but duty called. Not only did she have to get some election paperwork finished in order to file first thing Monday morning, but she had to get ready for closing arguments in a case that was slated to go to the jury by Tuesday. So work on a Saturday summoned her.

Kay eased out of bed, yawned, stretched, then willed herself to her feet. She'd had a late night—after working until midnight, she'd played Romper Room with her husband until three in the morning. So her bed was begging her to snuggle just a little while longer. But it was already 8 a.m. She could sleep in her casket. Right now there was work to be done.

"Good morning, Mommy."

If God had needed a person to accompany His sunrise every morning, Kay's four-year-old daughter, Leslie, would be the perfect candidate. With deep dimples and a head full of natural light brown coils, Leslie was the pulse that kept Kay's heart beating.

"Good morning, Sunshine," Kay said, kissing her daughter on the cheek. "Why aren't you dressed for piano practice?"

"Daddy said I didn't have to go." Leslie jumped up and down on the bed, her signature rainbow tutu fluttering as she bounced. "Daddy said I could stay home with Miss Selena," she added, referring to their nanny/housekeeper/cook.

"Well, Daddy was wrong. Miss Selena is off today. And stop jumping on my bed. Go get dressed." Kay lifted her daughter up, set her back onto the floor, and then playfully swatted at her to exit.

Kay couldn't help but smile as she thought about her picture-perfect life. A life that she'd fought hard to achieve. She stepped into the shower, recalling something her father used to always tell her. *It doesn't matter where you've been. All that matters is where you end.* That was one of the few things Robert Matthews had ever said that Kay would agree with. Neither her father nor her mother, Gwen, had left her much else that she wanted to remember.

Twenty minutes later, Kay was making her way into the kitchen, where her husband was at the counter cooking the kids' breakfast. She and Phillip shared domestic duties, a gesture that made her love him even more. As a defense attorney, Phillip worked just as hard as her, but he believed in equitable distribution of duties. That's something that she couldn't say for most men, especially the men whom she'd dated before saying "I do" to Phillip.

"Good morning, honey," Kay said as she walked over and planted a ferocious kiss on her husband. After ten years, his kiss still gave her goose bumps. His chiseled bare chest made her almost forget that she needed to work. "Why didn't you wake me up?"

"Because you looked so beautiful sleeping there."

She picked up a piece of turkey bacon off the plate on the counter, took a bite, then leaned back against the cabinet. Leslie, now dressed for piano lessons, was sitting at the kitchen table, coloring.

"What are you watching?" Kay asked her husband when she noticed his eyes glued to the small television perched at the end of the counter.

Phillip removed the last of the bacon from the pan, then turned the fire off. "Sad story out of Jasper. Apparently, these kids were hanging out at a convenience store. Cop comes out. Some kind of altercation ensued. Long story short, one of the boys was recording. The cop told him to stop. He wouldn't and a scuffle broke out. The cop ended up getting shot and killed."

"Wow," Kay said, shaking her head at the TV. They'd frozen the video of the young boy as the anchor talked.

"Police have not yet identified the suspect, but they do believe he is a Jasper resident. All three suspects remain at large," the anchor said.

"So, the kid is on the run?"

"Looks like it," Phillip replied. "He hasn't been arrested."

Kay opened the refrigerator and took out a pitcher of orange juice. "When did that happen?" she asked as she poured four glasses of juice.

"Last night. About one in the morning." Phillip set a plate on the table. "Leslie, go get your brother and tell him to come eat breakfast."

Kay slid into a seat at the table. "Doesn't surprise me. What kind of kid hangs out on the corner at one in the morning?" She tsked. "But let me guess, the community is going to go crazy and say it was the cop's fault."

The look on his face said Phillip was not pleased with her comment. Even though he was biracial, with a white father and a black mother, Phillip completely identified himself as a black man and he hated when she made those kinds of generalizations. But as a black woman, Kay felt completely entitled to speak the truth as she saw it. And as a prosecutor for Harris County, the largest county in Texas, she saw a lot of truths on a daily basis.

"We don't know whose fault it was, Madam Prosecutor," Phillip said.

"I'm sure it's the criminal who is on the run, Mr. Defense Attorney," Kay countered with a smile.

Phillip didn't return her smile. She hated that he got so worked up over these kinds of issues. But if it dealt with young minority males, he was passionate about it. He worked at a downtown law firm but he spent just as much time volunteering with at-risk teens.

"I'm just saying, how about we reserve judgment until we know the whole story?" Phillip added.

"Maybe if the little thug had a curfew, this wouldn't be an issue." Kay shrugged nonchalantly.

Phillip stopped fixing her plate and stared at her. His right eyebrow inched up just a bit, the first sign that he was about to get upset. "Why does he have to be a thug?"

Why did she even start this conversation? If Phillip had his way, every wayward minority kid in the country would get a second and third chance.

Still, as passionate as he was, so was she. And she was just as committed to ridding the streets of riff-raff. "You said the shooting took place at one in the morning, on a street corner? And did you see that tattoo on his neck? Ugh. Yeah, he's a thug."

The look on her husband's face was one of disgust.

"What?" she said.

"Really, Kay?"

"Oh, don't be so sensitive." Kay flashed a smile, hoping to ease the building tension.

"I'm not being sensitive," Phillip corrected. "This is just a really sad case. That boy looks about fifteen or sixteen. I can only imagine how he's feeling."

Kay rolled her eyes. "Forgive me if I'm not moved. The feelings I care about are those of the family members of the poor officer he killed."

Their discussion was interrupted when Kay's fifteen-year-old stepson walked in.

"What's up, fam?" Why he tried to be cool was beyond her. Ryan was a self-proclaimed nerd, so the slang talk didn't even fit him. While most kids would still be in their pajamas, Ryan was already dressed, in a polo buttoned all the way up, khakis, and spit-shining penny loafers.

"Good morning, Ryan," Kay replied, patting her stepson's cheek as he sat down at the table. His real mother, Phillip's first wife, had been killed when Ryan was just two years old. So, really, Kay had been the only mother he'd ever known. "Maybe if that boy hung around people like Ryan, he'd have a different path in life."

"Aw, come on, Ma," Ryan said, ducking out of her reach.

Even though Kay had become his stepmom when he was five, she loved that boy with all of her heart. He was the exact opposite of the boys she prosecuted on a regular basis. Ryan had his head on straight. An ambitious, studious child, he'd never been in any trouble. Granted, they sent him to the best schools, but he was still self-motivated, with a 3.9 GPA in all advanced courses. And even though he was only a sophomore, two Ivy League scholarships already awaited him.

"Ryan is just like that boy on television," Phillip said.

Kay frowned. "Uh, Ryan is nothing like that boy on television."

"His circumstances could be different, but that doesn't make him any less of a person."

"What are you guys talking about?" Ryan asked, digging into his food.

"Your father has such a bleeding heart."

"What happened?" Ryan asked as he pulled out a book to read while he ate, a habit they'd tried to get him to break and then eventually stopped fighting him on.

"Some hoodlum on the news. He shot a police officer," Kay replied.

"Dang," Ryan said. "For real?"

"And back to your point," Kay continued, returning her attention to her husband. "Number one, Ryan wouldn't be hanging out at a gas station at one in the morning. Number two, Ryan knows that when an officer questions him, he obeys, right, son?"

"Right." He chomped on his food and continued reading.

Phillip looked like he didn't even feel like arguing about it any longer so he just let the conversation drop.

Ryan didn't look up from his book as he said, "Dad, Mom's right. That's not me. I'm a good kid." He stated that like it was an undisputed fact.

"I know that, son." Phillip sighed. "I was just making a point with your mother."

"No need to make a point with me," she replied. She knew she could be a little harsh, but in eleven years in the DA's office, she'd seen her share of ungrateful young men with no home training trying to take advantage of the system. And no, the system wasn't geared in their favor, but as she used to always tell them, if they stayed out of trouble in the first place, they'd never get caught up in a system that meant them no good.

Luckily for her, Ryan had listened and she never had to worry about him becoming a statistic like that kid on TV. That kid had made a bad decision and now his life was ruined. Watching her children as they sat at the breakfast table, Kay couldn't help but feel grateful that they were destined to go down a different path.

3

"Gloriaaaaaa!"

The bellowing sound of her husband's voice confirmed it. Elton knew.

As soon as she heard the screech of his tires in the front driveway, Gloria knew that he knew. She didn't know if he'd seen it on the news or if someone at church had told him about it. But he knew and was about to raise holy hell.

"You know, don't you?" he yelled before he even got all the way in the door. She stood in front of him, not saying a word. "You saw it on TV. That's what you were watching." It was a statement, not a question.

Gloria shook as he spoke. "I . . . I . . ."

"Since when did you start lying to me? And how could you let me walk out of here when this was going on?" he barked.

At one time, back when he was wooing her in high school in Baton Rouge, Louisiana, Elton had been a handsome man. But as much as she loved him, over the years his ugly ways had diminished everything she'd found attractive back then. It wasn't the thinning hair or even the forty pounds he'd put on—it was how any and every thing caused him to lose his temper. Gloria had spent many years living on edge because of that. And now his anger was about to go full metal jacket.

Gloria couldn't help it. She lied again. "I . . . I wasn't sure. I was praying that it wasn't Jamal and I . . ."

"Where is he? You said he went with Brian!"

She opened her mouth, but nothing would come out.

Gloria had been crying since Elton left. She had committed the video on the news to memory. Frame by frame, she knew it well.

"He didn't come home last night," Gloria confessed. "I didn't discover it until this morning. I was just so scared. I was hoping that he'd fallen asleep over at Brian's or something. I've been calling all morning, but I keep getting voice mail on his cell. Nobody's answering at Brian's house, either." Gloria sank down into Elton's favorite chair and sobbed. "Oh, my God. Where is my son?"

She expected Elton to fuss some more, go ballistic, anything. But he stared at her for a moment, then walked over and grabbed the remote.

"Deacon Wade said that it's on every channel." Elton flipped through the news channels. The first two were talking about something else. But the third, the local CBS affiliate, had just begun playing the video. Again.

Elton watched in horror. "My God," he muttered.

When the part where Jamal turned the camera on himself came up, Elton pressed pause on the DVR, then spun around to face his wife. "You weren't sure?" he screamed. "There is no doubt that's our son."

Gloria cowered in her seat. Her whole world was unraveling and she had no idea what to do about it.

"They don't know who he is, but it's just a matter of time! Everyone in Jasper knows that is our son!"

Gloria responded with more tears, but Elton wasn't moved.

"I knew I shouldn't have listened to you," he shouted as he paced back and forth across the living room. His six-foot-three frame was shaking. Gloria was sure that it was more anger than fear. "Always babying him," Elton continued. "I've been telling you for years you making him into a mama's boy." She wanted to ask him what did that have to do with anything. Their son was wanted for killing a cop. What did being a mama's boy have to do with that? He must've read the expression on her face because he continued yelling. "He needed a foot in his behind! But you were always taking up for him. 'Go easy on him, Elton.' 'Just let him go with his friends, Elton,'" he said, mocking her from yesterday. "'He'll be okay, Elton.'" Elton jabbed the remote in the direction of the television. "Does that look okay to you, Gloria?"

She flinched at his tone. But before he could say anything else, someone started banging on their door.

For a moment, her heart fluttered, praying that it was Jamal. But that thought was quickly dispelled when she heard, "Police! Open up!"

Elton shot his wife one last disgusted look, then walked over to the door. He swung it open. Gloria stood, her heart dropping at the sight of the two plainclothes police officers on her steps. In back of them were several uniformed policemen.

"Mr. Elton Jones?" the first cop, a short, stocky black man, asked.

Jasper only had one black police officer on the entire force of thirty, so of course, they'd send him out.

"Yes, that's me," Elton replied.

The second officer, who wore a scowl across his face, quickly stepped up. He was a bald man who looked like he'd spent two minutes too many in a tanning salon. His too tight polyester suit squeezed his robust frame.

"We're looking for your son, Jamal Jones."

"He's not here," Elton said.

The scowling officer leaned in to try to look over Elton's shoulder. "You sure about that?"

Elton stepped aside, not bothering to hide his aggravation. "You're more than welcome to come in and see for yourself."

That's all the cop needed to hear because he motioned for the other officers to enter. And come in they did. Four entered first, barreling like Jamal was waiting for them in a back bedroom. Two more followed and went into the kitchen.

"Hey!" Elton said when one of the uniformed officers knocked over a picture frame. "Can you ask your men to respect my home?" Elton said to the scowling officer.

The officer took a step forward. "You'll have to excuse us. When we're hunting for a cop killer, decorum isn't our strong suit."

The black officer quickly stepped forward. "Mr. Jones."

"Reverend Jones," Elton corrected. Even in their darkest time, Elton wanted to make sure he was revered.

"Reverend Jones," the officer said. "I'm Detective Joseph King. This is my partner, Billy Martin. I'm not sure if you know what's going on."

"I just saw the news."

"So you know your son is a cop killer?" Detective Martin's voice dripped with sarcasm.

"Martin!" Detective King snapped.

Elton wasn't rattled. He was unblanched in his reply. "I know from the news that my son is *alleged* to have shot a police officer. But I'll let a court of law determine his innocence or guilt."

"No court needed when you have video." Detective Martin sneered, as he opened a hall closet door and looked inside.

"You'll have to excuse my partner. As you can imagine, we're all on pretty high alert," Detective King said.

"If my baby did what they said he did, he didn't mean it," Gloria said, her voice quivering.

"Gloria, be quiet," Elton snapped.

"We need to bring your son in, so we can get to the bottom of exactly what happened," Detective King said.

"Well, we can't help you with that," Elton replied. "Because like I said, we haven't heard from our son since he left home yesterday evening."

Detective Martin continued grilling Elton. Exactly what he was saying, Gloria didn't know. She actually felt like she was going to pass out and all of the words had become jumbled.

"Ma'am, are you all right?" Detective King asked. His gentle tone snapped Gloria out of the daze she was slowly drifting into.

This was not going to end well. While Detective King looked calm, all of the other officers looked like hungry wolves. Then the expression on Elton's face only made her stomach knot up even more. Elton was a private man and this inquisition from police would surely send him over the edge.

"I told you, we have not seen our son," Elton said, his agitation evident.

"So, you mean to tell me that he has not been in contact with you at all?" Detective Martin asked. This time he looked directly at Gloria.

"I haven't heard from him." A sob escaped her even though she'd been trying her best to stay strong. "I just want to hear from him."

"If you'll excuse us, this is very upsetting to my wife," Elton said, finally coming to Gloria's side. "I'm sure you're going to leave a police officer outside of our house. You'll know if he comes here."

"You're sure he hasn't called you?" Detective Martin asked again, his glare penetrating Gloria. "We already have his two little friends, Brian Waters and Dix Jacobson, in custody. They were with him at that store. And I assure you, they'll give your son up if you don't."

"I'm also sure you will have our phones tapped soon," Elton snapped as he stood protectively in front of Gloria. "So, you'll know if and when he calls. But he has not been in contact with us. I don't know how many more ways we can tell you that."

"You do know harboring a fugitive is a federal offense?" the detective asked.

"What part of 'we haven't heard from him' do you not understand?" Elton yelled. This time it was his voice that was on the verge of cracking.

"Reverend Jones," Detective King calmly said. "We understand that this is very difficult for you. We're just trying to do our job."

Elton took a deep breath. Gloria didn't think she'd ever seen her husband so rattled. "I understand that. Believe me, I want to find my son," Elton said, his voice leveling off. "I want to make sure he's safe, and if we hear from him, I assure you, we'll let you know."

Gloria remained silent. She wasn't about to make that promise. The way the cops were swarming around her house, the anger that she saw in Detective Martin's eyes, she wasn't assuring anyone of anything when it came to her son, especially not this man who seemed like he'd have no greater pleasure than to kill Jamal with his bare hands.

4

———

Harris County Courtroom 101-B was deathly quiet as the jury foreman stood and cleared his throat. As if he knew every eye was perched on him, the salt-and-pepper-haired man slowly spoke.

"On the charge of murder in the first degree, we, the jury, find the defendant, Dwayne Murphy"—he paused for effect—"guilty."

Dwayne's side of the courtroom erupted in chaos. His elderly mother wailed, while his three baby mamas loudly sobbed and cried about how unfair the verdict was. Forget the fact that Dwayne had tied up and robbed an elderly couple, shooting the poor old man in the head when he tried to escape. As far as the family was concerned, Dwayne deserved a second chance. But Kay wasn't a second-chance kind of chick. That's why she had an impeccable record as a Harris County prosecutor.

"Yes!" Harold, the assistant district attorney sitting next to Kay, muttered. He'd been second chair on this case. And although he had nicknamed Kay "Stone Cold Sally," he was grateful to secure a conviction.

The judge made his final declarations and as they led Dwayne out in handcuffs, he glared at Kay. He didn't say a word, but his eyes belied his hatred. How in the world was he mad at her when he'd committed a heinous crime?

Kay didn't give Dwayne the satisfaction of letting him bother her. She was used to hate-filled stares. She'd put away enough bad guys that she didn't let any of them faze her.

"Good job, as usual, Mrs. Christiansen," Dwayne's severely tanned public defender said as he shook her hand. He really hadn't put up much of a fight, but at the last minute he had tried to trot out some witnesses to cast reasonable doubt on the real killer. Truthfully, he acted like he just wanted to get back to whatever beach had torched his skin.

"You know how I do," Kay replied with a smile.

"Yes, I do," he replied. "You go for the jugular. That's why you're going to get my vote for mayor." He lowered his voice. "But don't tell anyone." He winked before turning and exiting the courtroom.

Kay sat and went over some last-minute paperwork, then headed across the street to her office. She knew that she had some extra oomph in her strut. Winning gave her a high. A sense of power over the bad guys. She was going to miss this part of her job. Putting criminals behind bars had been her sole purpose for the past decade. With a ninety percent conviction rate, Kay was a sought-after prosecutor and had fielded offers from all over the country. But she was happy with her life in Houston. She did let the Democratic National Committee convince her to take that winning record to the city's top spot and that's what she was poised to do next. And even though the election was almost three months away, if the early polls were any indication, she was well on her way.

"Another win for Mrs. Christiansen."

Kay smiled as her boss, Sam Turner, walked into her office. It wasn't often that the Harris County district attorney himself paid a personal visit to his prosecutors. And yet, here he was.

"Thank you very much, Mr. Turner. Just doing my job," Kay replied.

"And you do it so well." Sam was a robust man, with thinning white hair and eyebrows that seemed like they met at the bridge of his nose. He boasted more than thirty years of legal experience, so he was well respected. While Kay didn't agree with some of his ways, he had her ultimate respect.

Sam walked in and headed over to a side wall, which was adorned with commendations, awards, and letters of achievement. He was looking at those things like he hadn't seen them many times. "We sure are going to miss you in this office."

"Hey, I haven't gone anywhere yet," Kay replied.

Sam turned to face her. "But you will. I can't believe you're about to become my boss."

"Let's not put the cart before the horse," Kay said, popping her briefcase open to remove some files. Lots of people thought she was a shoo-in for the mayor's job, but her competitor, Marty Simon, was a man not to be underestimated.

"I'm just speaking the truth," Sam said.

"Well, there is still a little thing called an election that has to take place."

He waved her off. "Yes, I know. You're going to win it hands down, though."

"I don't know about that. Marty Simon is a pretty viable candidate," Kay replied. There were two other people running, some hippie whose only mission was to legalize the use of marijuana and a self-proclaimed civil rights activist who believed all nonblacks were the devil. No one paid either of those two any attention.

"Marty Simon is also a prick and a snot-nosed Texan who thinks he should be handed everything on a silver platter, including the mayoral position." Sam's contempt was obvious. As someone who worked hard and had pulled himself up through the ranks, Sam had little respect for "privileged fools," as he called them.

"Well, Marty is definitely some competition," Kay said.

"You got this. I can't believe you're staying on the job, though, through this whole election. You sure about that?"

"Yes, I'm sure. I love what I do and I'm not mayor yet. And until I win an election, I'll keep prosecuting."

"And that's why you're my number-one girl." Sam patted the back of the wingback chair in front of her desk. "Well, I have to go. I just wanted to stop in and tell you good job on that Murphy case. Should get a nice little feature in the paper for that one."

After decades in an office that was besieged with negative publicity about overturned DNA rape cases, Sam welcomed any positive media coverage.

"Thanks a lot," Kay replied. "His sentencing is in a few days and I'm sure he'll get life."

"That's what I'm talking about," Sam said. "Kudos to you, soon-to-be-mayor Christiansen. You've ensured that the city has one less criminal on the streets."

Kay smiled. "That's what I do. Make the city a safer place."

He headed to the door. "And soon you'll be doing that as mayor. You just make sure you remember the little people. And give us big raises." He winked as he left her office.

5

The crinkle of the blinds caused Gloria to turn her head toward the window, where Elton was once again peering out.

"Dag-blasted cops driving by here all day." He slammed the blinds as if they'd done something to him. "If they're not driving by, they're posted up just sitting for hours. We're lucky Jasper has a small police force or they'd have somebody staked out here twenty-four/seven."

Elton straightened his tie, a scowl etched across his face. He'd been at that window all night, watching the police watching their house. He paused when he noticed Gloria's velour jogging suit. "Umm, don't you think you need to be getting ready for church?"

Gloria slid her feet into her comfortable nursing shoes that Jamal used to always tease her about. "I'm not going to church and I can't believe you are."

"Well, that's ludicrous. Where else would I be going?"

She stood from her seat on the sofa. "Elton, our son is missing and you want me to put on my First Lady face? I don't think so. Jesus is just gonna have to give me a pass today."

"Don't get flippant with the Lord," he chastised.

She exhaled a weary sigh. "Elton, you do whatever you need to do." She walked over and grabbed her car keys off the counter.

"See, this situation has you turning into someone I don't even know," he snapped.

When she spun around to face him, a mixture of anger, fear, and frustration covered her face. "I'm not like you! I can't pretend everything is fine when it's not. I can't fake the funk in front of our congregation when I don't know where my son is!"

Elton took a deep breath. "Maybe being in the Lord's house is what we need."

She threw up her hands to let him know she was done talking. "What I need is to find out where Jamal is. I'm going up to the jail to see if Brian or Dix can tell me anything."

"I told you, when I talked to both of their families last night, they said they don't know anything," Elton said. He'd spent over an hour on the phone with Dix's grandmother, Helen, a member of their church. She was distraught over his arrest. Gloria had wanted to scream. At least she knew where Dix was.

"Elton, I can't sit around and do nothing," Gloria said as she headed to the door. "I *won't* sit around and do nothing." She didn't give him a chance to say anything else.

The drive to the Jasper County Jail had seemed like one of the longest of her life, even though it was only a few minutes from their house.

It felt like a small rodent was gnawing on Gloria's insides as she made her way into the old rundown building that housed Jasper's county jail.

"May I help you?" a male officer greeted her as she walked up. He looked agitated by her presence.

"Yes, I'd like to see Brian Waters and Dix Jacobson," Gloria replied.

The officer hesitated, glaring at her, before finally turning around to another officer who sat at a corner desk reading the newspaper. "Hey, Kenny, are those boys back there taking visitors? Somebody wants to see them."

Kenny glanced up from his newspaper, stared at Gloria for a minute, then said, "That Dix boy and his loud mouth don't get to see anyone. We had to put a muzzle on him."

"So she can see the other one?" the officer asked.

"I guess." Kenny forcefully pushed back from his desk like he was upset that his important work had been interrupted.

"Have a seat till we call you," the officer said.

Gloria nodded then went to sit in one of the hard chairs lined against a back wall. She clutched her purse tighter as her eyes darted around the small jail. A newspaper was tossed on the seat across from her, the headline so big that she could see it from her seat. COP KILLER ON THE RUN. Her son's picture—it looked like they'd used a menacing photo he'd taken when he was on the wrestling team—was plastered across the whole top of the paper. It took up all six columns.

Gloria refused to pick the paper up and, thankfully, the clerk called her so she didn't have to be tortured by even seeing it any longer.

"You can go back." He motioned toward a side door.

This was Gloria's first time ever setting foot in a jail. She would've thought they'd check her for weapons or something, but the door just buzzed to signal that it was unlocked and she walked to the back.

"He's in there," Kenny said, pointing to a box-sized room.

Gloria eased the door open and stepped inside the bare room, which only had a raggedy table and two chairs. She couldn't imagine her son ever being in a place like this. The sight of Brian sitting there, his butterscotch skin pierced with a large brownish red bruise on his face, hurt her heart. "Oh, my God, what happened?" she said, sliding into the chair across from him.

Brian cut his eyes over at the guard perched near the door. "They're just showing me love in the Jasper County Jail." He held his shackled hands up. "Can I at least get these things off?"

"Nope," the guard said, not bothering to move.

"Dang, you got my legs all shackled like I'm a slave or something!"

"How are you?" Gloria asked, trying to keep any more trouble from brewing.

He huffed. "No disrespect, Mrs. J., but how do you think?"

"I'm sorry, that was a crazy question."

"Have you talked to my mama?" he asked. "Are they trying to get me and Dix out?"

Like Dix, Brian was from an impoverished family. Last night, his mother had told Elton that she had a warrant out for her arrest so she "couldn't go anywhere near the jail." Gloria didn't have the heart to tell Brian that, but she didn't want to lie, either.

"They're working on it." That much she knew was true, because Helen asked for the church to pitch in for Dix's bail. Since Mount Sinai was barely keeping the lights on, that wasn't an option.

Gloria weighed her next words carefully. The guard acted like he wasn't paying attention, but she had no doubt that he was soaking in her every word.

"Do you have any idea where Jamal is?" she asked, her voice low.

She had hoped that he would cut his eyes at the guard, blink, anything that would reveal that he did indeed know, but just didn't want to say. But his eyes bore no answers and he confirmed it by saying, "Honestly, Mrs. J., we don't know where Jamal went. We all just ran and went our separate ways. They caught me and Dix at his cousin's house." Brian did look over at the guard when he added, "We didn't do nothin'! That cop came messin' with us." He turned back and looked Gloria in the eyes. "It was an accident. I swear to you. Jamal ain't mean to kill nobody."

"But how did . . ." She stopped. There were so many questions that she wanted to ask him. But she knew that here, under the heavy listening ear of the guard, and probably a bugged room, wasn't the time or place.

"They talking about I'm an accessory to a murder," Brian continued. "We ain't murder nobody. That shooting was an accident. If anything it was self-defense."

Gloria saw the guard roll his eyes and sneer and she knew they needed to end this conversation. "Okay." She patted his hand, trying to will some words of comfort to come out. "You stay strong in here. Everybody's working to get you out. And please, if you get any idea where Jamal could've gone, call me. Collect. I'm just sick with worry."

Brian tried his best to smile. "Don't worry, Mrs. J. Jamal may be a square, but he's a smart dude. Street smart. He's okay. I know my boy. He's probably long gone," Brian added and she could tell that was for the officer's benefit—at least she hoped it was.

6

The bright light shone directly in Kay's face. She squinted as the cameraman mumbled an apology, then adjusted the lights.

"Sorry about that," said Ming Vu, the reporter who was positioned right in front of Kay, ready to conduct her *Dateline*-style interview. "But you'd better get used to being in the spotlight."

Kay smiled. One of the first things her publicist, Loni, told her was not to appear too smug or cocky. As a strong black woman, she had to be careful of the dreaded "angry black woman" stereotype.

"Well, we'll just see how everything turns out," Kay said, flashing the "gentle look" Loni had spent two hours working with her to perfect.

"Thank you for staying late for the interview. I like to do these in-depth interviews when we don't have the hustle and daily activity of an office."

Ming Vu was known for her hard-hitting interviews. Loni had grilled Kay for hours, getting her prepared for anything Ming might throw her way. That's why it surprised her when Ming leaned in and whispered, "Between you and me, your win will do wonders for the minority and female agenda, so we're all rooting for you."

"I appreciate that. And while I will focus on those issues, I want to make sure that Houstonians know I represent all constituents, no matter what their race, religion, or creed," Kay said, fully aware that the mics could always be open.

Ming leaned back and winked. "Good answer." She looked over her shoulder. "So, Todd, are we ready?"

"Ready to roll," the cameraman replied. "I got the mic check while you ladies were talking, so I'm rolling."

"Awesome." Ming sat up straight and dove into the interview. "Kay, we're going to skip all the basics, as people already know you're a Stanford graduate, MBA and law degree from Rice, so your pedigree speaks for itself, but people want to know the real you."

Kay released a comfortable laugh. "What you see is what you get. I'm just an ordinary girl doing extraordinary things."

"An extraordinary prosecutor," Ming said. "That's right on the money." She crossed her long legs in her seat and Kay could tell the tone of the interview was about to shift. "So tell me, what drives you? Some would argue that you're incredibly hard on minorities."

"I treat all of my cases the same," Kay coolly countered. "Unfortunately, I do have a lot of cases from people of color that come through my office. I'm in the business of righting wrongs and there is no color driving that."

"Civil rights activist Reuben Muhammad said in a recent interview that you are worse than some of the"—she looked down at her notes—"and I'm quoting here, 'redneck prosecutors who revel in putting young black boys behind bars.' How do you feel about that?"

Kay inhaled, then let out a slow breath. She'd seen that interview, and while she had never addressed it, those words had sliced her heart. She took pride in her work and tried to be fair, but it seemed she could never make some people happy.

"Honestly, those words hurt," Kay admitted. "I have a son."

"Your stepson, Ryan?"

She paused. "Yes. And so it gives me no pleasure in throwing people, especially young minority males, in jail. But I also don't think the color of your skin should give you a pass because a system is flawed."

"So you admit that the system is flawed?"

Kay had to take a moment. Ming had almost tripped her up. "Of course, any system can stand some improvement, but right now it's the only system we have."

That answer seemed to satisfy Ming because she nodded, then tossed a few more questions at Kay—on topics ranging from the budget to employee discontent to crime. But Kay could tell by the look on both her publicist's and campaign manager's faces that she was handling the interview like a pro.

"So are you worried about Marty Simon?" Ming asked after wrapping up the city-related questions.

"I don't think about Marty," Kay replied. "I could spend my time telling you all the bad things I know about him, but I'd much rather spend my time telling you all the good things about me. I know Marty has engaged in some mud-slinging, but I have taken and always will take the high road."

"Very admirable," Ming said. During her entire interview, Ming had never looked at her notes, other than getting the direct quote from Reuben Muhammad. Kay made a mental note to see if she was tired of TV and wanted to become her press secretary. If she won. No, *when* she won, Kay mentally corrected herself.

"Tell us about your home life," Ming continued. "You know you and your husband are the talk of the town. Not many people can battle it out in the courtroom, then maintain a happy home afterward. But you've successfully done it for ten years."

"Well, my husband and I have only gone up against each other in the courtroom four times. And while we give our careers our all, when we cross that doorstep into our home, we hang our legal hats at the door. We don't let our work, especially when we're on opposite sides of the bench, come home with us, and that makes for a happy home."

"Amazing."

"I guess when you spend all day arguing, the last thing you want to do is come home and do it some more," Kay added with a laugh.

"Do your children know what you do?" Ming asked.

"Our youngest, Leslie, couldn't care less. She's four. So her biggest issue is which tutu to wear today. But the oldest, Ryan, he knows. And since he's such a scholar, he does try to weigh in, but again, we don't bring our work home and we don't discuss our cases."

"At all?" Ming asked.

"At all," Kay replied.

"Well, this picture-perfect life is just going to have us all a tad jealous."

"I do have a great life," Kay said. "But I work hard for the life I have."

"And I bet the only thing that would make it better is becoming the next mayor of Houston."

"You said it, I didn't."

Kay was glad to wrap up the interview. Per Kay's insistence, Loni had made sure that the reporters knew to stay away from the subject of her childhood. Loni let the media know how difficult it was for Kay to discuss her parents' deaths, twelve years ago, at the hands of a drunk driver. As an only child, there wasn't much else to investigate in her past. And that's just the way Kay wanted to keep it. When she had left for college at Stanford, which was as far away as she could get from her strict parents, Kay hadn't kept in touch with family much. Then, when her parents had died her senior year, Kay had completely cut everyone off. As far as Kay was concerned, she had reinvented herself. Her father and mother had died. So there really was no reason to connect with anyone else. Her life began the day she enrolled in Stanford University. And that's as far back as she ever wanted to go.

"Great interview," her campaign manager, Jeff, said. He'd sat quietly in the corner the whole time.

"Of course it was great," Loni said, handing Kay a piece of paper. "I taught her very well. Here's your media itinerary for the rest of the week. I've given a copy to Valerie so she can make sure it's all on your calendar."

Kay nodded her appreciation. Between her fantastic assistant, Valerie, and Loni and Jeff, Kay had the perfect team by her side. Perfect life. Perfect team. Perfect family. What more could a woman want?

7

Even the Word wasn't bringing her peace. That alone told Gloria just how hard this hit. Ever since she was a little girl, church had been her place of refuge. It had been where she sought—and received—comfort. But today, God's Word did little to heal her hurt. And for the first time in her life, she felt her faith wavering.

It had been eight days and God had not seen fit to bring her son home. Eight days and she had no idea where her only child was.

Images of her son's body beaten and buried in a shallow grave filled her mind. Just last year, another black Jasper resident, Alfred Wright, had come up missing. He was gone for eighteen days before they found his body, stripped down to his shorts and one sock, with his throat cleanly slit and one ear gone. His front teeth were broken and missing. The police had ruled it an "accidental drug overdose." Everyone in Jasper knew better, but police had still closed the case. Nothing inside her would let Gloria believe that things would be any different with Jamal.

Elton had told her to stop thinking the worst, but at eight days, what else was she supposed to think?

The cops had been following them all week. There was even a marked unit outside the church today (she knew she'd hear about that later). Elton couldn't stand to be embarrassed in his church, so this was going to add a whole other layer of stress to their already stressful marriage.

Gloria had come to church today in search of solace, for comfort that her son was all right. But so far, her nerves had only gotten worse. Sitting in that sanctuary allowed her mind to wander into the worst places. She should've been paying attention, but she couldn't keep the horrible thoughts from coming. She couldn't stop thinking about Jamal and what would happen if the police found him first.

The thoughts clouding her mind were exactly why Gloria had been doing anything she could to keep moving all week long. She'd washed every dish in the house, rearranged the pots in the cabinet, scrubbed the baseboards . . . she just had to keep moving. Because if she didn't, she would die. If she didn't keep moving, she'd be reminded that her son was out there somewhere, scared to death. At least, she hoped that he was still out there. She hoped that some robocop or vigilante hadn't gotten to him first. They'd dragged James Byrd Jr. for no reason. Shot Trayvon Martin for looking suspicious. Gunned down Michael Brown, even though people said he had his hands up. Jamal Jones had given them reason to kill. There was no way he'd be safe.

Gloria tried to refocus and stop her mind from traveling down that "what if" road. She watched her husband from the pulpit as he spouted off something about the faith of a mustard seed. Once again, he hadn't even addressed the Jamal situation. He just pretended that the two strange white men in the back of the sanctuary were visitors, not reporters. She knew who they were because they'd been nosing around before service and the gossip train had met her at the door this morning. Gloria had told Elton about them, but he'd just grumbled and walked off. Now he was in the pulpit doing what he did best—pretending all was well in the Jones household. It was a character flaw that Gloria had long ago given up trying to change.

Elton had just wrapped up his sermon and summoned the organist to begin playing for the altar call when Gloria felt a tap on her shoulder. She turned to see one of the ushers hovering over her.

"Sister Gloria?"

"Yes, Lena," Gloria replied, wondering why this woman would disturb her in the middle of service.

"Can you step out in the vestibule?" Lena whispered.

Really? Everyone at Mount Sinai Missionary Baptist Church knew Elton didn't like people moving around during his altar call, which was evident by the irritated look he was giving her right now.

"Please, it's Sister Naomi. She's sick," Lena said.

Naomi Tucker was one of the church members who often babysat Jamal when he was young. Gloria flashed an apologetic look at Elton, then stood and followed Lena out.

Naomi was sitting on the bench in the vestibule, laid back, her plump legs spread eagle, one usher fanning her, another holding her hand.

"Naomi! Are you okay?" Gloria asked, sliding on the bench next to her.

Naomi groaned.

"She peeked in the sanctuary, then she just collapsed," one of the ushers said. "She said she's feeling dizzy."

Gloria put her hand on Naomi's forehead. "You don't have a fever. What's hurting you?"

Naomi's voice was weak as she said, "I just feel faint. Can you take me home?"

Gloria was about to reply when she noticed the two nosy reporters stepping out of the sanctuary.

"Is everything okay?" one of them asked.

She tried her best not to be rude, but their intrusion was definitely unwelcome and they hadn't come out here for any other reason than to see what was going on. "One of our members is sick," Gloria snapped. "Is that newsworthy enough for you?"

As if on cue, Naomi moaned again. "I think . . . I'm going to throw up."

"Get her to the restroom," Lena said, grabbing her arm. Gloria took Naomi's other arm and helped her up.

The usher who had been fanning Naomi spoke up. "Service is about to let out. Can you take her to the restroom in the back?"

Gloria nodded as she and Lena began walking away

The reporters watched for a moment, then made their way out the front door.

As soon as Gloria and Lena got Naomi around the corner, Naomi turned to Lena. "Sister Lena," she said, her voice weak and raspy. "Thank you, but I think I just need to go home." She clutched Gloria a little tighter. "First Lady, do you think you can take me?"

Gloria raised an eyebrow. "Really?" All that she was going through and this woman wanted her to play taxicab?

"I can do it. It's no problem," Lena said. "The First Lady is dealing with a lot right now, I can take you."

Naomi seemed like she was about to topple over and she

grabbed Gloria's arms. Her fingernails dug into Gloria's arm to the point that it made Gloria wince. And then, it hit Gloria. Naomi knew something. This whole passing-out, moaning act was so out of character for her. So it could only mean one thing.

"I'm fine," Gloria said to Lena. "I can use the air and I know my way around Naomi's place. I'll take her home, get her settled, and come back. Can you just let Elton know?"

Lena hesitated, then nodded. "If you're sure."

"I am."

"Ohhhhh, I feel so dizzy," Naomi moaned.

"Do you need me to help you to get her to your car?" Lena asked.

"No. I'm okay," Naomi quickly said. "Thank you, Sister Lena."

Lena patted her hand. "You just go get some rest and let us know if we can do anything for you. I make a mean chicken noodle soup."

Naomi nodded her appreciation, then turned and draped her arm further in Gloria's as they walked toward the back.

"Let me get my keys," Gloria said, trying her best to stay calm.

Naomi glanced back over her shoulder, making sure Lena was gone. "Let's take my car."

The sudden urgency, and miraculous healing, shut down all of Gloria's questions and she followed Naomi out through the kitchen, into the side alley, and to her car.

"Get in," Naomi said, suddenly moving fast as she motioned for Gloria to get in on the passenger side. Her eyes darted around the alley, then she climbed in the driver's seat.

A thousand questions ran through Gloria's mind.

"Do me a favor and lean down," Naomi whispered as she started her 1990 Lincoln.

Gloria's heart began to race, but she did as she was told as Naomi's eyes darted around to make sure no one was following her, then she turned down the gravel street on the side of the church, instead of through the normal exit.

"Sorry for the performance, but I didn't know how else to get you out of church," Naomi said, her lips barely moving as she stared straight ahead.

"You know where Jamal is, don't you?" Gloria whispered as she crouched down in the seat.

Naomi didn't say a word as she turned the corner.

They rode in silence for the five minutes that it took to get to Naomi's house and as soon as Naomi pulled into her garage, then closed the door, Gloria was ready to bolt out of the car.

"Wait," Naomi said, putting her hand on Gloria's forearm. "He's okay. And you know I love Jamal like he's my own. I'll do anything for him." She paused. "Except go to jail. He showed up here on my way to church. Apparently he's been hiding out in my storage shed."

Gloria's heart plummeted into the pit of her stomach. Her son had been in a storage shed for a week?

"He begged me to get you," Naomi continued. "I don't know what to tell you to do. But he can't stay here. These police ain't playing and I just can't—"

Gloria stopped her. "Don't worry. I'm gonna get him to come home. I have to get him to come home." Gloria didn't know how she would make that happen. All she knew was that she had to. She raced from the car to see her son, tears of relief flooding her face. Her son was safe. At that very moment, nothing else mattered.

8

Gloria couldn't stop shaking. Naomi had directed her to a back room that was full of sewing supplies. The room smelled of mothballs and dust and looked like it wasn't used for anything other than storage.

"Sorry he had to stay in here. He wanted to stay in the attic but I told him with all that asbestos, he didn't need to be up there," Naomi said as she eased a dresser away from in front of what looked like a closet.

"No, I understand." Gloria knew she should help Naomi move the dresser, but she was too stunned to act.

Her heart raced as Naomi grunted with her last push. When the dresser was far enough out of the way, she moved to open the closed door.

Gloria stood, holding her breath, and her stomach muscles tightened when she saw Jamal cowering inside the closet in fear. His face was dirty with caked-on mud. His clothes were filthy and torn.

"Oh, my God, Jamal!" Gloria fell to her knees in front of her son. She looked him over, then pulled him into a tight embrace.

"Mama, I'm sorry," he cried. Hugging her brought an onset of tears and Jamal sobbed. His grip told her just how scared he'd been.

Gloria's tears mixed with his as she rocked back and forth, holding him like she never wanted to let him go. She could only imagine what he'd mentally endured for these past eight days.

"I'll give you a minute," Naomi finally said. "But we can't stay long. We have to go before people start looking for you. We all have to go."

Gloria nodded at Naomi, then pulled back and studied her son. In just a matter of days, it was as if every ounce of her son's innocence had been lost. "Are you okay? I've been scared to death." She touched his face, his chest, everything to see if anything was out of place.

"I'm okay. I-I just don't know what to do." His voice was weak and he looked like he'd made an excursion to hell.

Gloria helped her son up off the floor and onto a bench seat out in the room.

"What happened, baby?" Gloria asked.

"I don't know, Mama." Jamal fell back against the seat. "I didn't mean to shoot him. I didn't. I was scared he was going to kill me. All I was doing was recording him harassing Dix and he jumped on me. I wasn't breaking the law."

Suddenly Gloria regretted every lesson she'd ever taught Jamal about being confident and having his own mind. She should have told him like her daddy told her brothers, *You are and always will be a black man. Treat white folks with respect. Don't question authority, and do what the hell they say.* Gloria had always hated that. She felt like her father wanted them to be cowards and she'd vowed that things would be different for her own child.

Now look what it had gotten her.

"Tell me what happened," Gloria said. "I talked to Brian, but it just doesn't make sense to me."

"I don't even know what happened. Me, Squeaky, and Dix were hanging out and this cop started harassing us, talking about we looked like we were up to no good and that we had robbed a liquor store. I swear, Mama, we were just hanging out. The store owner was fussing but we weren't doing anything bad. And the cop started messing with us and roughing up Dix. And I started recording him. He got mad and told me to put the camera down. I wasn't in his way. I was standing off to the back recording. And he just charged me . . . and I . . . I don't know, he slammed me, and we struggled and some kind of way, I got his gun. I swear, Mama, I didn't mean to shoot him."

Jamal burst into tears again.

Gloria pulled him close. "I know, baby. I know that."

Tears streamed down Gloria's face as she held her son. Memories filled her mind. Childhood memories of an innocent little boy. A trouble-free little boy who once busted Old Lady Lewis's front window with a baseball and had cried for days. But this was no childhood game. This was real life. This was murder.

"I saw the news," Jamal finally said. "They're gonna kill me. They think I shot him on purpose and the cops are gonna kill me."

"No. We can work through this." Gloria tried to sound reassuring, although she didn't even believe her own words. "We'll get through this. I'll just go get your father and—"

"No!" His eyes widened in horror. "You can't tell Dad that you saw me!"

"Jamal!"

"Daddy will want me to turn myself in. If the cops get me, I don't stand a chance. I need some money. I've got to get out of town." Panic filled his voice.

"Out of town? Jamal, what are you saying?" Gloria said.

"I have to go. I just . . . I needed to see you before I left."

"Oh, Lord. You can't spend your life on the run." That thought alone gave her an unexplainable amount of pain. "Let's see what your dad—"

"No," he said, cutting her off again.

"Baby, I don't like keeping stuff from your father. He'll know what to do." Gloria didn't think even Elton could figure this one out, but they needed to be working through this together.

"You know he's going to do what's right. He always does what's right." Jamal sneered.

"Jamal . . ."

"Mama, I'm begging you." He stood and paced across the small bedroom. His voice and body reeked of desperation. "Just get me some money."

"I can't."

"I'm out, then." Jamal headed toward the door.

Gloria jumped up to stop him. "Wait. Please don't go. I'll get it. Just stay in your hiding spot and I'll come back. Just please don't leave. I'll work all of this out. I promise."

Jamal stared at her; his eyes were puffy and red. "Okay, Mama, I won't leave yet. But I have to go."

She nodded her understanding, then kissed him on his forehead. "Mama is here. I'm always here," she said.

He didn't have to say a word but the look in his eyes told her that he believed her. Yet, as her son crawled back into the closet, Gloria wondered how in the world she was going to keep her promise.

9

Tension had set up camp in the Jones household. Elton was still seething that Gloria hadn't initially told him about Jamal. Or maybe he was angry because she had talked him into letting Jamal go out in the first place. Or maybe it was the embarrassment that he hated most. Since the police had identified Jamal, the Joneses had been subjected to hate mail, their telephone rang constantly, and the media stayed camped out in front of their home.

And Elton resented every minute of it.

When the media came, so did the Black Panthers, and the Ku Klux Klan. The outrage far outweighed the support. Even some of their own church members had turned their backs and tried and convicted Jamal. There were supporters—many of whom they didn't even know—coming to Jamal's defense before even hearing his side of the story. The color lines had been drawn.

"Gloria!"

The sound of her husband's voice shook Gloria out of her

trance. She set the mop down and rushed into the living room. "Yes. What's wrong?"

He looked flustered and irritated as he tossed his sports coat across the sofa.

"Dang reporters blocking my driveway!" he snapped.

"What are you doing back?" She'd been grateful when he left about thirty minutes earlier. She was going to take Jamal some food, money, and clothes, but she already had to figure out how to get around the cop parked outside, she didn't need to have to figure out how to get away from Elton, too.

"I forgot the papers for the budget meeting. This nonsense with Jamal has me all discombobulated." Elton was shaking.

"You sure you're okay?" she asked.

"No," he huffed. "I'm worried sick about that boy. I know we haven't had the best of relationships lately, but I don't want any harm to come to him. Deacon Wade said rumor around the police station is that the cop who finds Jamal will get a bonus if he brings Jamal back—in a body bag."

Gloria gasped, clutched her chest, and fell back against the wall.

"Now, now," Elton said. "I'm sure it's just rumors."

"What if it's not?" she said. "They don't want my son alive. They don't even know what happened and they're out for my baby's blood."

"They know what happened," Elton said. "They got him on videotape, Gloria."

"You know Jamal, Elton. You know he's not a murderer. It was an accident."

He paused and looked at her. "Is that what his friends told you?"

46

This was the first time he'd asked her anything about her visit with Brian.

"Brian told me. But he didn't have to because I know my son."

Elton shook his head. "Well, all I know is ever since he started hanging around those boys, he's been headed for nothing but trouble."

Gloria knew that she needed to tread lightly, but after hours of blaming herself, she wanted to share some of the blame. "Have you ever thought if we had tried to be there for him and not chastised him so much, he wouldn't have been caught up in something like this?"

"No, ma'am," Elton snapped. He wagged a finger in her direction. "You will not make this about me. Every mistake that boy makes is of his own accord. I kept my foot on him to keep him on the straight and narrow and it didn't do any good."

This wasn't the time to get Elton riled up again. "What do you think they're going to do when they catch him? Do you really think that stuff about the body bag is just talk?"

That caused him to stop his rant. The look on his face sent a ripple of fear through her body.

Elton released a defeated sigh. "Well, I called Perry," he said, referring to their old attorney. "Even though he doesn't practice anymore, he still has connections."

"What did he say?"

Elton looked like he was weighing his words. "Gloria, it's probably best that you don't know," he finally said.

The look on his face caused her voice to rise an octave. "What did he say?" she repeated.

Elton Jones faced his wife. "The police are indeed out for blood, Gloria. Perry said the cop that died was a well-liked veteran police officer. I just wish I knew exactly what happened. How Jamal could do something like this."

Gloria's first instinct was to confess everything, tell him where their son was so he could talk to Jamal himself. But something wouldn't let the words escape from her mouth.

Elton let out a long, disheartened sigh. "Perry said when they find him, if they don't kill him first, they will be going for the death penalty."

Those words caused her to lose her balance. She fell against the sofa and Elton's rarely seen sympathetic side sprang to the forefront.

"It's okay, honey." He took her into his arms. "God's got this. He's not gonna let them hurt our son. Prayerfully, we'll make it through."

It felt good to have her husband hold her and although she didn't really believe his words, she relished the rare time of togetherness. So much so, that at that moment Gloria wanted to take Elton straight to Naomi's to see their son. But just as quickly as the thought entered her mind, she reminded herself that Elton would demand they go directly to jail.

Death by cop or death by the state. Her son's options were slim.

After a few silent minutes, Elton said, "Do I need to call someone to come sit with you? I have to get back to the budget meeting."

She wanted to scream at him, "Screw that church!" For once she wanted him to put his son first, but right now, she needed her husband gone so she could think with a clear head. That way, she could figure out her next move.

"You go on. I'll be okay," Gloria finally said. "Mama should be over any minute now."

"I love you." He planted a kiss on her forehead.

"And I love you, too," she said, trying her best not to break out in tears.

"We'll get through this. We'll find our son and we'll get through this," Elton said, stroking her hair.

She nodded. Even though she'd found Jamal, she wasn't at peace. In fact she didn't know if she'd ever be at peace again.

Gloria had just closed her eyes when she heard Elton say, "Hello, Mama Hurley."

"Elton."

Gloria's mother didn't say anything else as she made her way inside. She had never been a fan of Elton. By now he was used to her cold and condescending ways. He didn't like it, but over the years he had learned to live with it.

"Hey, Mama," Gloria said.

"Hey, baby," Erma said as she set her designer bag on the coffee table. At seventy-eight, she still had her independent streak and in fact had moved to Houston three years ago when she married her third husband. That marriage had only lasted eight months because she said she wasn't "anybody's maid." She'd gotten the house in the divorce and had stayed in Houston and only came to Jasper once a month to see family and friends.

"Did they catch my fugitive grandson?" she asked. Erma Hurley was one of those old people who say what they want, whenever they want. But Gloria wasn't in the mood for any quips about her son.

"No, Mama."

"Hmph. Better not let me know where he is. The news said they got a reward for five thousand dollars."

Gloria side-eyed her mother. "So, you would turn your own grandson in for five thousand dollars?"

"Hell! I'll turn him in for some bingo chips." She strutted her petite frame into the kitchen.

Gloria shook her head. Unfortunately her mother wasn't joking. She didn't play when it came to the law. She turned her own brother in when he robbed a bank saying she had "no tolerance for criminals."

"Well, it's not all that it seems," Gloria said.

Her mother reappeared in the den, a glass of tea in her hand. "Seems like to me he shot a cop."

"No. On the video, you heard some ruffling and you heard a gunshot go off. But you don't know who shot whom."

Erma sat down across from her daughter. "I'll take the dead cop as the one who got shot for one hundred, Alex."

"This isn't funny, Mama. It was an accident."

"I'm not laughing, Gloria." Erma sipped her tea. "And how you know what happened? Were you there? No, you weren't. The only way you know what happened"—she stopped, studied Gloria, then slowly went on—"is if you talked to him." She peered at her daughter again. "Gloria Hurley Jones, you know where that boy is, don't you?"

Gloria looked away. "Mama, I went to the jail to talk to Jamal's friends, the boys that were with him that night. They told me it was an accident."

Erma cocked her head, studied Gloria for a minute. Finally, she said, "Then why couldn't you look me in my face and say that? Why'd you have to walk away?"

"I don't know what you're talking about." She busied herself by opening her curio cabinet and straightening her Annie Lee figurines.

"I bet you don't," her mother replied. "That's why at this very moment, you have to adjust your dolls instead of look me in my face and talk to me."

"These are not dolls, Mama."

"And you're not being truthful."

Gloria sighed, closed the cabinet, then turned around. Even though she was almost fifty herself, Gloria still had a hard time lying to her mother.

Erma stood, walked over, and took Gloria's chin in her hand. She looked her daughter straight in the eyes. "You never was a good liar. Look here, I know you love that boy from the bottom of your soul, but don't let him ruin your life."

Gloria pulled her chin away. "Mama, you don't know what you're talking about. And you're the one always talking about how you'd do anything for your kids."

"I sure would, except break the law. I'm too old and too pretty to be in jail. Now those folks are going to string that boy up and if you get in the way, they're going to string you up, too."

"So, Mama, what am I supposed to do? Just hand Jamal to them?" Gloria whispered. She didn't believe her house was bugged, but she could never be too sure.

"I can't believe that Reverend Do Right, I'm sorry Do Right *Now*, is going along with this," Erma said, going back to her seat.

Gloria didn't reply.

Erma stopped just before sitting down. "Holy Mother of Mary. He doesn't know, does he?" That made Erma laugh. "It took your son killing a cop for you to finally stand up to that man."

"Mama, me keeping a secret from him doesn't mean I'm standing up to him."

"Well, at least you aren't being his puppet for a change."

That was another discussion she wasn't going to have with her mother.

"I'm just trying to figure out what to do."

Erma threw up her hands to stop Gloria from talking. "You know what? Don't tell me nothing else. I don't want to have to testify against you. So, I don't know nothing about nothing." Erma picked up the remote. "I wonder is *Jeopardy!* on yet."

10

There was something about family dinners that brought Kay joy. Probably because it was something she didn't have growing up. Kay used to watch those people on *Leave It to Beaver* and other popular TV shows where they all sat down as a family, and feel a longing inside. As an only child, she was often left alone to eat by herself. Her father was always too busy at church and after her six-year-old brother drowned, Kay's mother was always in a state of depression in her room. So everyone ate their food in solitude.

That's why Kay told Phillip from the beginning that despite their hectic schedules, she wanted to make sure that they sat down together and ate as a family at least once a week. It was a tradition that Phillip had gladly upheld, especially because most of the time Selena prepared an awesome meal and all they had to do was sit down and enjoy it.

"So, Mommy, can I go to the fair on Saturday?" Leslie asked. "Pretty please with a strawberry on top?"

"I told you I would think about it. We'll see if Daddy can get off and make it a family thing," Kay said, blowing a kiss at her husband.

"Yay," Leslie said, clapping her hands.

"Ryan, are you okay?" Kay asked. He had been picking over his food. He was probably bummed out because he got a B on a test or something. Bad grades usually sent him into a state of depression.

"I'm cool," he mumbled.

Kay turned to her husband and smiled. "He's cool."

Phillip shook his head. "One day we'll get an extensive conversation out of our son."

"He talks to Charlie," Kay joked. Charlie was Ryan's best friend. And since Charlie's mother, Camille, was her best friend, Kay was happy that the two boys were so close.

"But we're not cool like Charlie." Phillip laughed.

Ryan rolled his eyes. "Whatever."

"Oh yeah, babe, congratulations to you," Phillip told his wife. "I saw the case with Dwayne Murphy. I knew they'd give him life."

"What? You approve of a life sentence?" Kay joked.

"Hey, I have no problem with locking up criminals who commit heinous crimes. It's the young boys I have an issue with."

They did discuss cases after they were over so Kay didn't mind telling her husband about this one. "It is really sad. Dwayne has four sons, two of whom have already been in jail. So the cycle will just continue."

"Yeah," Phillip replied, his mood turning melancholy, "that's why I do what I do. Hoping to stop the cycle. I just wish there was some kind of way we could give these boys better opportunities."

"I do, too," Kay said, "but some people you just can't help. They don't want to be helped. Now the case you just wrapped up," she continued, "that boy, he deserved a second chance. So, I'm glad you got him off."

Phillip had also emerged victorious in a case against an honor roll student who was shot after police mistook his black marker for a gun.

"Just curious, why do you think he deserves a second chance?" Phillip asked.

"Because that cop was trigger happy, with a history of complaints, and that boy just happened to be in the wrong place at the wrong time."

Phillip let out a deep sigh. "That's what I'm trying to tell you, there are a lot of boys in the wrong place at the wrong time."

"There is a difference. Take Trayvon Martin," Kay countered. "He didn't deserve what he got at all. He was minding his business. Michael Brown, on the other hand, he took some cigars."

Phillip looked at her, stunned. "*Alleged* to have taken some cigars, which the police officer reportedly didn't know at the time. Regardless, you think that was worth him dying over?"

"Absolutely not," Kay said. "Make no mistake about that, but what we have to get these young boys to understand is that when you place yourself in these precarious positions, then you're asking for trouble; right or wrong, you give people reason to justify shooting."

"It's so much deeper than that, Kay. I don't know if you could even understand. I would think with the number of young men you see coming through your courtroom, you'd be a little more sympathetic."

"No, I'm actually able to look at it from the other side because I've seen several young men who have been given chance after chance. Men who tried to use the 'system wronged me' excuse and then they got right back out there and did the same thing."

"Well, there's a number of reasons; lack of jobs, for one."

"Okay, we're not gonna start with the 'I got an excuse 'cause the white man keeping me down.' It's time we stop waiting for other people to lift us up and try to lift ourselves up," Kay replied.

"This conversation is soooo boring," Leslie chimed in. "Can we talk about something else?"

Phillip and Kay looked at each other and smiled. Their daughter was right. Their passionate debates were one thing they loved about each other, but this was family time.

"What would you like to talk about, Sweet Pea?" Phillip asked.

"Justin Bieber," she answered, her eyes wide with excitement.

"Really?" Phillip raised an eyebrow at his wife. "Why is our four-year-old into Justin Bieber?"

"Just be glad it's not Chris Brown or someone like that."

"I don't want my four-year-old into anything but *Teletubbies*," Phillip said.

"What's a Teletubby?" Leslie asked.

Phillip and Kay laughed. They really were out of touch. That had been Ryan's favorite cartoon when he was a little boy. It was at that point when Kay noticed Ryan hadn't said a word as he sat picking over his food.

"Are you sure you're okay, Ryan?" Kay asked.

"Yeah," he replied.

"You don't look okay," Phillip said. "Son, how's school going?"

"It's all right."

"Well, did you make the lacrosse team?"

"Nah," he said. "I didn't try out. I was thinking it would take away too much time from my schoolwork."

As much as she loved her stepson and how studious he was, Kay really did wish he would learn to relax and have some fun. Maybe she'd look into taking him and Charlie to an upcoming concert or something. She needed to show Ryan how to enjoy his childhood and just have fun.

"So, is it your night to do the dishes? Or is it mine?" Kay said, as she stood and started clearing the table.

A mischievous grin spread across Phillip's face. "How about we do them together and then go find some way to entertain ourselves later?"

"Ugh," Ryan said. "Can you two not?"

Kay giggled.

"How are you going to entertain yourselves?" Leslie asked. "Can I come, too?"

"No, sweetie. That's Mommy and Daddy time," Kay replied.

"On that note," Ryan said, standing up, "I'm out." He pushed away from the table and walked off.

Phillip lost his smile. "You know," he said to Kay, "I'm a little worried about him."

"Oh, you know your son. It's probably nothing," Kay said, dismissing his concern. "When it comes to Ryan Christiansen, you don't have anything at all to worry about."

That was one thing Kay was willing to put money on.

11

Gloria didn't know if she was making the right choice, and she prayed that Jamal didn't hate her for it, but she didn't know what else to do. She didn't want to keep the lies going with her husband and at this point they needed him to do what God had called him to do—lead their household.

She'd made the decision to tell Elton about Jamal after she saw the news this morning. The local media had been covering the case nonstop. Gloria had watched in horror as the reporter interviewed a Jasper resident named Mickey.

"Why are you out here protesting?" the reporter had asked.

"'Cause that boy gunned down one of Jasper's finest, who only wanted to protect and serve." The man leaned over and spit out some of the snuff that was stuffed in his bottom lip. "And the good folks of Jasper are waiting on him to be brought in—dead or alive."

His words, and the way he'd peered into the camera with beady, evil eyes, let Gloria know that her son was in serious danger. If they had any hope of working this out, they needed to come together as a family.

"Woman, are you gonna tell me where we're going?" Elton said as they turned into Naomi's neighborhood. He'd been griping since he'd gotten in the car and Gloria wanted so bad to tell him to just shut up and ride.

She'd tossed and turned all night after her mother left. She'd prayed, then prayed some more before telling Elton. Well, she hadn't told him—yet. She'd fixed him a hearty breakfast, complete with his favorites—smothered biscuits and sausage and hash browns. Then, when he'd finished, she told him to come with her and ask no questions. Of course, he'd been asking questions ever since.

"You know I got a million and one things to do." He leaned out the window to survey their location. "And are you driving around in circles?" he said, noticing the 7-Eleven they'd passed five minutes ago. She had already stopped at a church member's house to drop off something, then taken a back route to Naomi's. Her stomach was in knots because she'd been worried about the police following her. But the short staff must've been taking its toll on the police force because for the past three days, there had been large gaps in between the time the marked units were parked outside their house. As soon as she'd seen the cop car pull off this morning, she'd grabbed Elton and instructed him to follow her.

"I'm not trying to ride around with you while you run errands," Elton said.

Gloria glanced in her rearview mirror as she made a quick right turn.

"Where are you going and why do you keep looking in the rearview mirror?" Elton asked. He was definitely getting agitated.

"I just want to make sure we're not being followed," she said.

"Okay, Gloria, you need to tell me what in the world is going on," he said, his voice firm. "Does this secret mission have anything to do with Jamal?"

When she was absolutely sure no one was following her, Gloria turned down the back alley that Naomi had shown her.

"Come on," she said, stopping the car and parking.

"I don't like all of this Double-O spy stuff," he huffed.

"Just come on, Elton. Trust me." She exited the car without giving him a chance to respond.

He followed her up Naomi's back walkway and stood looking around nervously as Gloria reached under a flowerpot and got a key.

"Why are you going into Naomi's house? Where is she?"

Gloria wanted to tell him to shut up, but she had never been disrespectful to her husband and she wasn't going to start now.

She pulled him inside and toward the back room, flipping on the main light in the hallway. He followed her but asked no more questions.

She repeated the scene that Naomi had played out, moving the dresser and all of the clothes on the floor in the front of the closet door. She opened the door and whispered, "Jamal, it's me."

"Jamal!" Elton bellowed.

Gloria motioned for him to keep his voice down. Jamal moved some clothes out of the way and peeked out, his eyes wide.

"You brought him?" Jamal cried. "I can't believe you brought him!"

"Jamal, what are you doing in there?" Elton hissed as he peered into the dark closet. "Come out here now!"

Jamal eased out of the closet. Thankfully, he'd cleaned up some and had put on a fresh T-shirt. He still looked weary around the eyes.

"Are you hiding him here?" Elton snapped at Gloria.

"Good to see you, too, Daddy," Jamal said, his voice a mixture of sarcasm and exhaustion.

Elton took a deep breath and pulled his son into an awkward hug, then quickly released him. "Of course I'm glad that you're all right, but somebody needs to explain to me what's going on."

"I just found out that he was here," Gloria replied as Jamal continued to look at her like he couldn't believe that she had betrayed him. "Baby, I'm sorry, but your dad needed to know."

"You're doggone right!" Elton said. "You got your mama running around putting her freedom on the line! How would you feel if they threw your mama in jail behind this?"

Jamal bit his bottom lip as a thin mist covered his eyes. Over the past year, he'd become defiant whenever Elton chastised him, but now, he'd returned to his childhood response to his father's wrath—looking away in shame.

"He didn't have me doing anything, Elton," Gloria protested. "We're trying to figure this out."

"There's nothing to figure out. You have to turn yourself in," Elton said.

"See, Ma!" Jamal exclaimed, a look of panic spreading across his face.

"You just have to cause havoc!" Elton said. He shook his head as he paced in the small bedroom. "Do you know the shame you have brought to this family?"

"It's all about the shame," Jamal mumbled.

Elton spun toward him, jabbing a finger in his face. "Don't you dare get smart. Do you know what the last few days have been like for us? A nightmare! And the police are following us everywhere. They're even at church! Defiling God's house. Harassing the members. Harassing us. They were convinced we were hiding you somewhere!" He turned and glared at Gloria. "Little did I know they were right."

"Dad—"

"Don't *dad* me," Elton snapped, turning his venom back in Jamal's direction. "Do you know your mama could've been arrested if they caught her coming here?"

"Elton, now is not the time!" Gloria snapped, trying to cut off his rant. "We need to help our son."

"This is ridiculous. I'm gonna help him all right. Let's go," Elton said, grabbing Jamal's arm.

"Go where?" Jamal asked as his father literally dragged him toward the door.

"We're about to go to the police station."

Jamal broke free and darted across the room. "Mom, see, this is what I'm talking about!" he cried. "This is why I didn't want him to know where I was!"

"So, on top of everything else, you wanted your mama to lie to me?" Elton said.

Panic swept through Gloria's body. "Stop it! Just calm down. Both of you," she said. "We need to talk about this."

"There's nothing we need to talk about." Elton looked back and forth between the two of them, then settled his gaze on Gloria. He took a deep breath and stepped toward his wife as if he desperately wanted to reason with her. "He has to turn himself in, Gloria. There is no other way. They'll come in here shooting at me and you." He turned back to Jamal. "I'm not going to let you ruin this family, son."

"I *am* this family," Jamal cried. "Does anyone care about me?"

"Of course we do," Elton said, "but we're not going to condone you shooting a police officer."

"I didn't mean to shoot him!" Jamal cried. "It was an accident." He turned to Gloria. "Tell him, Mama. Tell him it was an accident."

"Okay, fine. It was an accident. We'll tell that to the police," Elton said, trying to remain calm.

"Mom . . ." Jamal turned to Gloria like he knew there was no getting through to his father. "I'm not going to jail. Those racist cops will kill me. I will never survive."

"Stop trying to make this about race," Elton said. "You did something bad and we need to deal with it."

Gloria stared at her husband in disbelief. Surely he couldn't be that delusional. If those Jasper cops got her son, this would definitely be about race.

"Are you serious?" Jamal said. "You know how these people are."

"Of course I know, son," Elton said. "But you can't run. Plain and simple."

"I'm not going to jail," he repeated.

Gloria stepped up and took her son's hands. She was glad when he didn't jerk them away. "Baby, no one's trying to make you go to jail. Your daddy will call Perry and he'll represent you, and we'll tell them. We'll get the police to understand that this was all a horrible accident."

Even as the words left her mouth, she knew better. The look on Jamal's face said he didn't believe her, either. But she had to stay hopeful.

"We're a family. We have gotten through things worse than this," she continued.

She glared at Elton. "Haven't we?"

He didn't reply.

"No, I'm leaving," Jamal said, reaching for something in the closet. He pulled out a pink and purple kiddie backpack, no doubt belonging to Naomi's granddaughter. "You can either help me or I'll make it on my own."

Elton must've decided to take a different approach because he said, "Son, a life on the run is not the way to go."

Jamal ignored his father. "Mom, I waited here because you told me to trust you. I thought I could."

"You can, baby. You can trust both of us." Gloria was trembling. She'd hadn't expected Jamal to run. "Your father will tell you, he's not gonna do a thing until we've all worked this out. Right?"

Elton just stood there.

"Right?" she demanded.

He nodded, although his displeasure was evident. "Fine, we'll work it out. I don't know how, but I guess we will. Let's just hope all three of us don't end up in jail before that happens."

Gloria felt sick to her stomach. Once again, she'd made the wrong decision. Telling Elton was the worst thing she could've done. Why she expected any reaction other than the one he was giving right now proved that this situation was causing her to lose all rational thinking. Now the question was, how was she going to clean up the mess she'd made?

12

For someone who was on the brink of what could be a very ugly divorce, Kay's best friend, Camille, was in a pretty good mood.

"Girl, I have to give you major props," Kay said, turning the volume up on her car phone speaker so she could hear Camille better. "I just could not have the same upbeat attitude as you if Phillip and I broke up."

"Of course, I'm sad about it. I gave this man fifteen years of my life," Camille replied. "But man sharing is against my religion so he had to go."

Camille and her husband, Vincent, owned a bail bonds company, so Kay had met them eight years ago through their legal interactions. The two of them were so close because Camille was everything that Kay was not—bold, outspoken, and vivacious. A gorgeous, statuesque woman, Camille was actually the brawn of their bail bonds business. Her father had been a private investigator, so she knew the art of tracking down people to collect her money.

They didn't get to talk as much as they used to, something Kay hated. But between her job and the mayoral race, Kay was always on the run. Their sons were both the same age, attended the same private school, so if Camille and Kay didn't manage to talk about things in general, they kept in regular contact because Ryan and Charlie were always together.

That's why Camille had called today, while Kay was on her way to speak to Phillip's mentoring group. Camille wanted to let Kay know that she was picking the boys up after school. Their conversation had quickly shifted as Camille started telling Kay some more details she'd found out about Vincent's twenty-two-year-old jump-off.

"Girl, she had the audacity to call me and tell me that she would be the new Mrs. Bailey soon and she wanted us to have a good relationship for Charlie and Zola's sake," Camille huffed. Kay knew neither Charlie nor Camille's seven-year-old daughter, Zola, was happy about the divorce. "Vincent hadn't even been gone two weeks and she's calling me with that mess," Camille continued. "I told Vincent he'd better get his hoes in check before he ends up having to post bail for me."

Camille was joking, or at least Kay thought she was, but knowing her quick-tempered friend, Kay wouldn't want to test her.

"What did you tell, what did you say her name was?" Kay asked, referring to the other woman.

"Misty. Sounding like a two-dollar stripper," Camille replied. "I told that trick not to ever call my house again. She can post all the Instagram photos she wants. I'm too old for that mess."

"For real, who does that?" Kay replied. "You post lovebird photos of the guy you're cheating with on social media?"

"Twenty-two-year-olds do that, that's who," Camille snapped.

"But it's cool. I told her karma would deal with her. Then I hung up on her."

Kay said a silent thankful prayer for Phillip. While she would never say never, she just couldn't imagine ever going through some mess like that with him.

"Okay, I have to go. I'm here," Kay said, pulling up to the Acres Home Community Center, where the mentoring luncheon was being held.

Kay made it a point to visit with Phillip's mentees at least once a year. She saw enough of the juvenile delinquents in the courtroom, but this was something that meant a lot to Phillip, so she came to this event each year.

"All right, girl. Thanks for letting me vent."

"You sure you're okay?" Kay asked, pulling into a parking space.

"Yeah, I'm fine. Or I will be. You just make sure you lock up your purse," Camille said. "You know those little deviants will see that Jimmy Choo and start calculating how much they can get for it."

"I doubt they even know who Jimmy Choo is," Kay replied. "Speaking of calculating. How much will you be donating to the Community Center for their annual fund-raiser?"

"Fifty thousand dollars," Camille said.

Kay gasped. She had no idea the bail bonds business was doing that well.

"And I'm gonna give you a pair of Jordan's, too, so that you can play with that bounced check I write," Camille added.

Kay cracked up laughing. "Girl, I thought you were serious."

"Child, all these felons jumping bail. And now this divorce; I need to hold on to every nickel I have."

"You need anything?" Kay asked.

"Seriously, I'm good. You just go in there and get your pin for sainthood and I'll talk to you later," Camille said.

Kay hung up and made her way inside. The program was just getting started, so she waved to her husband and slid into her seat at the front table.

She watched with pride as Phillip gave a brief introduction, then proceeded to talk about his reasons for working with the center.

It was moments like this that Kay understood why Phillip did what he did, why he would leave his cushy corporate job to provide defense to indigent young men. His passion for these young men was evident in every word he uttered.

As Kay looked around at the sea of black and brown faces, she felt a small tug at her heart. Being a prosecutor had taught her to automatically think the worst when she saw boys who looked like this, the baggy pants, the tattoos, the backward hats. But seeing these young boys here, she wondered, if they had been like Ryan and given half a chance, would their circumstances have been different?

The second speaker in the youth empowerment seminar wrapped up. A former gang member, he had held the group's attention by talking about life behind bars. At first Kay balked when her husband asked her to be one of the speakers for this event. But because he didn't pull that card very often, she gave in. Now she was glad she did. A police officer had gone first and now it was her turn and these young boys seemed poised and ready to ask questions.

"Okay, boys," Phillip said as he came up to the podium, "let's give Officer Robinson another round of applause and, hopefully, you all learned something valuable from him." Phillip turned and smiled at Kay. "Our last speaker this afternoon is actually my wife."

Several of the kids started oohing and aahing. One little boy yelled, "Mr. Christiansen, your wife is hot!"

Phillip looked at him and grinned. "I know." He turned back to the crowd. "Please join me in welcoming my wife, Harris County prosecutor and the next mayor of Houston, Kay Christiansen."

The boys clapped. Kay could tell it was them being polite and not because they were really interested in what she had to say. She took a few minutes and told them about her job. That part was easy. But on the next part she knew she was going to catch it.

"Okay, anybody have questions?" she asked. Several hands went up.

She pointed to a teenage boy with cornrows sitting in front. "My cousin got caught up on a case," the boy said, "and he was supposed to have a jury of his peers, but it wasn't but a bunch of old white men and women on the jury. That ain't his peers. What's up with that?"

Kay flashed a sympathetic smile. "Unfortunately, our jury rolls are chosen from people who are registered to vote and in the African American and Latino communities, many people don't register. They don't realize that decision has far-reaching effects."

"I don't get it," another boy said.

"It simply means that if you don't register to vote, you'll never be called to be on a jury," Kay said.

"So, you mean if I don't turn in that voter registration card Mr. Christiansen had me fill out, I won't ever get called for jury duty?"

"You can't vote," the little boy sitting next to him said.

"Yes, I can. I'm eighteen."

"Eighteen and in the ninth grade," a boy sitting next to him said, laughing. "Dumbo." The guy swung at him, but the smart-mouth kid ducked.

"Settle down," one of the mentors standing near them said.

"He's right. He can vote," Kay continued. "He's eighteen. And yes, if you don't register to vote, you'll never be called for jury duty."

"I don't know why y'all waste your time with trials anyway," another teenage boy said. "Y'all just gonna find the black man guilty."

"Shoot, least y'all get a trial," a young Hispanic boy chimed in. "They threatened to deport everybody in my family if my cousin Oscar didn't plead guilty to something he didn't do." The boy scowled in Kay's direction.

"No," Kay countered, shifting under his unwavering glare. "There really isn't a conspiracy to throw black and Hispanic boys in jail. We like to think that everyone who comes through our courts will have a proper defense. Although we know that's not always the case."

"Especially when you're giving them the janky public defenders," the boy said.

"Unfortunately our public defenders are overworked and underpaid," Kay said, "so you might not always get the best defense. But most of them are good people who are committed to their jobs."

"The system sucks. All the prisons are filled with minorities. We ain't the only ones committing crimes. So you can't tell me it ain't something jacked up about it," he argued.

"Yes, the system has its flaws," she said, "but it's the only one we have."

Several of them moaned.

"Why the cops always harassing us?" someone from the back asked her.

"Yeah," another boy added. "Like that dude out of Jasper. Five-O messing with him when he wasn't bothering nobody."

Kay didn't want to touch that one, so she stepped back and looked at the officer who spoke first. "Maybe you can answer that."

He stepped up, answered the question, and fielded a few more. When they were done, Kay couldn't help but feel that she hadn't made any inroads with these young men. Phillip must have known she was feeling down because he came up to her afterward.

"They're a hard group," he said, rubbing her arm. "But believe it or not, some of what you said will stick."

"You think so?" Kay said. "Because it sure doesn't seem like it."

Phillip nodded. "We do just have some straight-up bad kids. But for the most part, everybody here wants better. Many of them just become victims of their circumstances. If they're not in a single-parent home, they're following in the footsteps of brothers and uncles who are in prison. We're trying to change that by show-ing them positive role models. You know I was even thinking of bringing Ryan over here. Let him hang out. See them."

Kay's eyes bucked. "They would eat our son alive."

Phillip glanced around the room. "Yeah, you're right about that."

"No, Ryan is just fine in our little world. We can ready him for the real world."

She saw a fight almost erupt in a corner of the room. Two of the organizers quickly broke it up.

"And this," she whispered to her husband, "is not his world."

Phillip's lips brushed hers. "Okay, I get it. Ryan is privileged. We are blessed to be able to give him a better life. I just hope that when you become mayor, you'll reinstate city funding for our program. These kids need it."

"I will," Kay promised. She planned to honor her commitment, and not just for Phillip. Something about these boys made her wonder if he was right. Maybe all they needed was a chance.

13

Gloria groaned at the sight of Detective Martin at her front door. The scowl on his face told her that this was not likely to be a pleasant visit. And since he hadn't tackled her to the floor, she could only assume that they didn't know that she knew where Jamal was.

Elton had been furious all night. He'd even gone as far as calling her a liar. She didn't dispute that, but she wasn't about to make apologies for it now. In fact, she almost let him know that she was sorry she even told him about Jamal in the first place. But no need in making an already tense situation worse.

Elton was on edge and wouldn't stand for them hiding Jamal for long. They'd spent a little more time with Jamal, then left with the promise to return tonight. Although Elton had finally settled down, Gloria knew the only thing he would support would be for Jamal to turn himself in.

Elton had gone to the church with an attitude this morning and told her they would have a serious discussion when he got home.

"Good afternoon, Detective Martin, may I help you?" Gloria asked.

"Yeah, by telling me where your son is," he snapped.

"I told you, I don't know." She wiped her hands on the dish towel that she'd been holding when she opened the door. Not that her hands were wet, but she didn't want Detective Martin to see them trembling.

"Cut the act, Mrs. Jones. We know you've been in contact with your son."

"You know no such thing," she replied, struggling to keep her voice steady. "I told you what I know." *If he knew more, he wouldn't be at your door chitchatting*, Gloria kept telling herself. "I will not have you coming to my house and harassing me."

He jumped in her face. "You do know that I will throw you in jail along with your murdering son."

Gloria was shaken but she didn't move. "I don't know what you want me to do," she said, not taking her eyes off of him.

He slammed an open palm on the door. "I want you to tell me the truth. Where is he?"

The rage in Detective Martin's eyes sent a wave of fear throughout her body.

"I. Don't. Know," Gloria said. "I told you that if we hear from him, we'll let you know."

"I just want to be very clear," he growled. "If I find out you had anything to do with hiding or harboring him, you and your husband are going down."

"If you don't get off my front porch and stop threatening my wife . . ."

Gloria had never felt so relieved to see her husband. She hadn't even heard him pull up. Detective Martin turned and sneered in Elton's direction.

"What? You gon' shoot me like your son shot Officer Wilkins?"

"Detective Martin," Elton said, his voice calm, "we are trying to be cooperative, but you will not harass my wife."

Detective Martin stood erect, trying to compose himself. He glared at both of them. "You'd better hope I don't find your son first. And that right there *is* a threat."

He stomped off the front porch.

Gloria sobbed as soon as he was gone. Elton moved in, closed and locked the door, then took her into his arms.

"It's going to be okay, sweetheart. I know you're scared. Shoot, I'm scared, but God will work all of this out," he said. "But we can't do this, have these people harassing us. We have to get Jamal to turn himself in."

"He's not going to do it," Gloria replied. She'd gotten Naomi to check on Jamal this morning. Of course, Naomi's main concern was when he was leaving. But she loved Jamal, and the desperation in Gloria's voice must've been enough to convince her to help. Naomi had reported back to Gloria that it had taken everything she had to convince him to keep waiting.

"Then we have to turn him in," Elton said, snapping her out of her thoughts.

"Turn in our own son? To these people? Are you crazy? Did you see the look in Detective Martin's eyes?"

"What other choice do we have? Jamal killed a man. A policeman."

"Jamal is not a murderer," she found herself saying.

"And the court will see that."

Gloria broke free and paced across the living room floor. "Really? You think with this high-profile case, our boy stands a chance?" The local media had been covering the case nonstop. TV and newspaper reporters from Houston and other Texas cities had been calling around the clock. Yesterday, they got a call from a CNN producer, which meant the story was about to go national.

"We have to stay prayerful," Elton said.

Gloria had the faith of a mustard seed. But she also knew God gave people free will. And that will was running rampant in the Jasper Police Department, which was hell-bent on stringing up her son. "I can't turn in my son," she said with finality.

"Do you really want Detective Martin to get a hold of him? At least if we turn him in, it'll be on record. We can even call, what's that activist's name in Houston that helps people turn themselves in?" He thought for a minute. "Tyriq X. That's him. We can get him to escort Jamal in. You know the cameras follow him everywhere. That way, they'll be less likely to harm him. But Jamal has to turn himself in."

"I know," Gloria said, her heart breaking. "But I can't do it. I can't just hand my son over to them."

Elton stomped away. "There you go babying him again. In case you haven't noticed, he's crossed over into grown folks' territory now. What are you planning to do? Help him run off so we can never hear from him again? Are we supposed to let the police harass us forever, showing up at our door and at church?"

"I don't know," Gloria cried.

Elton removed his wallet from his pants pocket and tossed it on the counter with his keys. "I'm going to change. Then I'm going back up to the church. Then, this evening, we're going to get our son and turn him in."

Gloria let him leave. The look in her husband's eyes told her he meant what he just said—it was over. He would no longer support anything other than Jamal turning himself in. And she wasn't ready to do that—yet.

It wasn't just a motherly connection, but she knew Jamal didn't mean to kill that police officer. And she bore some guilt at how it all went down. Maybe if she had kept a tight rein like Elton wanted . . .

I just need some money.

Jamal's words rang in her head. Maybe if she got the money, he could disappear and let the anger die down. If he just went away for a while, police would calm down and they could turn Jamal in. The more she thought about it, the more she felt that was her answer.

Gloria tiptoed to the safe in the back closet and opened it, careful not to make any noise. There was two thousand dollars there that Elton kept in case of an emergency. She would pay for this later, but Elton's wrath was a price she was willing to endure to help her son. Gloria took all the money, then closed the safe and eased out of the room.

14

_____

I t was official. She was a criminal. Not just for harboring a fugitive, but for drugging a police officer. Well, Gloria hadn't actually drugged anyone, but she had taken the officer parked outside her house for the past hour a cup of coffee. She'd done it once before, so it's not like it was anything unusual. But this time, she'd been praying he'd take it because the sleeping pill she'd crushed up in the coffee was the only way she'd be able to get out of the house and get to her son. It had taken less than thirty minutes, but the minute she saw the officer dozed off in front of her house, Gloria grabbed the duffle bag full of supplies and darted to her car, which was parked in the garage. Elton had been gone an hour and she needed to act fast before he got back.

Fifteen minutes later, Gloria pulled into the same spot in the alley behind Naomi's house. She reached in the back and grabbed the duffle. As soon as her hand touched the bag, a wave hit her consciousness. Was she really about to help her son run?

"It's only temporary," she muttered to herself. If Detective

Martin hadn't threatened her, all but told her he would kill Jamal if he ever got his hands on him, maybe she'd have some faith in the system. But right now, they didn't even have an attorney. Perry wouldn't be back in town until tomorrow and Jamal was right. The only option he had right now was to run.

It hurt Gloria's heart to think of her son out on his own, in fear for his life, dodging the authorities. Where would he go? What would he do? Gloria had gone to a pay phone near the beauty salon this morning and called her cousin in Florida. Of course her cousin didn't want to get involved, but she had a friend who would be willing to put Jamal up until they worked all of this out, got an attorney, and found some way to keep him safe.

"Jamal, it's Mom," Gloria called out once she made her way to the back of Naomi's house. She prayed that he hadn't decided to go ahead and bolt already.

Naomi had been staying with a friend because she said she didn't want to risk being in the house if Jamal was found. She'd given them until today to get Jamal out. Everybody was in fear.

There was some rattling in the closet, then Gloria said, "I'm by myself." She pulled the door opened and saw Jamal still cowering in the corner.

"Have you been like that the whole time?" she asked.

He nodded.

"Have you eaten?"

He nodded again. "I had some crackers."

"Well, I brought you a plate," she said, pulling out chicken and dumplings, his favorite. He grabbed the plate and devoured the food. He ignored the plastic fork and picked up dumplings with his hand, stuffing six in his mouth at a time. Before he even finished chewing those, he gnawed off a big piece of the chicken leg. The sight of him eating like a caveman broke her heart.

"Okay, you know we have to leave today. Naomi is terrified. We can't put her at risk any longer," she said after a few minutes of watching him eat.

Jamal took a moment, chewed, and swallowed before speaking. Even at his lowest point, he still had his manners.

"I know. I don't want to get Ms. Naomi in trouble anyway."

"Oh, honey." She handed him the duffle bag as she fought back tears. She had never felt a pain like this. It felt like a hole was growing deep in her soul. "There are some clothes in there for you and some money. I also bought you a bus ticket to Florida. My cousin has a friend you can stay with for a while until this all dies down. But let me at least take you to the bus station."

"No, Mama. I don't want you to do any more than you have already done." He sucked the last of the meat off the chicken leg.

She let out a heavy sigh. She'd promised herself that she'd stay strong for her son, but it wasn't working. "Jamal, I don't feel right about this."

"Would you feel right if they killed me instead?" he asked matter-of-factly.

How was she supposed to do this? How was she supposed to "do the right thing" if it meant her son would be harmed?

"Well, I gave you everything I could. There's enough money in that bag to get you through for several weeks." Her voice quivered. "When you get to Florida, my cousin's friend will put you up for a while. But this is only temporary. We're going straight to work to try and get you an attorney."

"Okay, Mom," he said. He set the now-empty plate down and

threw his arms around her neck. "I love you, Mama. I'm so sorry I did this to you."

She pulled back and wiped the tears that were trickling down his face. "Baby, I know it was an accident. A horrible tragic accident."

"I feel so bad about that police officer. I never meant to hurt him. I just thought he was going to kill me and I grabbed his gun . . ."

"I know." She picked up his bag. He didn't have to tell her all the details. She knew her son. He wasn't a killer. "Come on, go change. The bus leaves in forty-five minutes."

She waited while he went to the bathroom, took a quick shower, and changed. Ten minutes later, he was back in front of her, looking more like the old Jamal, except for the puffiness around his eyes. Gloria knew she would never have the old Jamal again.

"Well, come on, baby, let's go."

Jamal grabbed the duffle bag and they made their way out through the side door and back out into the alley.

"You're sure you're not going to let me give you a ride?" she asked.

"No, Mama," he said. "I'm just going to cut through the woods to get to the station. I'll lay low till the bus comes." He was trembling, like the first day he rode the school bus and didn't know what lay ahead. "I'll be okay. I love you so much." He hugged her tightly one last time. And just when he turned to walk away, they heard, "Police! Freeze!"

Gloria gasped as she threw her arms in the air like she was on a TV show. Jamal slowly put his arms up as well. He looked back at her and she could tell from the look in his eyes that he was about to run. "Don't, Jamal!" she cried. There was no doubt that if he took off, they would shoot her son in the back.

"Jamal Jones! Do not move!"

Gloria's eyes moved in the direction of that voice, the voice that had haunted her for the past week. Then she saw the eyes of Detective Martin. His gun was aimed directly at Jamal's head. His finger poised on the trigger as if it was itching to move. Before she knew what was happening, Gloria jumped in front of her son. "Noooo!" she screamed, holding up her hands to shield her son.

"Gloria!"

Gloria's mouth dropped in horror as her husband appeared on the side of Detective Martin. "Honey, don't!"

She had so many things to say to her husband, but right now, she could only focus on her son.

"Mrs. Jones, you'd better move," Detective Martin hissed.

"No!" Gloria cried. "So you can kill him? No! You'll have to kill me, too."

It was then that Elton stepped directly in front of Detective Martin, his back to the gun, his attention focused on Gloria. "Sweetheart, it's over." He looked at Jamal, who was trembling behind his mother. "Son, do you want them to shoot your mother?" He motioned to what now looked like every police officer in Jasper. Each of them had a gun pointed in their direction. "They will gun us all down right here."

Gloria could barely speak, but she managed to say, "Did you bring the police?"

Before Elton could answer, an officer came from the side and tackled Jamal to the ground.

"Jamal Jones, you're under arrest," the cop said as he wrestled Jamal down, turned him over, grabbed his hands, and put them behind his back. "You have the right to remain silent. Anything you say can and will be used against you in a court of law." He read Jamal his Miranda rights as he slapped on the handcuffs, then jerked him up from the ground.

"Stop it! Don't hurt him!" Gloria screamed as Elton tried to hold her.

"Ma'am, we got this." It was the black officer, Detective King, who was in their house that first day. "Let us do our job."

Gloria ignored him and spun to face her husband. "I can't believe you," she said, her voice trembling as she broke free. "You called the police? On your own flesh and blood?"

"I did what I thought was right." Elton's eyes were watering, but she didn't care. "We're not going to let our son run. We're not going to ruin his life or ours," he said, his voice hoarse. "They agreed not to press charges against you if I led them here," he added.

Gloria heaved, trying to catch her breath, as tears ran down her face.

"Mama!" Jamal called out as they tossed him in the back of a patrol car and slammed the door.

"I'm coming, baby!" she cried as an officer and Elton held her back. "You'd better not hurt him!" she screamed at the officers.

They ignored her as they got in the front seat and sped off.

Gloria sobbed as she turned to her husband. Her whole body was shaking. "I will never forgive you for this. Never," she said before racing off to her car to follow her son to the police station.

15

All her life she had been taught not to hate. But right about now, there was no better verb to describe her feelings. Gloria didn't know how she'd ever be able to get over the contempt she had for her husband at this very moment.

"Honey, please understand," Elton said, trying to approach her.

Gloria was shivering with anger. "I'm not going to tell you again. Get away from me," she said through gritted teeth. She stepped out of his reach. She didn't want his touch. She didn't want him sharing the same air as her.

"I just want to see my son," she said, her voice cracking. They'd been in the Jasper police station for an hour now and no one had told them anything. Elton had gone to try to get answers. "Why won't they tell you how he is?" Gloria snapped. "How he's doing? Since you're in cahoots with them now, you should be able to find out what's going on."

Elton ignored her dig and kept his voice calm. "Detective King said it's going to take a while for them to process him in.

We're not going to be able to see him. Let's just go home and talk about it."

"Elton Jones. I'm going to tell you again. Leave me alone," Gloria said. Her words were dripping with venom.

"Look, I know you don't understand why I did what I did—"

"You're right," she said, cutting him off. "I don't understand and if something happens to my son behind those jailhouse doors, I will never, ever forgive you."

"Gloria, it's in God's hands now."

She jabbed her finger in his face. "Don't give me that crap about God. I know my God. This ain't about Him. This is about you. You don't want to be shamed. You don't want to be bothered with cops and reporters. Your selfishness led you to turn our only son in. Our only child," she cried.

Elton's lips pressed together. His chest rose, then fell. He exhaled, then simply said, "He was wrong. Our only child committed a crime and was wrong."

"And we could've figured out how to make it right. But instead, you just turned him over to these racist cops. Knowing they got a death warrant out for him." The thought of what those cops were doing to Jamal behind those doors was tearing apart Gloria's stomach.

"I did what I had to do," Elton repeated.

"No, you did what you *wanted* to do. You did what was best for Elton because that's all that ever matters. Jamal was right. You never wanted him. He brought shame to you since the day he was born."

"Don't go there," he said.

"Don't do what? Tell the truth? Our son has fought all his life for your love. And you're the one that's wrong." She stopped before she said some things she would regret. Right now she had no words for him. There was nothing more that she wanted to say to him. Gloria marched back up to the front desk. "Has your supervisor come in yet?"

"Ma'am," the bleached-blond desk clerk said as she chomped on a piece of gum like a cow chewing on hay, "I told you my supervisor is having dinner with his family. He don't like to be disturbed during dinner."

"Well, did you tell him it's an emergency?" Gloria said.

"Well, what constitutes an emergency to you," she said, not bothering to hide her attitude, "don't necessarily constitute an emergency for everyone." She leaned back, the buttons on her uniform looking like they were holding on for dear life.

"Look, lady—" Gloria said, banging the counter.

"No, *you* look." The woman leaned forward and pointed her pencil in Gloria's face. "Unless you want to join your son in jail, I suggest you back up away from my desk."

"Gloria." Elton eased up behind her and took her by the elbow. "Come on."

She snatched her arm away and tried to calm down as she talked to the woman again. "Look, all I need to know is has my son been checked in? I need to make sure he's all right."

"Well, I don't know what to tell you," the woman said. "He ain't been processed in the system and until he's in the system, he ain't here!"

"It's not like Jasper has some big high-tech system. Go ask somebody. Hell, go look! See if he's back there!" Gloria was yelling now. Yelling and crying.

The woman folded her arms and glared. "'Cause that's the way you get stuff done, by acting a fool with folks, right?"

"Gloria . . ."

Gloria ignored her husband. She shook her hands to calm herself. "Okay, I'm sorry," she said to the woman. "If you have children—"

"I got six of them," the woman said, cutting her off. "Which is the only reason I'm sittin' here letting you talk to me crazy. Cuz I can't afford to cuss you out and get fired."

"So then you can understand my frustration," Gloria said, pleading. "If one of your sons . . ."

"My son wouldn't shoot a cop." The woman turned her lips up.

"Gloria," Elton said, "I told you this isn't going to get us anywhere."

"I need to know if he's okay."

At that moment, Gloria noticed Detective King walking from a back room. He motioned to the woman Gloria was arguing with to let her know he would take over. The woman rolled her eyes at Gloria, then stepped away.

"Mrs. Jones," Detective King said, "I need you to calm down, okay? You're causing quite a scene."

"Is Jamal here? Is he okay?" Gloria asked. She didn't have time to hear his admonishments.

"He is okay. Nobody touched him. I made sure of it. I promised your husband that I would look out for him."

"Are you going to stay here with him? Are you going to spend the night in his cell?" Gloria asked. She was grateful to hear that he was okay, but she would get no peace until she saw it for herself.

"No, but all we can do is pray for the best."

Pray, pray, pray. Everybody wanted her to pray. Obviously, her prayers weren't working. She wanted action, not prayers.

"Just understand that I'm doing all that I can to keep him safe," Detective King continued. "There's a lot of attention on this case. I reiterated that to my fellow officers. So, if something happens to Jamal, they know they're under scrutiny. Maybe that will keep them calm."

"Maybe?" Gloria snapped. "You want me to trust my son with some maybes?"

"Look, just go on home," Detective King said. "Find you an attorney and let's go about trying to take care of this with your son the legal way."

Gloria took a deep breath. She knew he was right. She wouldn't get anywhere acting a fool in this police station. If anything, she would just aggravate these people even more and they'd take it out on her son.

"Come on, Gloria, let's go home," Elton said again.

Detective King nodded. "I suggest you listen to your husband."

Gloria cut her eyes at Elton but ignored him. "I'll go home," she said. "But I'm gonna be back in the morning and I'll be back every single day until somebody tells me something."

"I understand that," he said. "I wouldn't expect anything less."

"Let's go," Elton said.

Gloria glared at her husband. "The only place you need to go, Reverend Jones, is straight to hell." She stormed out of the building, angrier than she'd ever been in her life.

16

The hustle of the Harris County District Attorney's Office was something out of a network TV show. Prosecutors scrambled, attorneys bargained, defendants prayed. Kay was going to miss this atmosphere.

She reminded herself not to get too cocky. This was a contentious election. But Kay had already begun noting some things that she would change. It's not that her boss, Sam, wasn't doing a good job, but he hated ruffling racial feathers, so she'd seen him come down on the lenient side too many times.

"So, you have the *20/20* interview at nine, then the *Houston Chronicle* at ten." Loni's hard-driving planning mode shook Kay out of her thoughts.

"Thanks," Kay said just as her boss tapped on her office door.

"Good morning, Kay," Sam said, walking in before she could invite him in. "Hello, Loni."

"Hello, Mr. Turner," Loni said as she headed toward the door. "Mrs. Christiansen, I'll go make sure the conference room is set up."

Kay waited until Loni was gone and smiled at Sam. "Wow. I get a visit from the boss twice in one month. I don't know if that's good or bad."

"Always good when it comes to you, Kay," he said. "I came to personally hand-deliver this." He handed her a thick manila folder. "Your last case before you become my boss. It's out of Jasper."

Kay took the folder, opened it, then began sifting through the stack of papers.

"Oh, I heard about this case on the news," she said.

"Well, they caught him and you know they're not playing," Sam said. "This thing will be fast-tracked. Seems like they're trying to ward off any racial unrest. Some civil rights folks have already gotten riled up. They have a march planned this weekend and everything."

"So, they are protesting? But isn't there video of the kid shooting the cop?"

"Doesn't seem to matter," Sam said. "Black kid, white cop, Jasper, Texas, equals a recipe for disaster. They're anticipating a change in venue and wanted to give us a heads-up to get ready for it."

"Should I be taking this case, though?" Kay asked. Granted, the election was just over two months away, but a trial like this could drag on for many months.

Sam nodded. "This is a high-profile case. Lots of media attention. Not only good for you for the election, but good for the department. Plus, they'll be less likely to scream about any improprieties if you're the prosecutor."

Kay hated being given cases because of the color of her skin.

"Why don't we have Brandon do it?" she asked, referring to one of her black colleagues.

"Because Brandon can barely win a seat belt violation case."

Kay wanted to ask why he was even on the team then, but she knew it was because Brandon's grandfather was one of Sam's biggest contributors. Kay wanted to name one of the other blacks in the prosecutor's office, but she knew it was moot. Yes, it was an added bonus that she was black working this case, but she knew Sam really wanted her because of her winning record.

"We need a win on this case. We've *got* to have a win on this case," he said as if he were reading her mind.

Kay studied the mug shot of the young boy and something drew her in. Something about him seemed familiar. Maybe it was the eyes. She'd seen a lot of criminals and this kid didn't have criminal eyes. But judging from the report, he was a criminal.

She skimmed the report some more. "So, he shot a decorated police office. Wow, and the cop had a newborn baby?" she asked.

"Yep. And even though he's guilty as sin, there's talk that the cop provoked him and you know with everything going on with all the police brutality cases, folks are already all riled up. I wouldn't be surprised if Al Sharpton, Jesse Jackson, and the rest of them show up."

Kay didn't know who "the rest of them" were, but she let it drop. She knew Sam well. He wasn't racist. He was scared. This case could create some serious problems.

"Okay, fine. I'll take a look at it and get to work. Who is his defense attorney?"

Sam shrugged. "Don't know yet. Kinda got this under the table. You think you can handle this one last case, and your election?"

She glanced at the crime scene photos again. "Not only can I handle this case," she said as she tucked the folder under her arm and stood up, "but it'll give me great pleasure to put this hoodlum in jail on my way to the mayor's office."

Sam's shoulders sank with relief. "Now that's what I like to hear. My ace ADA is on the case, so old Sam can rest easy."

17

God was testing her. Truly testing her to see just how much she could handle. That's the only thing that could explain this latest blow she'd just been delivered.

"Bail is denied." The white-haired judge in the tweed blazer and wrinkled white shirt slammed his gavel.

"Judge Humphries . . ." Perry Roberts began.

"Boy, what part of denied do you not get? The de or the nied?" the judge asked, his bushy eyebrows narrowing as he peered over his rimmed glasses.

Gloria wanted to pass out. She knew when the judge walked into the small Jasper courtroom, minus a robe, looking like the leader of the "good ol' boy" system, they were in trouble.

She glanced over at her terrified son. When they'd brought him out and she saw the bruises on his face, the way he looked beaten and broken, her heart felt like someone was doling out their own beating on her.

Gloria knew that Perry had tried his best. A longtime member of Mount Sinai and a friend of the family, he was retired but agreed to come back and help them with this case. It had been two weeks since Jamal was arrested. Two of the longest weeks of her life, second only to the eight days she didn't know whether her son was dead or alive.

Gloria had spent the first week after Jamal's arrest refusing to speak to her husband. The first two days he'd given her space. But by day three, he was demanding they talk. When she refused, his frustration turned to anger. And when she declined to go to church with him on the Sunday following Jamal's arrest, that anger had turned to fury. But Gloria didn't care. He had betrayed their family in the worst possible way and she never planned to forgive him for it.

The only reason she had let some of the anger go was because Perry had returned to town and told her it was crucial that they present a united front at today's bail hearing.

But as Elton reached for her hand, Gloria once again drew it away. It was going to take a lot of prayer to ever truly forgive her husband.

"Please transport the prisoner back to his cell. Court is dismissed," the judge said, motioning toward the bailiff.

"Mama . . ." Jamal reached for her like he used to do when he was a baby and she was the only one who could comfort him.

The tears Gloria had been fighting back came at full force at the sound of her son's childlike voice as the bailiff dragged him away.

"It's okay, baby," Gloria called out after him. "We're gonna get you out of here!"

And just like that, he was gone. Whisked back to his cell, as Detective Martin, whom Gloria hadn't even noticed in the back of the courtroom, grinned his approval. This time, when Elton went to hold her, she let him. Otherwise, she would've collapsed to the floor.

"Let's go in the conference room and talk," Perry said once the judge had dismissed them. He led them into a small conference room right outside the courtroom.

"What just happened?" Elton asked.

"What you can expect in a place like Jasper." Perry sighed as they all sat down around the table. "Overall, we've got some good people in this town. But we have a lot of folks with the old way of thinking. That's why we have to ask for a change of venue. I have no doubt they're going to expedite this trial. There are only three judges in Jasper. Two of them are just like Judge Humphries."

Gloria knew that was coming. The national media had caught wind of the story and somehow her son had become the poster child for both police harassment and "Young Thugs Gone Wild." She didn't want to lead a cause. She didn't want the attention.

Gloria just wanted her son home and their boring life back.

"Okay, so a change of venue should be good, right?" Elton asked. "We don't need a jury full of folks who have already condemned Jamal."

"Oh, you definitely need a change of venue. But I can't do it," Perry said.

"I know you're retired and came out of retirement just for this," Elton said, "but we need you, man."

"I know that," Perry replied. "And I wish that I could deliver." He patted a folder that was in front of him. "But this is more than I can handle. I'm old, Reverend Jones."

"Yeah, but you used to be good."

"*Used* to be," he echoed. "I'm sixty-eight years old. I haven't tried a case in five years."

Gloria hadn't been able to speak. She just clutched the wad of tissue in her hand as she rocked back and forth.

"I can file the change of venue for you," Perry continued. "It's best to go to Houston. If I were you, I'd work on finding someone there right away."

"We can't afford one of those pricey attorneys," Gloria said.

"We're struggling to hold on at the church as it is," Elton added. "You know the economy has hit us especially hard and tithes and offerings are way down and it's just by the grace of God we're even still hanging on to the building."

"I'm so sorry," Perry repeated.

"We don't know any attorneys in Houston," Gloria cried, the sinking feeling in her stomach intensifying.

"Shoot, we don't know any attorneys but you," Elton said.

"And I simply can't do this justice," Perry said with finality.

"So what are we supposed to do?" Gloria asked.

Perry pushed a card in their direction. "This is an attorney named Riley Manning. He got his start in my office and I've kept tabs on him. He's a good guy and real good at what he does."

"But he doesn't know Jamal like you do," Gloria protested.

"He's good, though," Perry replied. "He'll represent Jamal well. I am so sorry and I wish that I had better news for you, but you have to get a change of venue and there's no way I can take on a criminal trial in Houston."

Gloria stood, clutching her purse to her chest. "Thank you, Perry." She turned around and headed out the door. She had to get out of there before she had a serious breakdown.

"Thanks, Perry. We'll call him," Elton said.

Gloria didn't say anything on the walk back to the parking lot. Once they were inside his pickup truck, Elton reached over and took her hand. "I'm sorry, honey. This is stressful on us all."

She wasn't interested in his apologies. She pulled her hand away. "What are we going to do, Elton?"

"I just don't know."

They sat in silence for a minute, then Gloria said, "Maybe we can do a fund-raiser at the church, like a legal defense fund-raiser."

Elton shook his head. "No. I can't go before those people and ask them for a dime."

"Why not? This is your son we're talking about."

"Because we have a small church, that's why. We'll raise what? At most, five hundred dollars? That won't even pay for the consultation, let alone a whole defense."

"So what are we going to do?"

"Well, we can just go with a public defender."

She quickly dismissed that idea. She couldn't let her son's life hang in the hands of an overworked public defender. "What about this Riley guy?"

"We can't afford him. Even if he works us a deal, we can't afford it."

"We can mortgage the house."

"That is my daddy's house," Elton said, horrified at the suggestion.

"And this is your son."

Gloria knew that most mothers were closer to their sons, but given their circumstances, she would've thought Elton would have a stronger connection. But since Jamal's birth, it was almost as if

Elton had animosity about the disruption in their lives. And now she was seeing a side of her husband that was the ultimate manifestation of that.

"My son had no concern for me when he decided to hang out with thugs. Now look at where it's left him," Elton grumbled.

She didn't bother responding to that and just turned and stared out the window.

After a silent ride, Elton turned the car into their driveway, turned the car off, and said, "Call the Riley man. But unless he's planning to do it for five hundred, or pro bono, or out of the kindness of his heart, then we just need to get ready because our son will be going away for a very long time."

Then he got out of the car like there was nothing else that needed to be said.

18

This had been the longest two hours of Gloria's life. That's how much time it took Gloria and Elton to drive from Jasper to Houston to meet with Riley Manning. Gloria had been thrilled that he'd agreed to meet them on such short notice. Elton hadn't shown much emotion, saying he didn't want to get his hopes up.

They rode in silence most of the way, the tension between the two of them unlike anything she'd ever felt before. Gloria prayed that this wasn't an indication of things to come. For the most part, she and Elton had always enjoyed a decent marriage. While he had his boorish ways, she knew that Elton Jones was a man who loved his family. He just didn't know how to show it. He didn't know how to move past the past.

Elton was also a proud man who hated for shame to be brought his way and this was the pinnacle of shame.

"Do I get off here, or keep going around on 59?" Elton asked as they approached downtown Houston.

Gloria had been struggling to forgive her husband. But until her son was safe, she just didn't see how that was possible. Her mother had, however, convinced her that holding on to anger right now wouldn't do Jamal a bit of good. That's the only reason she was trying to work with Elton—for her son.

Gloria glanced down at the directions that she'd printed out. "You're supposed to get off on Highway 59 and take that first right. His office is between Main and Fannin."

They didn't say anything else as Elton navigated off the freeway. They pulled up in front of the high-rise building and were met by the parking valet.

"Can you tell us where self-parking is?" Elton asked, making it clear they weren't interested in the valet's services.

The valet pointed to the left as Gloria rolled her eyes. Heaven forbid her husband shell out fifteen dollars for valet parking. But she knew that right about now she didn't need to be saying anything about money. Even with their retirement, they wouldn't have money to cover a lengthy trial. She'd spent years as a secretary for a local insurance company, but they'd shut down two years ago and she hadn't worked outside of the church since. So their money was tight.

They parked in the self-parking garage and made their way inside.

"He's on the thirteenth floor," Gloria said, looking at the card that Perry had given her.

Elton still didn't say a word as he pushed the up button.

Gloria was just going to let her husband have his moment because her attention here needed to be focused on convincing this man to take her son's case.

She and Elton made their way into the upscale office and were greeted by elegant furniture and contemporary art. Awards touting the firm's record adorned the walls, as did newspaper clippings about several of their cases.

Elton said what she had been thinking. "This man is not about to work for us pro bono," he mumbled as he looked around the office.

"Shhhh. We're going to think positive."

"Hmph," he muttered.

Gloria took the lead as they approached the receptionist's desk. "Good afternoon, we're here to see Riley Manning."

"Is he expecting you?"

"He is. We have a one o'clock appointment. We're a little early."

"No problem." The receptionist smiled. "Have a seat. I'll let him know you're here."

Gloria nodded, then motioned toward the lobby sitting area for Elton to take a seat. They both sat down and the look on Elton's face said he'd rather be anywhere but here. But Gloria wasn't going to concern herself with her husband's discomfort. Right now, they were on a mission.

"Hello."

They both stood to greet the man who had just walked over to them.

"I'm Riley Manning." He extended his hand. His demeanor was commanding. With strong features and an athletic build, Riley was one of the nicest-dressed men she'd ever seen. Gloria could see why he would be powerful in the courtroom.

Elton shook his hand. It wasn't often that anyone intimidated him, but Gloria could tell that her husband was nervous. "Elton Jones. This is my wife, Gloria."

"Nice to meet you. Sorry it's under these circumstances." He pointed to a conference room. "We can just go in here and chat."

Gloria led the way as the three of them moved into the room. After they were seated around a long mahogany table, Riley jumped right in.

"So tell me a little bit about your case. Perry filled me in on the details. He was an awesome mentor to me, so when he tells me this is something I should consider, I need to consider." Riley tried to smile to relax the tension in the room. And while Gloria tried to feign a smile, Elton didn't bother.

"We don't have any money," Elton blurted out.

Gloria wanted to die. He was always talking about embarrassing someone and that was the epitome of embarrassing.

Riley chuckled. "Yes, Perry explained the situation to me. How much do you have?"

"Nothing. We have nothing. We're barely making it now," Elton said a little too quickly.

"Well, there are some legal funds that can assist, but we're not at that point yet. I've read up on your son's case and I want to be clear: he does admit to shooting the police officer, right?"

"He doesn't have any choice but to admit it since he filmed it," Elton snapped.

"Yes," Gloria interjected, darting hard eyes at her husband. "He admits it, but it was an accident, and happened only after the officer attacked him. He was scared for his life, and that's what we want to make sure comes across. The jury has to know it was an accident, brought on by a cop that was harassing and threatening him, even though he wasn't breaking any laws. My son isn't a murderer. He's a good boy who got caught up in a horrible situation."

Riley held his hands up. "Okay. No need to convince me. If Perry vouches for the kid, then I'm on board."

Gloria got excited. "So you'll take the case?"

"Whoa, hold up. We have to be clear on this. If Perry vouches for your son, this is something that I would consider. Unfortunately, I just don't know if I can do your case justice."

Those were not the words that she wanted to hear. "Please, Mr. Manning," Gloria pleaded. "You're our only hope. They're expediting this case, trying to make sure it's resolved quickly."

"I get that, and I understand your need for a defense, but my issue isn't whether I think this is a case worthy of representing, because I do. I'm hesitant for other reasons. Number one, my caseload is already overwhelming."

"Isn't this a big firm?" Gloria asked. She wasn't trying to be snippy, but she didn't know what could be bigger than this case.

"Hold on," Riley said. "That's not my main problem. My main issue is that I'm getting married in three weeks and I promised my fiancée I would not take any new cases. We're taking an extended vacation so I will be out of pocket for a month. You can't afford that."

Gloria knew it was wrong, but she wanted to tell him that he could get married anytime, that right now, her son's life was on the line so that should take precedence over everything else.

He must've seen the dejection on her face because he said, "Let me see what I can do and I'll get back to you."

"But we have to move fast," Gloria replied.

"I know, Perry made that very clear. The change of venue has already been approved and it's going to the grand jury next week."

"A jury already?" Gloria exclaimed.

"No, it's not like that. A grand jury. They're a group of people who gather to decide if charges should be filed."

"So, there's a chance that this could not even go to trial?" Elton asked.

"Could they really decide to do that?" Gloria added, feeling a sliver of hope.

Riley shook his head, shattering her momentary elation. "Nah, I'm pretty sure they'll indict. They're going to want this case to run its course because of all the attention it is already getting, and of course, the dynamics involved."

"You mean the fact that my son is black and the cop is white? I bet if it was the other way around, he'd get off," Gloria snapped.

"Well, we can't live in a world of what-ifs," Riley said. "But let me work some things and I'll get back to you in the next couple of days."

"That's all we can ask for," Elton said, standing. "Thank you."

Riley stood as well and shook Elton's hand. "Don't thank me yet. Whether I take on this case or not, there's a lot of work to be done."

"And we're committed to doing it," Gloria said, her voice trembling.

Riley smiled, trying to comfort her. "I believe you are. The love of your son is evident in your eyes. He's lucky to have a mother like you."

Those words reignited her firestorm of tears. Elton ushered her out of the office and back to the parking garage. He didn't say anything as he pulled out.

Gloria watched the downtown skyline fade from view. Elton grumbled as they slowed because of backed-up traffic. She knew what he was thinking—the same thing as her. They needed to get used to this Houston traffic because it looked like they'd be caught up in it a whole lot more.

19

R iley Manning patted his stomach as he leaned back in his chair. He, his fiancée, Michelle, Kay, and Phillip had just finished dinner and Kay was bringing out key lime pie for desert.

"Kay, you really put your foot in that jambalaya," Riley said.

"Why, thank you. I try," Kay said as she set a piece of pie in front of him.

"Yeah, she put her foot in the checkbook that she wrote to the caterer," Phillip joked.

"I don't know what you're talking about. I can cook." She removed his dessert plate. "Just for that, no pie for you."

Phillip took his plate back. "I know you can cook. That's how you got me. But you don't."

"That's because she's too busy throwing criminals behind bars and getting ready to be the next mayor of Houston. Do you think you're ready to be the First Gentleman?" Riley took a bite of his pie as he winked at his friend. Phillip and Riley had met while undergraduates at the University of Texas at Austin and remained the best of friends.

"Yeah, maybe I'll retire and just sit at home and take care of the kids," Phillip replied.

They laughed some more, talked about the latest news and world affairs, and as the men turned their conversation to sports, Kay turned to Riley's fiancée. "So, Michelle. Did you enjoy your dinner? You barely ate anything," Kay said. "And I can't believe that you aren't getting any pie."

Kay had only met Michelle Moore a few times, but Riley was clearly in love with her. And if he liked her, Kay loved her.

"I did enjoy it," Michelle replied. "Just watching what I eat because I have the most to-die-for wedding dress and I can't afford to gain a pound."

"I can't believe you two are going to elope," Kay said.

"It's the second marriage for both of us, so we don't need all the fanfare," Michelle said.

Riley, who had jumped back into their conversation, pulled her close. "Yeah, the money we would've spent on a wedding will be spent touring the Riviera for four weeks."

"Honey, do you see how he took four weeks off from work? It is possible," Kay joked as she stood and began removing plates.

"Look who's talking," Riley replied. "Both of you guys are workaholics. That's how you ended up together."

"Yeah, I know." Phillip pulled his wife down on his lap. "But we really are trying to get better because we both know that as much as we love our work, family really is what matters most."

Her husband was right about that. They'd found that as busy

as they got, they always made time for family. So one of them was always at a game, dance recital, open house, whatever.

She kissed Phillip, stood back up, and went into the kitchen, where she dropped their plates in the sink, then took her seat back at the table. Phillip filled all of their glasses with dessert wine, and as they sipped Riley said, "Have you guys heard about the kid who shot the cop out of Jasper?"

"Yeah, saw it on the news when it first happened," Phillip replied. "Kay is actually prosecuting that case."

Normally, Kay wouldn't have liked her husband sharing that information with anyone, but they were having a press conference tomorrow anyway. Besides, Riley was one of the few people in the world whom she trusted.

Riley sat up in his seat, shocked. "Really? I didn't even know that the change of venue was public knowledge."

"What rock have you been under?" Kay said. "Everyone is talking about it. It was inevitable."

"I've been under this rock called getting ready to wrap up my cases so I can get married in peace," Riley said, blowing a kiss at Michelle.

They laughed.

"But seriously, how do you know about the change of venue?" Kay asked.

Riley exchanged glances with Michelle and she sat back as if to let him do his job. "The parents of the boy came to me to represent them," Riley answered. "You remember that lawyer I worked for when I first got out of law school?" he asked Phillip.

Phillip thought for a moment. "Oh, yeah. Perry something. He was a nice old man. We all wondered why you would go work for him in that country town."

"Because that nice old man was good at what he did. I heard him speak at an event and was mesmerized. I learned a lot under that old man," Riley replied.

"What does that have to do with the Jasper kid, though?" Kay asked.

"Well, like I said, Perry knows the kid's family. He referred them to me since it looks like they're moving the trial to Houston. But I'm not going to be able to do it because of the wedding." He turned to Phillip. "That's what I wanted to talk to you about. I was going to see if it was a case you'd be interested in."

Kay raised an eyebrow as she glanced at her husband. "Wow, he's been fascinated with this case since he first heard about it," she said.

"I have," Phillip said, the eagerness evident in his voice. "It raises so many issues, the right to record, police harassment."

"The dangers of a police officer's job," Kay added.

"Okay, okay," Riley replied. "Why don't y'all save this for the courtroom?"

"It's an open-and-shut case, though," Kay added with a smirk.

Phillip smiled at his wife. "Hmmm. Might be nice to go up against my wife again."

They hadn't faced off in a courtroom in two years, but it was an exhilarating experience. They both were so driven and passionate, it made for an interesting case. They were tied in terms of their records against one another. She'd won two and he'd won two. This case would be a tiebreaker. Of course, that wouldn't trivialize things if Phillip took the case on, but it would add another layer of dynamics.

"You know you want to take the case," Riley said. "I see the way your eyes are already dancing."

"I just might have to consider that if my wife says okay," Phillip said. "I mean, I actually did some digging already, just trying to get information on this kid."

Kay hadn't known her husband had gone to that extreme, but it didn't surprise her. "Fine by me. Bring it," she joked.

"I just might," he replied.

Kay wasn't sure if her husband would really take the case since he had his hands full with his mentoring group and his current cases, but it would be fun to be back in the courtroom against him. Fun and challenging—and a great way to wrap up her tenure in the DA's office before moving on to become mayor.

20

Yet another analyst was dissecting her son's case. Gloria sat watching the news as the newscaster stalled for time. They were waiting on the press conference, announcing the trial was officially being moved to Houston. She assumed a change of venue would give them a fighting chance. But from the tone of the anchor, to the reporter in the field, to the commentators discussing and analyzing this case, her son had already been convicted in the court of public opinion.

It didn't help that there were protests last weekend. She hadn't organized a single one, but somehow ten, then twenty, then thirty people had gathered in front of the Jasper Police Department demanding a fair trial.

Gloria didn't understand it. No one had asked her how she felt about this. No one had asked her opinion on any protests. Dix and Brian were out on bail and milking their fifteen minutes of fame. She'd seen them interviewed many times. In fact, a reporter had just finished speaking with Dix, who reminded viewers that they "weren't bothering anyone when the cop racially profiled them and got into a fight with Jamal and made Jamal shoot him." Of course, that sent the crowd into a frenzy, but Gloria wanted to scream. That idiot didn't even realize he was further convicting her son!

She just wanted it all to go away.

The meeting with Riley had gone well and she prayed that he would take on their case. Gloria wished that he had already signed on so they could have a press conference of their own. The picture of Jamal as some careless thug was already being painted and she wanted the world to know the truth.

The sound of the telephone snapped her out of her thoughts. Her phone had been ringing incessantly and were it not for Jamal, she would've cut the ringer off altogether.

Gloria picked up the phone. "Hello?"

"You have a collect call from the Jasper County Jail. Press one to accept," the automated system announced.

Gloria's heart fluttered and she almost dropped the phone as she pressed one. "Jamal?"

"Hey, Mama." His voice sounded weak, childlike.

"Hey, sweetheart."

"Daddy's not there, is he? I tried to call when I knew he wouldn't be there."

Gloria struggled to stay strong. He had to be having a hard time. Hearing her fall apart would only make it worse right now.

"He's at the church," she managed to say. "Jamal, I know you're angry with your father but—"

"Ma, no disrespect, but please don't talk to me about him."

She inhaled, knowing it would be useless to push the issue right now. Jamal was just as stubborn as his father and it was hard to ask Jamal to forgive Elton when she was still mad herself.

"Well, son, just know I'm working as hard as I can for you."

"Thanks, Ma."

A beat passed, then she asked, "You okay?"

"Not really. They couldn't put me in a juvenile facility? I'm in here with some hard-core criminals, Mom. And I'm scared."

She swallowed the lump in her throat. "I know, baby. We're working as hard as we can."

Someone in the background yelled, then there was a loud scuffle and it sounded like Jamal dropped the phone.

"Jamal?" Gloria called out, her heart going into panic mode.

It took a minute, but he finally said, "I'm here."

"What happened?" Gloria asked.

"A fight broke out. I thought they were gonna make me hang up."

Gloria didn't think she'd ever heard her son sound so scared. She had never so much as set foot in a jail so she could only imagine what was going on. "Oh, it just sounds horrible in there."

"It is. It's only about twelve guys here, but three are in for murder. A couple for gang banging and the rest drugs. These dudes are hardcore, Ma. But they say Houston is worse. They're moving me there tomorrow."

"Perry got you moved. The criminal element may be worse, but I'd rather that than some racist gun-toting cops hell-bent on revenge. None of us can rest with you there."

"Yeah, because these cops are looking at me like they want to take me out back and hang me from a tree."

"But no one has done anything to you, right?"

"No." He released a long sigh. "But it's just a matter of time. So Mr. Perry said y'all gotta find another attorney. Have you found anybody yet?" Jamal said.

"We're working on it. We met with this man in Houston and we're just prayerful that he'll take the case," Gloria replied.

"What if he doesn't?"

"We're just going to think positive thoughts, Jamal."

He was quiet again. "Mama, I didn't mean to bring you shame."

"You know I'm not the least bit worried about shame."

He sounded like he was crying. "I know I have to do some time, but I'm not a cold-blooded killer."

Gloria swallowed the lump in her throat. "I know it's hard and we'll find just the right person to prove that you aren't."

"I love you."

"I love you, too."

She hung up the phone just before a river of tears began flowing.

21

I t was showtime!

Kay took one last glance in the floor-length mirror in her office's conference room. She gave herself a thumbs-up. Her navy Christian Dior suit complemented her size eight frame and her shoulder-length haircut added just the touch of femininity without messing with her authoritative look. She was ready to show the world that she was ready.

Of course, she'd handled many cases in her ten years as a prosecutor, but this would be the most high-profile case she'd ever had, and she knew that with the election looming, extra attention would be paid to how she handled this situation.

"Are you ready?" Loni asked, giving her the once-over.

"I stay ready," she replied.

Loni nodded her approval. "That you do."

Kay's assistant appeared on the side of her and handed her a tip sheet. "I wrote down some of the highlights of the case," Valerie said. "Not that you need it, since you're so good, but better to be prepared."

Valerie was right. Kay had studied this case backward and forward over the past week. Cramming wasn't her nature, but between the campaign and trying to wrap up her other cases, she'd had to take a crash course in Jamal Jones. At least the case itself. She'd been so swamped that she hadn't gotten around to his personal life. She did learn that he didn't have a record, but she wanted to know everything about him—he probably was from a broken home and would try to use that as an excuse for ending up in a life of crime.

"Thanks, Valerie. Make sure you pull the personal info on Jamal. I want to know what his grades were like, his mama, his daddy or lack thereof, everything you can find. I want to be prepared for whatever they throw at me." She wasn't worried about today's press conference because it was just about the case moving to Houston. Technically, she didn't "officially" know that until two days ago.

"You got it," Valerie replied. "But what if it doesn't go to trial? I'm hearing the tape is pretty cut-and-dry so he might just plead out to avoid the death penalty."

"Hoping he will," Kay said. "But I want to make sure we get out front and be ready in case they try to throw a curveball."

"Well, we're ready to do this," Loni said. "They have you set up at the podium. They've blown up the pictures of the suspect. And get this, the officer's family is here."

"Oh, great, so they drove up from Jasper?" Kay asked.

"Yes, it's television gold, complete with his elderly parents, the teary-eyed wife, the cooing baby boy, the adorable little girl with perfect pigtails. Oh, my goodness, the family is so going to up the sympathy factor. I've already instructed the photographers to make sure they get good shots of the family. We've positioned them at the front, at just the right angle to include your photo in all of their shots."

Kay felt slightly uneasy about using these people's time of grief to further her campaign, but she knew it was pretty much standard procedure in such a case, so she would let Loni and her team do what they did so well.

"Hopefully, like Valerie said, this won't even go to trial." That would be perfect for Kay. She'd get the publicity, make her boss happy, and shut the case down without a tedious trial. "Where's the boy now?"

"He's being transferred as we speak," Valerie chimed in.

"Wow, that was fast," Kay said.

"The family requested that he be moved because they were worried about his safety in the Jasper jail," Valerie said.

"As well they should be." Kay wanted justice in a court of law, but she was no fool. Some of those vigilantes in Jasper wouldn't hesitate to dispense their own brand of justice. "Valerie, can you gather up all that information by the end of the day?"

"I'm on it." Valerie scurried out of the room.

"The officer's family wants to have a word with you before we start," Loni said. "Is it okay to bring them in?"

"Yes, we have a few minutes," Kay replied. "I'd love to meet them."

Loni opened the door and motioned for the Wilkins family to walk in. Just like Loni said, they were an all-American family. The pain they were feeling lingered over them like a dark cloud.

Kay extended her hand to the young woman who was clearly Officer Wilkins's widow. "Mrs. Wilkins, nice to meet you. I'm sorry it's under these circumstances."

"Thank you for seeing us," Mrs. Wilkins said. "This is my mother- and father-in-law." She pointed to the elderly couple, who nodded their greeting.

"We just, we just wanted to ask that you get this to trial as soon as possible. We can't take much more of this," Mrs. Wilkins said.

"I want you to know I won't stop until I get justice for your husband. I've taken prosecutorial discretion and he will be tried as an adult."

"Thank God," Officer Wilkins's father said.

The look on Mrs. Wilkins's face crushed Kay's heart. Her eyes were sunken and hollow and it almost seemed like her soul was empty.

"Keith was my everything," she said. "We've been together since we were fourteen. My babies," her hand went to her stomach, "including the one I'm carrying, will never know their father."

Kay was speechless. "I'm sorry. I didn't know you were pregnant."

Slow tears trickled down her face. "Neither did Keith," she said. "I found out the day before I buried him."

Kay felt someone pulling at her skirt. She looked down to see the dimpled little girl tugging at her hemline.

"Are you gonna lock up the bad man that killed my daddy?" she asked.

Kay knelt down to get eye level with the little girl. "Yes, I'm going to do everything I can to make sure we get justice for your father."

"Please," the little girl cried as she clutched a teddy bear. "I'm sad. Who's gonna take me to Daddies and Donuts at my school now?"

Mrs. Wilkins pulled her daughter close as Kay stood back up.

"Please, just help us get some closure," Mrs. Wilkins said, trembling as she held her daughter tight.

Kay took her hand. "I promise you, I will put your husband's killer in jail. I will make him pay, if it's the last thing I do."

Kay took each case seriously, but for some reason, seeing this fatherless family, she couldn't help but feel this one had just turned personal.

22

Gloria watched in anticipation as the TV news anchor announced that the prosecuting attorney was approaching the podium. The well-dressed prosecutor ignored the flash of bulbs as she took her place at the front of the room. Her shoulder-length hair was pulled back out of her face and she had on just enough makeup to bring out her beauty, but not seem overbearing.

"Good evening. And thank you all for gathering here," the prosecutor began.

Gloria leaned in and peered at the television. Where did she know that woman from? After a moment, a memory flashed. *Could it be?*

Gloria shook the thought off. Desperation was making her delusional.

"Good afternoon, I'm Kay Christiansen with the Harris County District Attorney's Office. Our office has been tasked with the controversial trial out of Jasper, Texas, involving sixteen-year-old Jamal Jones." Jamal's mug shot appeared on the screen. "Jones is accused in the shooting death of a decorated Jasper police officer, Keith

Wilkins. Jones will be tried as an adult by this office. We want to assure the community that justice will be served." The camera panned over to what must've been Officer Wilkins's family.

"We want Officer Wilkins's family, his beautiful daughter, his precious baby boy, and his lovely wife to know that their loved one's death will not go unpunished."

"Excuse me," a reporter said, raising her hand. "Are you fighting this hard because crime is a platform you plan to pursue if you're elected mayor?"

"I'm fighting this hard because the family of Officer Wilkins deserves nothing less. Yes, I am running for mayor. But currently I am a prosecutor and until the suspect in this case is brought to justice, my only focus is prosecuting this case to the fullest extent of the law," Kay replied.

To the fullest extent of the law.

Each word cut at Gloria's core. Her son didn't stand a chance. No way could a defense attorney go up against this woman. When she first saw her, Gloria thought that maybe since she was black, they'd stand a chance. But this woman looked like she didn't play and race would play no factor in anything she did.

Gloria studied the woman as she continued talking. When the camera zoomed in closer, all thoughts of delusion were gone. "Oh. My. God," Gloria mumbled. She bolted from her seat and raced into the back study, where Elton was working. She swung his door open, causing him to jump.

"Gloria, what are you doing? You know I don't like to be disturbed when I'm working on my sermon."

"You've got to see this," she said, grabbing the remote for his nineteen-inch office TV. She clicked the on button.

"Look at the prosecutor." She jabbed toward the TV. "The lady that will be trying Jamal's case."

Elton stared at the TV, confused. "Okay, so a black woman is prosecuting him?"

Gloria paused the TV and said, "Look closer."

Elton studied the TV screen for a moment, then shrugged. "I don't know what I'm supposed to be looking for."

"It's Kayla," Gloria said.

Elton's eyes grew wide and he dropped the pen he'd been holding. "Oh my Lord."

They hadn't seen or heard from Kayla Matthews in years.

"That's a good thing, right?" Gloria paced back and forth across the room, struggling to contain her excitement. "I mean, she's the prosecutor. God is looking out for us! I need to go see her."

"No, you will not!" Elton said, pounding his desk as he stood up. His tone caught her off guard.

"What?" Gloria lost her smile and looked at her husband, stunned.

"I forbid it."

"This is our son we're talking about," Gloria said in disbelief.

"What do you think she's going to do? Just let him off? Put her job at risk? To help us out?"

"But . . ."

"But nothing," Elton said with finality. "Leave this alone. Now, we can find Jamal an attorney, but you talking to her is not going to do anyone any good." He was actually shaking as he slid back into his seat. "Digging up the past won't help anyone."

"Elton, I don't believe you."

He slammed his palm on his desk again. "You betrayed me by

going behind my back and hiding Jamal." He stood again, then moved around the desk to face her. "As God is my witness, if you approach Kayla, there will be hell to pay."

He stormed out of the room, leaving her stunned and trying to figure out what just happened.

23

Kay hadn't been able to get that little girl out of her mind.

Who's gonna take me to Daddies and Donuts now?

"Just one more game, Mom. Please, please, please?"

Kay could only laugh at the sight of her son jumping up and down, acting like a child for a change and not some studious college student. That's why she gladly reached in her purse and handed him another twenty so that he and Charlie could go play another game of laser tag.

"Thank you so much!" Ryan exclaimed as he darted back to buy another game.

Camille walked over and set a Diet Coke down in front of Kay. They'd been at laser tag for the last hour and a half and both of them were ready to go. But Kay loved seeing her son relaxed, so she was willing to give him another hour, plus it had given her a chance to catch up with Camille.

"Are they playing again?" Camille said as she slid into her seat. "This is what, game number four?"

"Yes," Kay said, taking a sip of her drink, "and the last one because I really do have to get home and get some work done."

"Yeah," Camille replied, "I saw the press conference. I thought you said you weren't doing any more cases because of the mayoral race."

"Believe me, I'd rather not. But my boss just kind of put this on my table because it's so high profile."

"Oh, so he needs his ace boon *coon* ADA to take it down?"

Kay laughed, ignoring Camille's obvious racial reference. "You got jokes."

"You know I'm just messing with you," Camille said. "You're the best ADA in that office, black, white, or purple. But that is a pretty sad case."

"For the slain officer, it sure is. And with the video, it shouldn't be hard to prosecute," Kay said.

"I just can't imagine Charlie being caught up in something like that," Camille said.

"Charlie wouldn't be caught up in anything like that," Kay replied. "Neither would Ryan. We got some good kids here. You and I might be busy moms but we make sure our boys are taken care of."

They watched as two little boys dang near knocked each other down trying to get into the laser tag area.

"I don't know, Kay. Sometimes this whole parenting thing has me questioning whether I really know what I'm doing, because my sister gave her son everything, did everything right, and he still took a wrong path, robbing a store when he had the world at his fingertips."

"Yeah, I know that happens," Kay replied. "But we're laying the foundation right for our children. And we just have to trust them. Continue what we've built on."

Camille looked unsure but nodded just the same. "So did the kid that shot the cop have a record?"

"Nope, he hadn't been in any real trouble, but if he's hanging out at one in the morning, looking the way he looked, I'll say it was just a matter of time."

"Didn't they have some kind of protest down there? I saw something about that on the news the other day."

"Yeah, that's what I don't understand," Kay replied. "Black folks get all up in arms behind the wrong causes. Civil rights activists get folks all hyped up and they put on their marching caps when clearly the kid was in the wrong."

"Oh, come on now, Kay. You don't think the justice system is just a little biased against black boys?"

"No, don't get me wrong. I do. I know there are a lot of things that need to be changed with the system. Our sentencing laws are unfair. But we can't continue putting ourselves into bad situations and then when we get capped for it, turn around and talk about 'the white man did us wrong.' I can't tell you the number of young men that come through my office, who are buying and selling dope left and right and the minute they get caught, wanna get mad because the cop is harassing him. Well, the cop is trying to keep the drugs off the street. Stay away from a life of crime and you won't get harassed."

"I wish it was that easy," Camille replied. "I mean, I think we're being unrealistic to think that Ryan and Charlie are exempt just because they're privileged. When a police officer pulls them over, they see a black boy and automatically assume the worst."

"I know that," Kay replied. "That's why I teach my son to obey the law and when you're not obeying the law, don't be defiant. Unfortunately, that's the reality. Until we change the mind-set, let's play it safe and just do what they say. What harm can be done in getting out of the car? It's when we try to be defiant that things always go wrong."

"Hmph," Camille said. "I think we're gonna have to agree to disagree because I don't want my son to become some pansy that shakes in fear every time a cop comes around."

"If he's not doing anything wrong, there's no reason to fear."

"Yeah, tell that to the countless black boys across the country who have been convicted and crucified because of the color of their skin."

"Well, I know you're right to a degree. And that's why I do appreciate the work Phillip is doing. And I want to change some of those things as mayor. I don't know how, but I would love to be able to change that mind-set."

"Girl, please. You're going to need some magic powers." Camille waved her hand like the mere thought was unrealistic.

Kay laughed. "How about we change the subject? How are you and Vincent doing?"

That caused a shift in Camille's demeanor. As hard as Camille tried to act, Kay knew that the divorce was tearing at her soul. "We're doing okay. You know I never thought I'd be getting a divorce. But we're trying to remain amicable for Charlie and Zola's sake."

"You don't think you can work it out?"

"Let's see . . . umm . . . his mistress is carrying twins. Not only do I not think I can work it out, I *know* I can't. I don't do baby-mama drama."

"Yeah, I can't even get mad at you on that one. I wouldn't be able to handle that, either."

Ryan and Charlie finally came bouncing back over. "Okay, I guess we can go now," Ryan said.

"Really? Are you sure? You don't want one more game?" Camille asked.

"We're good," he said with a laugh. "Because I know you're just kidding anyway."

"You know me well," she replied.

"I gotta get home and study anyway," Ryan replied.

"Me, too," Charlie echoed.

"How did we raise such studious young men?" Kay asked.

"We're just some blessed mamas, I guess," Camille said.

As Kay watched them gather up their belongings, she couldn't help but smile. She turned to her friend. "Yeah, we're some of the lucky ones. We have some good kids and we just need to keep on counting our blessings."

24

Gloria had been trying to keep her mind together; right now, laundry was helping her do that. She had just finished the second load when the doorbell rang. She prayed that it wasn't more reporters—they'd been turning away a slew of media requests left and right. But when she glanced outside, Gloria saw a black man standing in a nice suit. Next to him was a bald man wearing a dashiki. There were two men who looked like bodyguards standing behind them. She slid the door open just a bit.

"Hello, may I help you?"

"Are you Mrs. Jones?" the man in the suit asked.

She nodded. "Yes, and you are?" They didn't look like reporters or police.

He extended his hand. "I'm Reverend Luther Clayborn from Greater Good Missionary Baptist Church out of Houston. You may have heard of," he pointed to the dashiki-wearing man next to him, "Minister Reuben Muhammad."

"As-salamu alaykum," he said.

Gloria had no idea what that meant, so she just nodded.

She hadn't heard of either one of the men and she didn't understand why they were on her doorstep.

"Is your husband home? We would like to have a word with you two," Rev. Clayborn said.

"He . . . he is. Hold on." She closed the door and went back to the den, where Elton was perched back in his recliner, watching television. He'd been in his own world since he found out about Kayla. And since Gloria was still salty with him, that was just fine with her. "Elton, there are some men at the front door."

"I'm not in the mood to talk to the police, Gloria." He didn't take his eyes off the TV.

"No, it's not police. These are some ministers from Houston. Luther Clayborn and something Muhammad."

Elton bolted upright. He must have known who they were because he jumped up and put his feet into his slippers and raced to the front of the house.

"Hello," he said, opening the door and vigorously shaking their hands. "It's such an honor to meet you, Reverend Clayborn. I've heard great things about you."

"I was wondering if I could come in and have a quick word with you?" Rev. Clayborn asked.

"Sure," Elton replied, stepping to the side and gesturing for the men to come in.

The men entered. Gloria offered them a glass of lemonade and both of them declined. The bodyguards stood at the door, like they were guarding it.

"Would they like anything?" Gloria asked.

The dashiki-clad man spoke up. "They're fine."

Gloria took a seat next to her husband. She had no idea what these men were here about. But the looks on their faces said they meant business.

"Well, Reverend Jones," Rev. Clayborn began, "let me get straight to the point. We've been following the case of your son, and Minister Muhammad and I think this situation is prime to spearhead our Black Justice Coalition launch."

"Excuse me?" Elton said.

Gloria's ears perked up. She couldn't tell if they were here to help her son or take advantage of him.

"What is a Black Justice Coalition?" Elton asked.

Minister Muhammad spoke up: "We are tired of seeing the black man denigrated and desecrated. And we are here to say we are not going to take it anymore."

Gloria frowned. He sounded like he was giving a prepared speech.

He continued, "We've been looking for the perfect case to launch our campaign and we believe this is it."

Gloria decided to speak up since her husband appeared to be too intimidated to ask questions.

"Why would you want to use my son's case?" she asked.

The two men exchanged glances, like they were trying to decide who would answer.

"Well, because there is video, and video makes this case visual, which paints a picture, if you will, of the battle that our young black men face," Minister Muhammad said.

Rev. Clayborn picked up from there. "We believe that your son, with his clean record, is just what we need to bring attention to our cause. Kind of like Rosa Parks. She wasn't the first person to refuse to give up her seat, but she was the prime candidate to spearhead the cause."

Candidate? Cause? Gloria frowned and looked at Elton. What in the world were these men talking about? And what did this case have to do with Rosa Parks?

"Not to mention the history that Jasper has," added Minister Muhammad. "As you know, this city is a hotbed for racial intolerance. It's a perfect platform to launch this nationwide movement."

"The protests are already in full effect," Rev. Clayborn continued in what now felt like a well-rehearsed presentation. "But right now, they're random. We'll take over, organize, execute, and take this to the national stage."

Gloria looked at her husband and then back at them. They were talking about her son as if he weren't a young boy sitting in a jail cell with real criminals. They were talking about him as a cause. He wasn't some poster child for black crusaders. He was just a frightened sixteen-year-old boy who wanted to come home.

"Elton, say something," Gloria mumbled. She wanted her husband to tell these men to get out of her house, that they weren't interested in what these men were selling.

"Reverend, I know that your church is going through some things," Rev. Clayborn continued. "This case could be just what we need to bring attention back to your church and get you some nationwide coverage."

"We're not interested in coverage," Gloria found herself saying since Elton seemed to have lost his voice. "We're interested in justice."

"And so are we," Rev. Clayborn said. "But justice comes to those who demand it. Have you hired an attorney yet?"

"Well, we're in the process of doing that," Elton replied. "We're just having a little trouble."

"Good, that you haven't hired anyone," Rev. Clayborn replied. "Of course we'll help with your legal fees and, in fact, have an excellent attorney, Jerome Woods. He's worked on several other racially motivated police cases. We've already spoken with him and he is anxious to get on board. Have you done any TV interviews?"

"No," Elton said. "That's not really our thing."

"Well, we have to change that. We have to be vocal and vigilant," Rev. Clayborn said.

Why is he answering these men's questions? Gloria wondered. Elton must have known she was about to lose it because he told the men, "Can we step back in my office to talk about this? As you can imagine, it's pretty difficult on my wife."

She wanted to tell Elton that there was nothing to talk about, ask him why he was entertaining this foolishness. At this point Gloria Jones had no words left for her husband or the men he had just welcomed into their home.

As she watched them walk into the back room, bodyguards included, the disgust she'd felt for her husband jumped to a whole new level.

25

Gloria was making this drive again, but this time she was by herself. It's not that she wanted to keep her husband in the dark, but she couldn't take the negative energy. Right now, her sole focus was on Jamal. She couldn't take the "if onlys" and "I told you sos" that Elton had been spewing lately. She just wanted to figure out how to save her son. And the way Elton had raved about how helpful the minister would be, Gloria knew that she'd have to do this alone because her husband had lost all good sense.

Gloria's mind drifted back to the conversation that she'd had with Riley yesterday, just minutes after the ministers left her home.

Her heart had stilled when his Houston office number popped up on her caller ID.

"Hello."

"Hi, Mrs. Jones. It's Riley Manning."

"Yes?" she said, it being the only word her mind could form. She wanted him to tell her he'd take their case. After the visit from those ministers, she *needed* him to tell her that he'd take their case.

"Well, after careful review, there is just no way I can take your case," Riley said.

Gloria fell back against the wall to steady herself. Her knees seemed to have lost all elasticity.

"But I'm not giving up," he quickly added. "I've reviewed the facts of your case. I've talked to Perry and we both agreed that a public defender would be a huge disservice to your son."

"But if you won't take the case, what are we supposed to do?" she managed to say.

"That's just it. I did talk with one of my colleagues and he—"

Gloria stopped him. "No disrespect, but I need someone who's going to believe in my boy."

"And I wouldn't give you someone who didn't," Riley countered. "My colleague, Phillip Christiansen, is very committed to a proper defense. I've talked it over with him and while he hasn't officially agreed to take on the case, he would like to meet with you," Riley said. "But we need to move fast. I don't know if you saw the press conference earlier this week, but this case is moving at monumental speed."

"I-I saw it."

"How soon can you get here?" he asked.

The sound of a blaring horn jolted Gloria back to the present. She'd been so lost in thought, she hadn't even realized that she'd weaved into another lane.

She gave an apologetic wave and focused her attention back on the road.

Fifteen minutes later, she was pulling into the parking lot of a small brick building that said CHRISTIANSEN & CARVER LAW FIRM. This was a huge change from the high-rise that housed Riley's office.

Gloria parked, then made her way inside. The receptionist greeted her as soon as the door chimed.

"Good afternoon and welcome. How may I help you?" the woman asked.

"I have an appointment with Phillip Christiansen."

She glanced down at a pad. "Is he expecting you?"

Gloria nodded. "He is."

"Okay. Please have a seat. Mr. Christiansen will be with you in a moment."

As Gloria sat, she struggled to keep her nerves from getting frazzled. She really liked Riley and hated having to try to convince someone different of her son's innocence.

She smiled when the handsome man who looked more suited for a magazine cover than a law office greeted her with a warm smile. "Hello, Mrs. Jones. Phillip Christiansen. It's a pleasure to meet you."

She stood to greet him. "Nice to meet you as well. Thank you for seeing me."

"Well, come on back. You'll have to excuse my office. It's a little cluttered."

She followed him down a small hallway. There were pictures and newspaper clippings, but these seemed more community oriented. He did appear to be successful, but the place just didn't seem as high class as Riley's office.

"Can I get you some bottled water, coffee?" Phillip asked once she was seated in his office.

"I'll take a water, please."

Phillip reached in a small refrigerator behind his desk and pulled out an Ozarka water. Gloria took the water, unscrewed the cap, and took a quick sip as Phillip got settled behind his desk.

"So, first question. Do you truly believe that your son shooting the police officer was an accident?"

"I *know* it was an accident. And the voice that yelled, 'You gon' die tonight, cop,' that wasn't my Jamal. It's one of the other boys," she said.

"That should be easy enough to prove."

"Jamal was just scared when the officer tackled him, instinct made him fight back, and then some kind of way, the gun went off," Gloria said. "I know that my son will face some type of punishment," she went on, "but he doesn't deserve a stiff sentence. He doesn't deserve the death penalty like the papers are saying he is facing. He's not a cold-blooded killer like they're trying to make him out to be."

"Has your son ever been in trouble before?" Phillip asked.

"No, but I don't see what that has to do with anything."

"Oh, it has everything to do with it. That's going to be the first thing the other side trots out," Phillip replied.

She sighed. "Other than recently skipping school, he's never had so much as a disciplinary write-up."

"Give me a second," Phillip said, glancing over a file in his hand.

"Take your time," she said. Gloria took in the scenery in the office. It was obvious from his University of Texas undergraduate degree and his Rice University law degree that this man was well qualified. What she didn't understand was why he wasn't in some big firm like Riley.

Gloria continued glancing around the room. She stopped when she got to a family photo. The image caused her to drop her bottle of water and gasp.

"Are you okay?" Phillip asked, looking up from his files.

"Y-yes," she said, reaching down and picking up the water, which didn't spill since she placed the top back on. She pointed to the picture. "Your . . . Your wife?"

"Yes, that's my family. My adorable children, Leslie and Ryan." He leaned back and smiled proudly. "And yes, my wife is Kay Christiansen, the prosecutor in your son's case."

Her eyes widened in shock.

"But let me be very clear," Phillip continued. "My wife and I met in the courtroom, going up against each other. We both respect what the other one does. We don't bring our work home. We don't discuss our cases. We take our jobs very seriously. And if I take this case, I will fight for your son like he's my own. I just want to be very clear."

"How . . ."

"How can we go against each other?" He picked the photo up off his desk and looked at it. The love he felt was obvious. "Well, because in the courtroom, we're not husband and wife. We're two attorneys who believe in the sanctity of the law. It just so happens that I'm on one side and she's on the other." He set the frame back down. "Is that a problem for you?"

Gloria didn't dare tell him what her real problem was. If he knew that, he'd never take this case. "No . . . no problem," she stammered.

"Good," he continued. "After reviewing everything, I will say I am afraid for your son. Not only is the media persecuting him, but the prosecutor will go for blood. But I will take your case and fight to not only get a fair trial, but even possibly get the charges dismissed."

"Thank you, Jesus," Gloria said, all thoughts of Kayla Matthews disappearing from her mind. "Did Mr. Manning explain our financial situation?"

"It's okay. There is a legal defense fund by the Save Our Boys Project that we'll tap into if necessary. Don't you worry about anything. Now, I can't say it's official until I meet your son and he agrees that he wants me."

"Oh, he'll want you," Gloria said with a huge smile.

"Good." Phillip stood and took her hand. "You just worry about staying strong for your son and staying prayerful that we have the best outcome possible. I want to set things up to see him as soon as possible."

Gloria had never felt so relieved. On the way up here, she'd told herself that if Phillip didn't take her case, they'd have to go with Rev. Clayborn and his militant friend, which she didn't want to do. She didn't have a good feeling about them.

"Thank you so much, Mr. Christiansen!"

He walked her out and she struggled to contain her excitement.

Now Gloria just needed to figure out how in the world she was going to tell her husband who their new attorney was.

26

———

"Come on, Ryan. Get off the computer and go to bed. It's past your bedtime," Kay said as she tossed Leslie's Barbie into the toy bin.

"Aww, Mom. Just five more minutes," he whined.

"That's what you said forty minutes ago."

"But I've almost figured out this chemistry equation." He peered at the screen as he scribbled in his notebook.

Kay walked over and stood behind him. She wouldn't know that stuff to save her life; it was just a bunch of equations that looked like a jumble.

"Why are you waiting until the last minute to do your homework anyway? I'm shocked at you," she chastised.

"Oh, this isn't for tomorrow. This is due next week but I'm trying to get a jump-start on it."

Kay stood smiling. How in the world could she be mad at that? Ryan was every mother's dream.

"Come on, son. You can finish working on that tomorrow." She patted his shoulder.

He shut down the computer, grabbed his notebook, and stood up.

"No, sir. Leave that notebook on the table. I know you. You'll be under the cover with a flashlight working on that chemistry equation."

He smiled. "Guess you got me." He dropped the book on the table, kissed her on the cheek, and darted upstairs.

Kay put away a carton of juice that someone had left out, then surveyed the kitchen. Thank God for Selena. Not only did she cook and watch after Leslie, but she kept the house immaculate so that when Kay got home, there was little housework to be done.

She turned the light off and headed down the hallway. "Knock, knock," she said, tapping her husband's office door. "What are you doing in here?"

"Just handling some business." He leaned back, removed his glasses, and rubbed his eyes. "Are you about to go to bed?"

"I am. I'm a little drained," she replied.

"Long day?"

"Yep."

Running this campaign was no joke. She, Valerie, Loni, and her campaign manager, Jeff, had spent all evening reviewing campaign strategies and preparing for upcoming debates.

"Well, go take your shower and I'll be waiting when you get out." He ran his tongue over his top lip in that LL Cool J way that always sent goosebumps up her spine. "I hope you can muster up just a little energy for Daddy."

"That I think I can do." Kay giggled before darting off to her room.

Kay showered, changed, then snuggled in the bed next to her husband, who, as promised, was waiting when she got out. This was her favorite time of the night, when they decompressed and just enjoyed each other's company.

"You seem a little stressed," he said, stroking her hair as she laid her head on his chest.

"I am. I know we don't talk about work," she replied, giving a disclaimer, "but I spent a great part of the day with Officer Wilkins's family."

Cheryl Wilkins had shown back up at her office this morning. Kay felt like she needed to help Cheryl find a good therapist because the woman was having the hardest time coping with her husband's death. Cheryl had cried and cried and Kay had once again assured her that she was going to bring Jamal Jones to justice. "I just feel really bad for her. It's such a shame to lose—"

"Ah," Phillip said, cutting her off.

She raised her hands in defense. "Okay, okay. I know we're not supposed to be talking about work."

"No. Not just that." He sat her up and turned her to face him.

"You know that thing Riley mentioned to us the other night?" Phillip began.

"What thing?"

"You know, about me taking on the case, your case?"

Kay sat back and stared at him. "Don't tell me you've agreed to it?"

He hesitated, then said, "Yes, I want to. Do you have an issue with me doing it?"

She thought about it for a moment. "You know I'll never tell you who you should and shouldn't represent."

"That's good to hear. This one is pretty high profile and I don't want it to cause any problems with us."

Kay thought about it for a moment, then said, "You know what? It'll be fun." She straddled him. "But you know I play hardball in the courtroom."

"I know. That's what turned me on about you. That's why I stopped you, though. No discussing the case once we get to 34 Andre Court, right?"

"Oh, you know this." She wiggled in his lap. "I can't let you use that magnificent body to woo my strategy out of me," she joked.

"Hmph. You're sure about that?" He pushed her down on the bed and started kissing her neck.

"Positive. May the best person winnnn . . ." She moaned as his lips met her breasts.

"He will," Phillip muttered between kisses.

Kay stopped him, then lifted his head to meet her gaze. "I love you."

"I love you, too." He removed a strand of hair from her face. "And nothing will ever change that."

He returned to finish the job of pleasuring his wife.

27

Who was this man that she'd married? That's the thought that ran through Gloria's mind as they stood in the middle of the living room, arguing. Again.

"Are you listening to me?" Elton roared.

Since the day she'd said "I do," Gloria had put her husband first. There was only one time that she'd put her foot down and stood up to him. Most of their marriage, she'd let him lead, even when she didn't agree. She'd taken care of him, often at the expense of her and Jamal's own feelings. And now, one simple tragedy had transformed her. She no longer cared what Elton Jones had to say.

She massaged her temples. "Elton, it's obvious that we aren't on the same page when it comes to our son." They weren't even in the same book, but Gloria was tired of arguing. Even if she understood his rationale for turning Jamal in, his behavior now caused her to question everything about her husband.

"I am thinking about this family," he barked. "I do not want to use Phillip Christiansen. That's just gonna create more drama. Now, the Black Justice Coalition has top notch people and I. . ."

Gloria tuned him out. He'd already given her 101 reasons why they should work with the ministers and their attorney. She was tired of hearing it.

"You work with whomever the hell you want!" she yelled, and headed out the door. "I'm using Phillip Christiansen!"

She'd driven back to Houston alone, struggling not to let Elton ruin her mood. She and Phillip were scheduled to see Jamal at the jail today and she wanted to be in the best spirits possible when she saw her son.

Gloria lucked out and found a parking spot right in front of the jail. A thought flashed through her mind. Maybe this was a sign that things were about to turn around. Okay, so maybe lucking out on a parking spot didn't necessarily mean anything, but she'd take every little blessing that she could.

Phillip had texted her and told her he was already inside, filling out some paperwork and to just wait in the lobby, which she did. The cold, bare walls of the Harris County Jail turned her stomach. This place was much bigger than the Jasper jail, but it definitely wasn't better. And it was packed. Sad faces, puffy eyes, and exasperated bodies filled the room of people waiting to see their loved ones.

Finally, after what seemed like an eternity, Phillip walked out. "Mrs. Jones, you made it."

He extended his hand to shake hers, but Gloria couldn't help it, she pulled him into a hug. He didn't seem surprised and simply smiled.

"So, did you get signed in and everything?" Gloria asked. "I'm amazed that you were able to get this meeting so quickly." Phillip had been on it and had set up a meeting with Jamal. Gloria was just grateful that she could attend.

"We're all set. I did have to call in some favors to let you be able to sit in on this meeting. But luckily, I cited a case law about a juvenile who had his case overturned because his initial counsel meeting was without his parents."

"Good thing you know your stuff." She smiled. Not only was this man on top of his job, but he also seemed to care about Jamal's well-being.

Phillip gave her a reassuring smile, then motioned for her to follow him back.

They walked into a small, dusty room that held nothing but a wooden table and four chairs. Phillip pulled out the seat for Gloria. He eased into the chair next to her.

They sat in silence for about five minutes, Phillip looking over paperwork, she praying incessantly.

The door clicked and both of them sat up. Tears raced to the front of Gloria's eyes as a uniformed guard brought her son in. Shackles adorned his wrists and ankles. The orange jumpsuit swallowed his frame. Fear covered his face. There was a bruise under his left eye.

"Oh, my God. What happened to you?" Gloria asked, jumping up and reaching out to touch his face. He moved his head out of her reach.

"I'm a'ight. This just ain't no party in here," he said with a raspy voice.

"Did a cop do that to you?" she said.

"Nah, Ma," Jamal said, sliding in the chair across from her.

"Some dude named Big Earl. But I'm okay, seriously." He looked at Phillip. "So are you my attorney?"

"That's what I want to talk to you about," Phillip said. "I want to represent you, but before I officially take on any new clients, I like to have a conversation with them and make sure I'm who they want on their team." Phillip leaned forward on the table. "I need you to be one hundred and fifty percent honest with me, okay? The only way I can help you is if I know everything. Got it?"

Jamal nodded.

Phillip took out a pad and pen. "Now, I need you to start from the beginning on what happened that night. Tell me every detail." He looked over at Gloria. "Does your mother need to step out?"

Jamal looked at Gloria. She would die if he asked her to leave, but thankfully, he said, "No, she can hear everything because I've already told her."

Gloria relaxed as Phillip pulled out a small digital audio recorder. "Hope you don't mind, I'm recording in case I need to refer back to my notes at any point."

Jamal nodded as Phillip pressed play. "Now, start from the beginning and don't leave out a single thing."

28

Jamal Jones couldn't understand how anyone would want to live in a small town. As soon as he turned eighteen and/or got a little money in his pocket, he was going to put Jasper, Texas, as far in his rear-view mirror as humanly possible.

"Yo man, why you so quiet?"

He looked up at his friend Dix, who was leaned up against his '79 Impala. They were in the parking lot of the Stop-n-Shop, the only convenience store in town that stayed open 24 hours.

"Hello? Am I speaking English?" Dix asked when Jamal didn't reply.

Jamal waved him off as he texted Shante, a girl from nearby Beaumont that he'd met at a football game last week.

"You know he's stressed out," his other friend, Brian, or Squeaky as they called him, said. "His pops probably givin' him a hard time again."

Dix shook his head as he shadowboxed, something he could always be found doing. He had dreams of being the next Floyd Mayweather, though he had never taken one boxing lesson in his life. "Man, if I was you, me and yo pops would be coming to blows, preacher or not."

"Yeah, Dix is right," Squeaky said. "Yo pops be for real trippin'."

Jamal couldn't argue with that. Ever since he hit thirteen, he and his father had butted heads. If it wasn't for his mother, he probably would've run away a long time ago.

"Why your old man be trippin' like that, though?" Dix asked the question he always asked. "He supposed to be a man of God."

Jamal shrugged. Like always, he didn't have an answer for his friend. "Just strict. And you know me and rules . . ."

Squeaky laughed as he reached in the car and pulled a beer out from the backseat. He didn't bother offering Dix one because Dix didn't think "an athlete in training" should drink. Squeaky didn't offer Jamal a beer, either, because Jamal hated the taste of beer and never indulged.

"Shoot, for real, it's like you allergic to rules, bruh," Squeaky said as he popped the top on his beer and took a sip.

Dix shook his head as he laughed as well. "I mean I ain't never met somebody as smart as you but refuses to go to school."

Jamal finished his text, then looked up at his friends. "It just ain't for me." He wanted to say neither is hanging out in the parking lot of a neighborhood convenience store, but since this was what his friends did dang near twenty-four/seven, he didn't want to insult anybody. They'd get real salty if he told them the truth; he really didn't care for hanging out with them anymore. He didn't know if he'd outgrown his boys or what, but hanging for the sake of hanging just no longer interested him. He wanted more out of life.

His mother tried to tell him that if he would commit himself to school, he could easily win a scholarship somewhere. She called him gifted, a genius, because he could skip school all year long and then show up for the final exam and ace it. He'd already tested at amazing levels. He'd also gotten interest from nearby colleges for his wrestling skills. Being on the wrestling team at Jasper High School was the one thing he did enjoy. But after his last suspension for skipping school, he'd been cut from the team. His father told him constantly that he was just going to let all of his talent go to waste. Jamal didn't know what he wanted to do with his life. All he did know was that he wanted out of Jasper, Texas. He hated being a preacher's son and if he was really being honest, he hated his dad. Once he made it out of this town he'd send for his mom to come visit him, but that's all he'd ever want from Jasper.

"No hanga out!" The high-pitched sound of the Korean store owner broke up their conversation. "I tell you ova an ova, no hanga out!"

"Hang, dude. There's no 'a' at the end of it," Dix said, laughing.

"You rude! You rude! You motha should teach you betta!" the shop owner said, wagging a finger in their direction. Even though they always came to this store, none of them had ever bothered to learn the man's name.

"Oh, you wanna talk about my mama?" Dix said, advancing toward him.

"Leave, leave now. It one in the morning. You should be home!" the store owner shouted as he scurried back into the store.

"And you need to be on dese nuts!" Dix yelled, grabbing his crotch.

"I don't know why he keep tryna run us off. It ain't like he got nobody coming into this busted-ass store anyway," Squeaky said.

They sat around and laughed and talked for a few minutes and then a police car came rolling up.

"Oh snap!" Squeaky said. He tossed his beer can to the side.

They watched as the lone officer pulled his patrol car to a stop, then got out and came over to them.

"Yeah, we got a call about some loitering," he said.

"We didn't call about anyone loitering," Dix said, stifling a laugh.

Squeaky leaned in and looked at his name tag. "Yes, Officer Keith Wilkins. We didn't make any calls but if we see anyone loitering, we'll definitely let you know."

"Oh, so you want to play games, huh?" the officer said.

"Nah, I gave up games at ten," Dix casually replied.

The officer took a step toward Dix. "Look you little smart-mouth punk, I don't know who you think you're talking to, but—" The officer's radio, which was attached on his shoulder, crackled, then dispatch said, "All units on alert. Armed robbery of Jake's Liquor on Tafferty. Black male suspect remains at large."

Officer Wilkins pushed Dix against the car. "You fit the description. Did you rob that liquor store?"

"Man," Dix said, his nostrils flaring in anger, "we ain't doin' nothin' and y'all always harassin' us. Racist pigs."

"Y'all punks always doing something," the officer said as he pushed Dix again. "Put your hands on the hood!"

Jamal took his cell phone out and began recording.

"You getting this, bruh? You getting this police brutality?" Dix yelled as the officer snatched him around and kicked his legs to spread them.

"Naw, you wanna be a Billy badass?" Officer Wilkins said as he patted Dix down. When he didn't find anything, he pushed Dix again. "Matter of fact, you know what? I think I need to haul all you in for that liquor store robbery."

"We ain't robbed nothin'!" Squeaky shouted. "We're law-abiding citizens. Why don't you go to the other side of the tracks and get those dudes smokin' meth?"

"I can't because I'm over here arresting you," Officer Wilkins said, moving in Squeaky's direction.

"Arresting me for what?" Squeaky asked as Officer Wilkins slammed him against the car next.

"For loitering, or suspicion of robbery. Or for being a pain in my ass. I'll figure something out."

"Seriously?" Squeaky said.

Officer Wilkins ignored Squeaky's protests as he jerked his arms behind his back.

"Police brutality!" Squeaky yelled.

Jamal held his Samsung Galaxy phone out, continuously recording everything. He didn't say a word as he zoomed the camera in.

"Get it all! Get all this police brutality on tape!" Squeaky yelled as he squirmed to try and keep the officer from putting handcuffs on him.

Officer Wilkins finally noticed Jamal. He stopped and stared at the camera. "Are you recording me?"

"Yep. I know my rights. I'm not violating any laws. I have a right to film." Jamal continued recording. "As long as I'm not interfering in your arrest, I have a legal right to film." Jamal turned the camera around to his face. "You see how they treat us? If you're young and black in America, you're guilty until proven innocent."

Officer Wilkins released Squeaky as he took a few steps toward Jamal. "I said, get that camera off me."

Before Jamal could respond the officer raced over and knocked the phone out of his hand. The phone tumbled into the grass.

"Hey! You can't do that!" Jamal said.

"I just did."

"Look, I ain't did nothin' wrong!"

The officer reached for Jamal, but he jumped out of the way.

"You can't arrest me. I didn't do anything. I'm going home."

Jamal turned to retrieve his phone and leave when the officer grabbed his arm, spun him around, and flung him to the ground.

"You little piece of—"

"Get off of me!" Jamal screamed.

He kept hearing his mother's voice. *It's a police officer, calm down.*

While he heard her voice, he saw his father's face. He saw the last time his father beat him, for skipping school. Jamal had promised that was the last time any man hit him.

"Get off of me!" Jamal screamed again. "Get off me!"

"I'm gonna teach you little punks a lesson!" the officer yelled.

From the sideline, both Dix and Squeaky continued yelling as well.

"Shoot that racist pig!"

"You gon' die tonight, cop!"

The words of his friends rang in his ears as Jamal struggled with the officer, whose rage was rising by the minute. At one point their eyes met, and Jamal knew, this officer was not going to let him live. As Officer Wilkins reached for his service revolver, every wrestling move Jamal had ever mastered kicked in. He managed to flip the officer over. All he was trying to do was get away before this man killed him. But the cop was no weakling. He grasped his revolver and as his fingers moved toward the trigger, Jamal summoned all his strength to wrestle it away.

They fought over the gun until one single shot penetrated the night air.

The sound of the gunfire was followed by silence, then Squeaky yelled "Let's get out of here!" and he and Dix took off running. Jamal wasn't mad at them, because he always knew those two were some "everybody for themselves" type of dudes. But Jamal couldn't think about them now. He hadn't meant to shoot the officer. As he saw the puddle of blood forming, he knew that he'd done just that.

"Oh, my God. Oh, my God."

"Hey, what's going on?"

Jamal looked up and saw the shop owner peering through the darkness and then Jamal did the only thing he knew how to do. He ran like hell.

. . .

Both Gloria and Phillip sat riveted as Jamal wrapped up his story. Tears ran down Gloria's face. Jamal buried his face in his hands and sobbed. "I didn't mean to do it. I didn't mean to do it."

Gloria wanted desperately to hold him, but the glare of the guard stopped her. She did, however, take his hands as Phillip said, "I believe you, son. Now, we just need to get a jury to believe you, too."

29

————

Gloria couldn't believe that she had been reduced to spying on her husband. But if she hadn't, there is no way she would have known what he was planning. Even listening now, she would have never believed it if she hadn't stumbled into the church sanctuary and been able to duck out of the way in time to hear.

"My wife is concerned that the Black Justice Coalition is really only about uplifting their own cause," Elton said.

"Of course we are," Rev. Clayborn replied. "And part of our cause is bringing justice to young black men who have been wronged. And our brother Jamal has been wronged. This is a town of deep-seated racism and we want to bring the fact that nothing has changed directly to the forefront."

Gloria couldn't believe Elton was even still talking to these men. They'd dang near incited a riot at a protest march, they'd spouted their cause and all the change they could do, yet not one time had any of them asked how Jamal was doing. She didn't trust these men, and the fact that her husband was even entertaining them was an-other crack in his already shaky foundation.

"H-how much money will my church get?" Elton asked.

"Well, our donations have already begun flowing in. We'll allo-cate a percentage for your family and church," Rev. Clayborn said.

"So, what exactly will you need me to do?" Elton said.

Rev. Clayborn smiled. "Well, we need to get our attorney down so he can get moving on the case. Then we have planned a full media campaign. CNN, MSNBC, Fox, local media, even *The View* and *The Talk*. We plan to hit all of the media outlets, including the morning shows. We will need you and your wife by our side sup-porting our efforts," he said.

The Muhammad man spoke up. "Reverend, the one thing we can't have is us being extremely vocal and then you all coming back saying you don't support our cause. So we need to make sure we're all in accord."

Elton didn't say anything, just shifted his body like he was unsure what to do. Gloria willed her husband to do the right thing. Give her a tiny reason to believe in him again. Yet he said nothing.

Rev. Clayborn's voice got stern. "You do support our cause, don't you?"

"Well . . ." Elton began.

"Let me be very clear, Reverend Jones," Rev. Clayborn contin-ued. "You said yourself that your church is struggling. The Black Justice Coalition is prepared to give a donation of twenty thousand dollars to the Mount Sinai Church to, shall we say, defray any costs incurred with our usage of your facility. We can call it an advance on our donations."

Elton's eyes danced and Gloria's stomach churned. Was her husband really about to sell out their son for a cash donation to the church? She'd had all that she could take. She stepped out so she could be seen.

"Ummm." She cleared her throat.

Elton jumped up. "Uh, hello, honey. I-I was just meeting with the ministers here." Elton had to have known he was wrong, because he didn't usually stumble around her. He took his job as head of household very seriously and she had never seen him the least bit intimidated—until now.

Gloria didn't say a word as she stared at the two men.

"Good day, Mrs. Jones," Rev. Clayborn said.

"As-salamu alaykum," Minister Muhammad added.

"Hello," Gloria said, only because her mother had taught her never to be rude.

"We were here just discussing—"

"I heard what you were discussing," she said, cutting off Elton before he started lying to her in the church. She turned to Ministers Clayborn and Muhammad. "But I just want to be very clear that we will not be needing your services. We have secured a wonderful attorney."

"You have?" Minister Muhammad asked, shooting a strange look at Elton, who simply looked away.

"Yes, Phillip Christiansen has decided to take our case," Gloria said.

"Mrs. Jones," Rev. Clayborn said, "I really do not think that is a good idea. Our attorney has an impeccable record."

She turned to him and snapped. "A record of inciting violence," she said. "I've researched your attorney and not only does he not win cases, but all he's good for is getting folks riled up and not in a good way."

"Gloria!" Elton said. He turned to Rev. Clayborn. "I'm sorry. You'll have to excuse my wife. This whole thing has been stressful on her and she's not herself."

"You don't need to speak for me, Elton." She knew she was catching him by surprise because usually she was the meek and timid pastor's wife. But that was before these people started messing with her son. "Thank you, gentlemen. Obviously, we can't stop you from doing what you need to do, but my husband and I would rather have your prayers than to become the face of your cause."

They looked appalled, but Gloria didn't care. She didn't care that she was being rude. She didn't care that she was making her husband mad. Right now it seemed like she was the only one who had sense when it came to her son.

30

After reviewing the evidence, Kay doubted that *State v. Jamal Jones* would ever see the light of day. If Jamal's family had any sense, they would take her offer of Manslaughter 1.

She knew her husband, though. He was going to fight this and want to take it to trial, but Kay was hoping she could get through to the boy's parents. A trial could get very ugly and with a videotape there was simply no way they could win. It's not like the cop shot himself.

"Knock, knock."

Kay looked up from her desk to see Valerie poke her head in the door. "Good morning, Mrs. Christiansen."

"Good morning, Valerie," she said, waving her in. "Are those for me?" she asked, motioning to the folders in Valerie's hand.

"Yes, ma'am." Valerie handed her the folders. "The top folder has all the info on Officer Wilkins's family. The next is some more case material and the one on the bottom is all the info you asked me to pull on the suspect's personal history. His parents, his school, all his personal information."

"Okay, great." Kay opened the first folder and her heart once again went out when she saw Officer Wilkins receiving his pin from the police academy. She closed that folder and pulled out the one with the suspect's personal info. She liked to get into the head of the criminals she prosecuted, understand what made them tick.

"Excuse me, Mrs. Christiansen," Kay's secretary, April, said over the telephone intercom. "I have Judge Raymond's office on the phone. She had something come up this afternoon and wants to know if we can move your pretrial meeting up."

"Up to when?" Kay asked.

"Up to now. Like in twenty minutes."

Kay silently cursed. They weren't supposed to meet until 3 p.m. She wanted to review these files first, but Judge Mona Raymond was not a person who liked the word *no*.

"Fine. I'll be there. Get Harold. Tell him to meet me in Judge Raymond's chambers in twenty minutes."

"Why are you stressing?" Valerie asked after Kay had hung up the phone. "You know you're prepared."

"I know, but I really wanted to go through these files. It's not like me to be unprepared, but this campaign has had me running."

"Hopefully, you won't need them. Maybe they'll accept your plea today, and all of this," she said, pointing to the folders, "will be moot."

"You're right." Kay stuffed the folders in her briefcase and stood. Valerie was great at keeping things in perspective. She'd hired the girl six years ago, when she was a junior at the University of Houston. It had broken Kay's heart when Valerie dropped out of school because she got pregnant. Valerie had kept promising to go back, but she'd told Kay that as a single mother, she had to keep working full-time.

"I'll make sure Harold gets over there," Valerie said.

"Great, I'm heading over now."

Twenty minutes didn't give Kay time to do more than grab a granola bar and head over to Judge Raymond's office. Kay liked to keep her energy up because she always wanted to stay on top of her game. No doubt Phillip would be on top of his.

When Kay walked into Judge Raymond's chambers, her husband was already there, chatting it up, using his undeniable charm to put the judge on his side. Kay had peeped his game a long time ago. Luckily, Judge Raymond was a hard-nose who might smile and chitchat with him, but when she banged that gavel, she was strictly business.

"Hello, Mr. Christiansen," Kay said.

"Hello, Mrs. Christiansen," Phillip replied.

"I just think it's so cute when you two go up against each other," Judge Raymond quipped, before turning back serious. "Thank you for getting here on such short notice. Are both parties ready?"

"Yes, we are, Your Honor," Kay said, sliding into a chair across the table from Phillip. Harold, the other assistant district attorney working with her on this case, eased in the door.

"Sorry, got here as soon as I heard," he said.

"You're fine," Judge Raymond said, motioning for him to take a seat. She turned to Phillip. "Are your clients on the way?"

"Yes, luckily my clients were already en route, so the change didn't affect them. They were pulling into the parking garage a few minutes ago, so they should be here any minute now. My client won't be joining us. The jail is on lockdown."

"Again?" the judge asked.

"Yep," Phillip replied. "So it will just be the parents."

"I know this is an emotional time for your clients," Judge Raymond said, "but the mother is aware that I don't do theatrics, correct?"

"Yes, Your Honor. I have informed her of that."

"So will you be taking our plea offer?" Kay asked. Her office had formally presented the plea agreement to Phillip's office yesterday.

"Absolutely not," Phillip replied.

"You do realize the video tells the story?" Kay asked.

"The video tells *half* the story," Phillip countered. "We're not exactly sure who fired the fatal shot. Maybe the gun just went off. Maybe one of the other boys picked it up and fired."

"So, that's your theory?" Kay asked.

"Reasonable doubt, that's all I need," Phillip said.

"Well, if your client hadn't gone on the run, we would have been able to have ballistics determine whether he fired or not."

"My client was a scared young kid who was raised in a city known for racial intolerance. So he was in fear for his life. But initially, he was doing nothing wrong. Shall I quote you the law: 'Members of the public are legally allowed to record police interactions. Intentional interference such as blocking or obstructing cameras or ordering the person to cease constitutes censorship and also violates the First Amendment.'"

"Okay, *War of the Roses*," Judge Raymond interjected. "We're going to save this until the defendant's parents are present."

Kay scribbled a few notes just as Phillip said, "Here are the defendant's parents now." He stood as the couple walked in. "Your Honor, this is Reverend Elton Jones and his wife, Gloria."

Kay looked up from her notes and every ounce of air drained from her body. If she had been standing, her legs would've surely given out. She stared at the Joneses in horror. This had to be some kind of sick nightmare.

"This is the prosecutor, Kay Christiansen," Phillip continued.

This could not be happening.

"Are you all right?" Judge Raymond asked.

Kay took short, deep breaths, trying to keep from passing out. Was this really Elton and Gloria Jones in front of her?

The judge looked back and forth between Kay and the Joneses. "Do you know them?" she asked.

"I—I . . . Excuse me, Your Honor." Kay stood and bolted out of the room, nearly knocking Gloria over on her way through the door.

Kay knew her husband would follow, because as professional as he was, he cared about her well-being more than anything else, so he would come and see what was wrong. That's why she ducked into the ladies' room.

Kay had never suffered from asthma. But right about now, she felt like she was having an asthma attack.

"Kay, are you all right?" Phillip called from outside the door

"Yes," she answered between breaths. "Just give me a minute!"

"Kay?"

"Just go back inside!"

"Kay! What's wrong?"

"Go!" She inhaled, trying to compose herself. But it wasn't working. She shook her hands like she was fanning herself. *Breathe, Kay, breathe,* she told herself.

This couldn't be happening. No way could she go back in that room. She *wouldn't* go back in that room.

Kay ducked into the bathroom stall when she heard the door open. She locked the door and leaned against the side of the stall.

"Kayla." The voice from her past called out to her. "Kayla, are you all right?"

"What are you doing here?" Kay asked from inside the stall, her voice trembling.

"Trying to save my son," Gloria softly said.

"J-Jamal Jones is your son?"

"Come out so we can talk."

Kay took a deep breath and eased the bathroom stall door open. She stood face-to-face with the woman she hadn't seen in almost seventeen years. Gloria hadn't changed. She had a few more wrinkles and a few more silver strands, but everything else was the same.

"Yes, the boy you're prosecuting is . . ." She paused. "Jamal is my son."

"Did you know I was the prosecutor?"

Gloria nodded.

"Did you know who my husband was when you hired him?"

Gloria didn't say a word.

"What kind of game are you playing?" Kay hissed, her shock now replaced by anger.

"I'm not playing a game. I'm just a mother trying to save her son." She took a step toward Kay. Kay took a step back. "Do you have children, Kayla?"

"Don't ask me any questions."

"Phillip said you do," Gloria answered for her. "What lengths would you go to for your child?"

Kay glared at her. She had so much that she wanted to say to this woman, but in the end, all she said was "I'm not doing this with you. I don't know what kind of game you and your sick husband are playing, but I'm not taking part."

"The only thing I'm trying to do is save my son. Save—"

"I'll call the judge and ask for a continuance." Kay stormed out of the ladies' room. She was usually strong and confident. Not much could rattle her, but this blast from the past was about to make her completely lose her mind.

31

Does someone want to tell me what's going on?"

Judge Raymond was pissed. Gloria didn't know much about the judge, but she could tell that this woman didn't play.

"Uh, Your Honor, I-I don't know." Phillip said, obviously confused. "I went to check and I don't know if she's sick or what."

"She is," Gloria said, easing back into the chair. "I heard her in the bathroom stall throwing up. Maybe it's some type of virus. I told her I would tell you all that she left."

"Oh, good Lord," Judge Raymond said. "I hope she didn't come in here and infect us all with something." The judge sighed, then looked at her notes. "So are you prepared to continue in her absence?" she asked Harold.

Harold blinked. "Ahhh . . . not really, Your Honor."

"Well, you're going to have to get ready. We will at least hear the argument from the defense." She set her pen down and leaned back, letting everyone know she was ready to begin.

"Your Honor, my client would like to have the case thrown out," Phillip began.

"And I would like to retire on a beach in Tahiti right now," she replied. "What do you have that's a little more realistic, Mr. Christiansen?"

Phillip pulled out some papers and slid them toward her. "My client, Jamal Jones, has never been in trouble before. This is an unfortunate incident that stemmed from a request to stop filming." He handed the judge an iPad, where she could watch the video. "According to *Housh v. People,* an arrest that fails to allege a crime is within jurisdiction, and one who is being arrested may resist arrest and break away. If the arresting officer is killed by one who is so resisting, the killing will be no more than an involuntary manslaughter."

"Okay, so someone's been reading up on case law," Judge Raymond quipped, as she pressed play. "So, why didn't he just stop filming?" she asked after watching a few minutes.

Elton turned and looked at Gloria. She answered, "Your Honor, because he believed he wasn't doing anything wrong and we taught our son to be strong in his beliefs and to be aware of his rights. He knew that as long as he wasn't in the way, he had a right to film."

Phillip added, "She's right. U.S. citizens have the right to record."

"Looks like he's being defiant here," Judge Raymond said, her eyes glued to the iPad.

Elton, who still hadn't said a word, let out a small murmur. Gloria couldn't make out what he was saying, but she was so disgusted with him, it didn't even matter. Today was his first time meeting Phillip and to say Elton was acting like an ass would be an understatement. He was standoffish and aloof, like he was irritated about even having to be here.

Gloria kept her attention on the judge. "The shooting was an accident," she felt the need to add.

"Well, that will be up to the jury to decide," the judge said.

"As you can see from the video," Phillip continued, "Jamal is at a distance from the officer. The officer came over to him."

"So, who's the one yelling 'You gon' die today, cop?'" she asked.

"It was one of the other boys. There were two boys with my client. They will be called as witnesses to support that my client felt attacked," Phillip said.

"He didn't feel attacked, he was attacked," Gloria countered.

"All right, settle down," Judge Raymond admonished. "Again, that is something the jury will have to decide. The grand jury has determined that there is probable cause and enough for us to move forward with the trial, so I'm going to let the ruling stand. Motion to dismiss denied."

Gloria's eyes watered up. She knew the chances of having this case thrown out were slim, but still, she'd held out hope.

"But Your Honor . . ." Phillip began.

"Don't worry, Mr. Christiansen," she said, cutting him off. "You all will get your day in court." She turned to Harold. "Do you have anything to add?"

"Ummm . . . no, Your Honor," the young man said. "We again urge the defense to take our plea of Manslaughter One."

"Not happening," Phillip said.

"Then we'll see you in court," Harold replied.

"Fine." Judge Raymond turned back to Phillip. "Get back to my court clerk after four tomorrow. We will get this expedited and on the books. Everyone from the mayor to the governor has contacted us about this case." She turned back to Harold. "And I suggest you find out what is going on with Mrs. Christiansen and you all get it together. One of you will be prosecuting the case soon."

"Yes, Your Honor."

The judge stood, signaling the conclusion of their meeting.

After it was over, Gloria fought back tears as Phillip talked with them for a few moments.

"Okay, we're in for a rocky ride," Phillip said.

"Can you handle this?" Elton asked. "Because the Black Justice Coalition—"

"Only wants to use our son," Gloria interrupted. She wasn't about to go down that road with her husband again.

"Mr. Jones, I assure you, I'll fight to the bitter end for your son. But if you're not sure I'm the one you want representing your family, then I can only respect that."

"Nonsense," Gloria said. "We're sure." At this point, she didn't care what her husband said. "Call us if you need anything else." This time it was Gloria who took her spouse's arm and all but pushed him out the door.

"We blindsided Kayla and I think we're going to pay big time," Elton said once they were back in the car and pulling onto the freeway. "And the look of horror on her face when she saw us. . ." He shook his head. "This is going to end badly. Mark my words, this is going to end very badly."

"Well, I'm going to think positively," Gloria replied. "That's what our son needs right now."

Elton pouted as he pulled onto Interstate 10, the freeway that would take them back to Jasper. "Dagnabit!" he said when he saw the bumper-to-bumper traffic. "As if I have time to be traipsing up and down this road."

Gloria was tired of him. So she said, "Well, when I come back, I'll just stay with Mama, so you don't have to be inconvenienced. You don't even have to come to the trial," she said, swallowing hard to keep from crying. She knew her husband could be a jerk, but he was taking it to a whole other level.

"Of course I'm going to be at the trial," he said. "Don't be ridiculous."

"Well, you're acting like . . ."

"I'm acting like . . . this upsets me because it does," he said. "This is a mess, a disaster. And yes, I'm furious with Jamal because if he had his butt at home like I wanted, none of this would have happened and that man would still be alive!" Elton seemed like he'd been waiting to get this all off his chest, because he kept going. "I have worked hard for this boy all my life. And for what? This? So you'll have to excuse me if I don't want to be embroiled in a highly publicized murder trial. People don't even want to come to church, because we got news crews camped out. People judging him and us, watching over our every move," Elton said with disgust.

"They're not watching us anymore."

"Well, they were and it wasn't a good look," Elton grumbled. "And then we finally have some folks that really want to help and you're giving them a hard time."

Gloria rolled her eyes. "Oh, yeah, your precious Black Justice Coalition. They don't care about us. They care about their cause!"

"I'm not going to debate this with you," Elton said.

Gloria stared out the window. "Are you going to go see Jamal?" she asked. "That's all I want to know. You haven't seen him since you had him arrested." There was no winning that conversation so she needed to just change the subject. "You need to go see him."

"I didn't have him arrested. He got himself arrested. I very well could've saved his life."

"Whatever, Elton."

A heavy silence filled the car before he said, "Jamal is still mad at me about the arrest anyway. He probably won't even come out to see me. And I guess you're still mad, too," he said, studying her. "Your lips all poked out, your eyebrows are furrowed. You're still mad."

When she didn't reply, he continued. "I am sorry that you don't understand that I will not support you and me being harassed, or our son being on the run for God knows how long. You saw the anger in those police officers' eyes. If they would have caught him, they would have killed him."

Gloria leaned her head back against the headrest. Elton was right. Even though she didn't have it in her heart to turn her son in, it was for the best.

She reached across the armrest and took his free hand. She didn't know how to forgive him, but she needed to try. She was tired of fighting and her son needed both of his parents. If they had any hopes of making it through this, that was the only way.

32

Kay took a deep breath as soon as she heard the door chime. She'd been ignoring Phillip's phone calls all day. She had sent him a text to let him know she was at home and resting. She'd been home, but she wasn't resting. Her mind had been in an absolute jumble for the past eight hours. Kay was grateful Phillip didn't come rushing home. He had allowed her time to pull herself together. And now it was time to give him some answers. The trouble was, she didn't know what those answers would be.

"Hey," Phillip said, setting his briefcase down on the dresser. "You all right? I've been worried sick all day."

"I told you, I'm all right," Kay said. She was lying across the sofa, an afghan tossed across her legs.

"Do you want to tell me what happened?" He sat down across from her. "One minute you were fine, the next you weren't."

"It's like I texted you. I think I had a stomach virus or something."

He narrowed his eyes and looked at her sideways. He knew

nothing short of the Ebola virus could keep her out of court. They'd had several arguments about it as she worked through the flu and even a case of the measles. She had even gone back to work two weeks after delivering Leslie. So the fact that some sudden illness had shut her down, she knew Phillip wasn't buying.

"So, did you know the Joneses?" he asked point-blank.

"What would make . . . why would you ask me that?" she stuttered.

"I don't know. You were fine until you saw them."

"No, the stomach virus, it just hit me all of a sudden," she lied.

He stared at her for a minute, making her feel like a witness under intense cross-examination. Finally, he said, "Okay, if you say so."

"I'll be fine."

"Well, did Harold call and tell you?"

She let out a heavy sigh. She'd gotten the memo. Harold had called her frantically at least twenty times before she finally answered. And he told her that the case was moving forward, with or without her.

Kay knew that he was nervous and afraid that he would have to prosecute the case, and they both knew he wasn't ready to do that. She had sent him a text and told him she was feeling better and would be in the office tomorrow. She definitely couldn't turn the case over to him, and Judge Raymond didn't seem like she was going to take any excuses.

But after what she had just discovered, there was no way she could move forward with prosecuting Jamal Jones. How in the world could she get out of it? How in the world *would* she get out of it? Her boss had already begun making a big deal. He had called another press conference for the end of the week, and then resigning from the case would look especially bad on her in the race for mayor. CNN had called and was planning on doing a story, as well as *USA Today*. What was she supposed to do?

Phillip stood up and said, "I'm going to change." He stared at her. "You do know that I'm not buying that you were sick?"

Kay forced a smile and shook away all thoughts of Judge Raymond and Harold.

"No, seriously, honey. It just came out of nowhere."

"Are you sure it had nothing to do with the Joneses?"

She faked a laugh. "No, no, it had nothing to do with that," she tried to reassure him. "I really did have this sickness just pop up suddenly."

He leaned back against the door frame and studied her some more. "But you look fine now."

"I'm feeling better. I actually went to the urgent care facility."

"And what did they say?"

"It's a bad virus going around and the only thing they can think is something hit me. But I seriously am okay. They told me to just take it easy the rest of the day, which you can see I'm doing."

He stared at her some more and then said, "Kay, you know I've been married to you for a long time, so I know when something's not right."

"Phillip, please," she began.

He held his hand up. "But if you say so, fine. I'll trust you." He blew her a kiss and walked out of the room.

Trust. The words made her cringe. Once her husband found out the truth, would he ever really trust her again?

33

With all the stares and mumbles she was getting, you would think the town of Jasper, Texas, had never seen a scandal. It was taking everything in Gloria's power to rise above the gossip and not respond to the sneers and snarky comments. There were a few people that were trying to be supportive and offered condolences for the whole situation. But there were some, like catty Helen Grainger, who needed to be put in their place.

Gloria had walked up on Helen cackling with some members right before service. She hadn't heard everything, but she'd heard enough.

"Helen, may I speak with you for a moment?" Gloria said. As if they wanted to see a show, a small crowd slowly gathered in the vestibule.

"For what?" Helen asked.

"Can we go in the pastor's study, please?" Gloria asked.

Helen folded her arms defiantly. "Really, First Lady? If there is anything you need to say to me, you can say it right here. Patsy is a dear friend of mine," she said, motioning to the lady standing next to her. "And so is Lizzie, Lois, and Ethel." The group stood smirking at her. And to think, before all of this, Gloria had considered these women her friends.

"Okay, if that's how you want to play it," Gloria said. She'd been on edge all week. She'd even started calling Kayla's office because she thought they needed to talk. Of course, Kayla wouldn't take her calls. "It's my understanding you're the main source behind the gossip spreading around the church that Jamal is going to, as you told Deacon Cole, rot in prison. I would appreciate it if you didn't try to convict my son before he's had his day in court."

"Well, I saw the video," she said.

"We all did," Patsy chimed in.

"Well, if you did, you would have seen your grandson on there starting the whole thing," Gloria countered. As far as Helen was concerned, her grandson could do no wrong.

"Dix didn't shoot nobody," Helen said.

"Since you saw the video, you saw he was the one that caused things to escalate in the first place by getting smart with the police officer," Gloria said.

"I beg your pardon," Helen snapped.

"I didn't stutter," Gloria snapped right back. Then she caught herself, deciding that the last thing she needed was church drama, so she took a different approach. "Look, none of us knows exactly what happened. How about we just wait before we pass judgment?"

"Ladies, my wife is right." Gloria hadn't even seen her husband enter the vestibule. "Not to mention, this is not the time or the place to have this discussion," Elton said.

Helen crossed her arms, then uncrossed them again. "It seems to me like you need to be worried about getting your house in order," she said. "No disrespect, Pastor, but some of the church elders were talking and we believe that the church anniversary program should not move forward until all of this is resolved."

Elton looked at her, dumbfounded. It shouldn't have surprised Gloria. Helen would seize any opportunity to make their family look bad. They had a beef that went back for years.

"Helen," Elton slowly began, "we've been having the church anniversary every year for the last ninety-six years. We're not about to change that."

"Well, seems like to me and several others that we don't need any more attention brought to our church. Your family is doing a pretty good job of shining a bright enough light."

"You know what I would think?" Elton continued. "I would think that in our time of need our church would be there for us." Several of the members looked down in shame. "Just like I was there for you when your son, Billy, was accused of raping that—"

Helen grabbed her chest. "How dare you."

"I'm just telling you the truth. When he was accused of raping that young girl over in Port Neches." He turned to Patsy. "Just like I was there when your son took your life savings and exchanged it for a twenty-dollar bag of crack. So, don't go there with me and mine's."

The defiant look was actually wiped off Helen's face. In fact, all of the women looked appalled.

"Now, if my son shot Officer Wilkins, and that remains a big if, it was a tragic accident, nothing more." He looked around at everybody standing around the vestibule. "Each and every one of you has known Jamal since he was a little boy. You know as well as

I do what type of kid he is, and yet you're buying into the hype that he's a thug."

Lois, another longtime member, stepped up. "Well, Pastor, someone showed me a website that had a picture from Jamal's Instagram where he was shooting the middle finger."

Gloria had seen that picture and was devastated. It was the one picture that Fox News chose to run over and over.

"And so?" Elton responded. "You know I don't condone that. But Jamal was doing stupid teenage things. He never had any idea that it would come back to haunt him. Now I know some of y'all got some perfect children around here," he said. That caused a few chuckles. "But the bottom line remains, we have no control over the things that our kids do and you know they don't listen to us, and these dang social media sites and that Internet got them acting plumb fools. But you all know Jamal. You know he ain't a plumb fool and you know he ain't a killer."

Helen actually seemed to be shrinking in size. "Sorry, Pastor," she mumbled.

"Now, I understand this is tense for all of us," he continued, "and I don't like bringing this kind of attention to Mount Sinai any more than any of you do. In fact, I probably despise it more. But it is what it is and the good Lord doesn't give us more than we can handle. So what I need each and every one of you to do is just pray for us. Don't gossip, don't talk to the media about us. Just pray. Can you do that?"

"Yes, Pastor," many of them mumbled.

For the first time since this whole ordeal began, Gloria felt something other than contempt for her husband. Maybe they could recover from all of this, she thought.

She'd just have to do like Elton said and pray.

34

H ell had officially frozen over. That's the only thing Kay could say to explain sitting in her private conference room across from the woman she had never expected to see again.

"Thank you for agreeing to come," Gloria said.

Kay had no words. She hadn't wanted to come, but Valerie, of all people, urged her to have the meeting. Gloria had been calling the office nonstop for the past two days. Kay knew Valerie was getting suspicious about why the woman kept calling and Kay kept refusing to talk to her.

Kay was here for one reason only, to find out what Gloria Jones was really up to. She didn't know if Gloria was going to try to blackmail her into a favorable outcome or what. All Kay knew was right about now she needed answers before she could determine her next move.

"Let's not pretend we're here to shoot the breeze," Kay said, taking a seat in the chair across from Gloria.

"Fair enough."

"So what's your game?" Kay asked.

"I told you. I don't have one. I was referred to your husband by Riley Manning. I didn't know there was a connection until after we met and I saw your picture in his office," Gloria said.

"So, you didn't put the name together? Phillip Christiansen? You said that you knew I was the prosecutor."

"Did you put the names together?" Gloria asked.

"There are a million Joneses out there," Kay snapped. "Of course I didn't."

"Well, truthfully, I didn't, either. My mind has been all over the place and I just didn't."

Kay studied her, like she was trying to determine if she was being truthful. "I bet you did a backflip when you found out I was the prosecutor."

"Quite the contrary. I mean, initially I did, but then I thought, I know you have a lot of bitterness," Gloria said.

"Ya think?"

Gloria fiddled with her purse strap. "I just want to make sure you don't take that bitterness out on Jamal. Elton—"

"Don't. Don't even . . ." Kay held up her hand to stop Gloria from bringing up that man's name, which would only make this conversation go south.

"Okay, okay. I'm sorry. I just want you to be fair."

"Fair?" Kay leaned forward. "Wow. First of all, I take my job seriously. I'm always fair."

"But I know you hate—"

"More than you will ever know," Kay interrupted her. She took a deep breath, leaned back, tried to calm herself, then continued. "But I'm past that. I moved on. I have a good life."

"We did, too. And Jamal, well, he's a good kid."

"I have a police officer's widow that would say otherwise."

"Does Phillip know?"

Kay glared at Gloria. So now they were getting somewhere. Gloria was slowly revealing her true intentions. "No one knows. And I'd like to keep it that way. Let me remind you that you stand to lose just as much as me."

Gloria didn't seem rattled. "Right now, the only thing I care about is Jamal."

So she wanted to play hardball? Kay needed to show this woman that she didn't get to this point in her career for no reason. "Let me stop you just in case you have any inkling of an idea to try to extort a verdict out of me."

Gloria looked shocked. Her hands went to her chest like she was clutching some imaginary pearls. "I would never in a million years do anything like that."

"Good. Because I would hate to prosecute you *and* your son."

Gloria was quiet, then she said, "So you don't feel anything?"

"Toward you? Your husband? Tell me, what should I feel?" she snarled.

"Not us. I don't blame you for hating us."

Kay was silent for a minute, then said, "I don't hate you. I hate your husband."

Gloria looked down. "He's made peace with that. He sought and received forgiveness."

Kay released a pained laugh. "Oh, has he now? That's how your God works? Your husband can do his dirt, say two Hail Marys, and all is forgiven?"

"That's how *our* God works," Gloria said matter-of-factly.

"You know what?" Kay stood. "You can save this speech for someone else."

Gloria stopped her. "I wasn't asking about us. Jamal. Do you feel anything for Jamal?"

She glared at Gloria. "I don't know Jamal."

"But if you did . . ."

"But I don't."

"Kayla . . ."

"My name is Kay!" she shouted, pounding the table. "Kay! Kayla stopped existing the day your husband raped me! And you, with your self-righteous, dutiful, naïve self, sat in that church and told those people that I seduced him! That I, a fifteen-year-old girl, seduced her pastor!"

Gloria's eyes watered and Kay took a moment to compose herself. She couldn't believe that she'd lost her cool.

"I-I'm sorry," Gloria mumbled.

Kay inhaled. Exhaled. "Like I said, I'm over it. Anything that pertains to this case will be done with pure professionalism. Other than that, I have nothing to say to you or your husband."

Kay turned and stormed out of the room. She had to get somewhere and get some air. Get out of sight before she burst into tears.

Instead of going right back to her office, Kay went to the left, out into the stairwell, and up to the roof. She went there sometimes when she needed to clear her head and focus on a case. She really needed to clear her head now.

The crisp October air was a welcome relief. Kay took deep breaths, letting the air fill her lungs. But try as she might, she couldn't keep the memories from coming back.

35

Kayla Matthews had always been a bit of a social outcast. She'd wanted desperately to fit in, but nobody wanted to be friends with the daughter of a super-sanctified couple. And Gwen and Robert Matthews were as sanctified as they came in Baton Rouge, Louisiana. They'd just started letting Kayla wear pants when she turned fifteen, two months prior. But boys, dating, and parties, Kayla could forget. So of course, that put her on the "least likely to get asked to hang out" list.

That's why when Maxine Lewis and her friend Tasha Gore asked Kayla to study and hang out with them, she'd jumped at the offer. It was probably only because Maxine went to New Hope Missionary Baptist Church, where Kayla had been a member since she was three years old. Maxine used to be quiet like Kayla, but for the last few months, it was like she had become a different person. She was loud, disrespectful to adults, and just had a really bad attitude. But Kayla was grateful to have a friend, so she jumped at the chance to hang with them.

"I'm tired of studying," Tasha said. They'd agreed to meet in one of the church Sunday school rooms so Kayla could tutor Maxine and Tasha in algebra. They'd only been at it for about twenty minutes, fifteen of which Maxine and Tasha goofed off.

"Me, too." Maxine closed her textbook, like there was no more discussion.

"So, I meant to ask you, what's up with you and your mama?" Tasha asked Maxine. "I saw y'all arguing when she dropped you off."

"Ooh, don't even talk to me about that ho," Maxine snarled.

Kayla was mortified. She couldn't stand her parents, but never in a katrillion years would she dream of saying something like that about them.

Tasha laughed like it was no big deal.

"Why are you mad at your mom?" Kayla found herself asking.

"Cuz her mama is a bi—"

"Uh," Maxine cut her off. "You are in a church, you know?"

"My bad." Tasha laughed as she hopped up on a utility table.

Maxine turned back to Kayla. "But she's telling the truth. My mama makes me sick."

"Her mama wanted y'all's pastor," Tasha said jokingly. "She thought she was gonna be the pastor's side piece, but he found him another piece." She chuckled, side-eyeing Maxine.

"Shut up, Tasha!" Maxine snapped.

Kayla was too stunned to pay much attention to their bickering. When she'd first met Maxine eight years ago, the two of them had been such introverts that they'd never really struck up a friendship. But while they weren't friends, Kayla did know her. Or at least she thought she did.

This girl standing here, calling her mother names and wagging her neck, was a completely different person.

"Why you looking at me like that?" Maxine asked, her attitude strong as she tossed her shoulder-length wavy hair.

"I'm just tripping on you, and you know the way you are," Kayla said. "Like, you used to be so . . . sweet and nice."

Maxine rolled her eyes. "Nice girls finish last. So I guess I gotta be bad."

She and Tasha gave each other a high-five before Tasha said, "Since we're being bad . . ." Tasha smiled as she pulled a pack of Virginia Slims out of her pocket, then waved the cigarettes. "Who's up for some smokes?"

"Yes!" Maxine said.

No! Kayla wanted to add. But she remained quiet.

"You smoke?" Tasha asked.

Kayla shrugged. "Sometimes," she lied.

Tasha motioned for them to follow her into the storage closet at the back of the room. As soon as Maxine closed the door, Tasha lit up. They giggled as they passed the cigarette around. Kayla tried her best to appear cool, like this was something she did all the time.

"I know that you young ladies are not sitting up in my storage closet smoking cigarettes!"

They had all been so deep in their act that they hadn't noticed the pastor, Rev. Elton Jones, open the door. One of the most respected men in Baton Rouge, Pastor Jones had to be pushing forty, although he didn't look like most creepy old men she knew. He looked like he might have been handsome when he was younger.

"Pastor Jones," Maxine said, pushing the cigarette behind her back. For a girl who had been putting on such bravado a few minutes ago, she looked more scared than any of them.

Pastor Jones stood in the doorway, his large frame towering over them. "Maxine, I am shocked at you." She cowered under his glare. He turned to Tasha. "And you, young lady, I don't know who you are, but this is not how we do things at New Hope." Lastly, he turned to Kayla. "Kayla. I am so disappointed in you, I don't know what to say."

Kayla lowered her head in shame. At least Maxine tried to speak up.

"We were just—"

"Don't add lying on top of everything else." He shook his head. "You girls need to get on out of here."

None of them needed to be told twice. They darted toward the door, but just as Kayla tried to step through, Rev. Jones grabbed her arm. "Kayla, you stay."

Maxine stopped and looked at her. She must have been scared that Kayla was about to get in serious trouble, because the expression on Maxine's face was one of absolute terror.

"Go on," Rev. Jones said, waving Maxine away. "I need to speak with Kayla."

Without another look, Maxine took off.

Kayla was trembling with fear as Rev. Jones motioned for her to step back into the storage closet.

"I can't believe you, Kayla," he began as he closed the door. "What do you think your parents are going to do when they find out what you were in here doing?"

"I-I . . ."

"I know your dad still believes in that belt. And if he doesn't tear your behind up, your parents will probably ground you until you're twenty-one."

"I'm so sorry."

He was quiet for a moment, then said, "You know I'm going to have to tell them."

"Please, Pastor. Please don't tell them," Kayla begged. Her father would try to kill her. And if she survived, she'd never get to go anywhere again in life.

He stopped and a small grin crept onto his face. "What you gonna do for me if I don't tell?"

She had no idea what she could possibly do for him, since he was one of the most powerful men in Baton Rouge, but still, she said, "Whatever you want. Just please don't tell."

"Whatever I want?" He took a step toward her, licking his lips, his eyes settling on her budding cleavage.

"Ummm . . ."

"I want you." He stepped closer. "I see the way you're filling out." He ran a finger down her arm. "You're so innocent. So pure. Not like all these other fast-tail girls around here."

"P-pastor, what are you doing?" she managed to say.

"I'm taking you up on your offer to give me whatever I want." He pushed her up against the wall.

"No. Please," she cried when she realized what he was doing.

"Shhhh," he said as he pinned her up against the wall with one hand and fumbled with his other hand to get his pants down. "Come on, Sweet Pea, settle down."

"No!" She squirmed. "Please, no."

That made him moan more and he seemed to zone out, as he covered her mouth to stifle her cries and penetrated her until she blacked out.

. . .

Kay didn't realize she was crying until she heard Loni say, "Kay, are you okay?"

"Huh? Yeah. Sorry. I was lost in thought." Kay quickly wiped her eyes and turned to face Loni.

"Are you crying?"

"No. No," Kay said. "The wind is making me tear up."

Loni eyed her skeptically as she waited to feel the nonexistent wind. "Okay. If you say so. I've been looking everywhere for you. Valerie said you might be up here."

Kay tried to compose herself. "Yeah, just taking a break. Getting some fresh air. What's up?"

"I just wanted to remind you about your meeting with the Urban League in the morning," Loni continued.

"Thank you, Loni. I don't know what I'd do without you."

"Hopefully, you'll never have to find out." Loni smiled. "But come on, these rooftop excursions scare me."

Kay returned her smile and was thankful that Loni had left it at that.

36

Gloria hadn't been able to stop crying since she left Kayla's office. Kayla's pain was so raw. After all these years, it was still raw.

Gloria cried for Kayla and the innocence that Elton had taken away from her. She cried for the lifetime of bitterness that Kayla had held on to. She cried for her son, praying that he didn't pay for his father's sin. And then she cried as her mind raced back to the past and she recalled the role that she had played in all of this.

Gloria was shaking, from both anger and embarrassment. Elton stood next to her in their living room with his head bowed. Standing in front of them were Kayla and her parents. Gloria hadn't been able to process the news that she had just been told.

"So how do you know her child is Elton's?" Gloria asked.

Kayla looked up in horror. It was at that point that Gloria saw the welts across her cheek. Gloria could only imagine the pain Robert Matthews had inflicted on his daughter. Anger blanketed both Robert's and Gwen's faces.

"Because she told us so," Robert snapped.

As angry as she was, Gloria still wanted to take Kayla in her arms, hold her, and tell the young girl she'd watched grow up that everything was going to be all right. Gloria was a little shocked that Gwen wasn't hugging and holding her daughter. But they just stood next to Kayla.

The Matthewses had shown up on the doorstep after calling to demand a meeting. Gloria had no idea what they wanted and when Elton had done everything under the sun to get out of the meeting, she knew something was up. She just never expected this.

"Well, our daughter will not have a child out of wedlock, especially with a married preacher. We're going to fix this," Robert said.

Kayla cried more and Gloria's heart dropped. "You're going to make her have an abortion?" Gloria asked, shocked.

Elton's eyes lit up. He'd looked hopeful and that sent a ripple of disgust through Gloria's veins. It was bad enough she had been unable to give him children. A bout with cervical cancer in her early twenties had left her barren. Elton had told her he was okay with that and they'd built a life with just the two of them.

"We are absolutely not having an abortion," Gwen exclaimed. "A great sin has been committed and we're not about to commit another one."

"Then what are you going to do?" Elton finally spoke.

"Well, first of all, I want to know what happened. Kayla won't tell us anything. It took a beating to even get your name out of her. We wouldn't have even known she was pregnant if my wife didn't know her womanly cycle." He glared at his daughter. Pure hatred resonated from his pores. "She won't tell us anything else. Only that she did not want this to happen. She has shamed this family and I will never forgive her." He took a step toward Elton. "Pastor, I'm going to ask you this and as God is my witness, you better tell me the truth. Did you force yourself upon my daughter?"

Elton's eyes grew wide as he looked at Kayla, then at Gloria, and back at Robert. "No, no!" he said. And then he buried his face in his hands and sobbed. "I am so sorry," he cried. "I did have sex with her. I was weak. She kept seducing me and coming on to me and in one weak moment, I gave in."

"What?" Kayla cried. It was the first word that she'd spoken. "That's not what happened!"

Gwen turned to her daughter and said, "Be quiet!"

"But Mama . . ."

Robert snapped, "You heard your mother!"

Elton ignored them as he turned to Gloria. "You know I have been true to you. I just had a weak moment. I tried to follow Second Timothy and flee from youthful lusts and pursue righteousness. Yet the lips of a seductive woman are oh, so sweet."

Gloria couldn't believe her husband was quoting Bible verses to justify his actions. She felt sick to her stomach. There had been lots of women who wanted Elton. Wilma Lewis had all but declared she was going to make him hers. There had also been rumblings of an indiscretion with an underage girl, but Gloria had never been able to prove anything. And Elton had always maintained that any advances to him were purely one-sided. And Gloria had believed him. He'd never given her reason not to.

But this confession now had her doubting everything.

Elton continued, trying to plead with both her and the Matthewses. "I never meant for it to happen. She was . . . she was in the storage closet, smoking."

"Smoking!" Gwen yelled. "You must be mistaken. My daughter doesn't smoke."

"There are a lot of things your daughter does that you aren't aware of," Elton said.

Tears just continued flowing down Kayla's face as her chest heaved up and down.

"Were you smoking?" Robert demanded. Kayla didn't immediately reply, causing her father to yell again. "I said, were you smoking?"

"Y-yes, but . . ."

"Lord, Jesus," Gwen muttered. She grabbed the back of the sofa to keep from toppling over.

"When I said something to her about it, when I caught her," Elton continued, "she begged me not to tell you all. She opened her shirt and said she would give herself to me if only I kept my mouth closed. It was wrong. But I was weak."

"He's lying," Kayla cried.

Gwen reached out and slapped her. "Don't you dare call the pastor a liar!"

Gloria knew her husband well, or at least she thought she did. Despite the advances, despite the rumors, in all their years of marriage he had never shown so much as an iota of interest in another woman around her. Could this little girl really be his seductress? Elton wouldn't lie about something like this, would he?

As Kayla sobbed, Robert took a step back.

"Well, we needed to know what happened. My wife and I will make proper arrangements and figure out what to do from here.

Pastor, I am very disappointed. As you know, my wife and I will not be able to stay at your church."

"I am so sorry to hear that. You have been a lifetime member." Elton was shaking. But Gloria couldn't tell if it was from fear or relief.

"Yes, we have been at New Hope all of our lives, which is why it pains us to have to leave," Gwen said.

"But we hold our pastor to a higher standard and we simply cannot continue receiving the Word from you," Robert added.

"I understand," Elton said.

Gloria took in a trembling Kayla. She looked like a little girl. But over the years, Gloria had seen many a woman all but throw herself at her husband. Could they simply be starting younger now? Then, as if to erase any doubts, a voice in Gloria's head spoke up. *She's not a little girl. She's. A. Woman. A woman who is giving your husband what you can't.*

That thought made Gloria's stomach feel like it was on the spin cycle of a Whirlpool washer and at that moment she didn't know who she hated more . . . her husband or the child who had seduced him.

.   .   .

"I know you're worried about him, but God will work it out."

The sound of Elton's voice snapped Gloria back to the present. He'd come out onto the back porch, where she'd been sitting. Of course, he would think she was thinking about Jamal. He'd long ago blocked out any memory of what happened with Kayla. And that had been his philosophy ever since. Pretend bad things didn't happen. Gloria hated that for years, yet she'd gone along with it.

"I hope you're right, Elton," she replied.

"I am. God gives His hardest test to the strongest." He sat down next to her and gently took her hand. Gloria didn't snatch it away, but the electricity she used to feel, the love that resonated through her body whenever her husband touched her, was gone. Right now, Gloria Jones felt nothing.

37

Kay sat at her desk in a daze. She was not one to goof off, but her mind had been mush since her visit with Gloria. When she shut out that part of her life she was sure that it was over. The death of her parents three years ago solidified that she would never have to revisit the entire thing again. And yet here was the past, perched on her doorstep.

"Knock, knock." Loni stuck her head in the door. "Good news." She walked in before Kay could reply. "The poll numbers are in." She waved a piece of paper at her. "And guess who's leading?"

Kay managed a smile. "That's good to hear."

Loni frowned and approached Kay's desk. "Well, you sure don't act like this is good news."

"No, just got a lot going on," Kay replied.

"Yeah, this case. I just don't understand why you took it on," Loni said.

"Uh, because you told me to. You said the publicity would help, remember?"

Loni waved her comment away. "I changed my mind. Can't you pass it on to someone else? It's just too time consuming and we've got to get you prepped and ready. These interview requests are rolling in left and right."

Kay thought for a moment, what she wouldn't give to pass this case on now. "You know, I may actually give that some thought," she said.

"Seriously?" Loni said, surprised. "Wow, I was just mouthing off. I really didn't expect you to walk away. You've never walked away from a case."

"I've never been up in the polls, either," Kay said, forcing a smile.

"Well, honey, let me know if you do because I will vamp up your marketing and publicity." Loni's bushy natural curls bounced with delight.

"Okay, I'll let you know. I'm going to give it some serious thought."

Loni strutted out of the room and Kay leaned back in her chair.

Walk away, that's what she had to do. But there was no way her boss was going to go for that. She'd have to tell him the truth. *The truth.* If she needed to be telling anyone, it was Phillip. Phillip didn't need to be blindsided by this. He would be so angry. When they were dating, there were many occasions where she started to tell him the truth about her past, but once those wounds had healed, she had no desire to open them up again. But what if Gloria was lying and did try to blackmail her for a favorable verdict? Gloria didn't seem like the blackmailing type, but there was desperation in her eyes. Over the years, Kay had seen that look in too many mothers' eyes. She knew at this point that Gloria Jones was capable of anything.

No, it was time. She needed to have a talk with her husband. She needed to be honest and then she needed to step down from this case and hope that her plans to be Houston's next mayor weren't completely derailed.

· · ·

Kay had practiced her speech all the way home, but as soon as she turned down the street into her neighborhood, the words didn't feel right. So she made a U-turn and headed in the opposite direction. She wasn't ready to go home. Not yet. Not until she figured out how her life had taken this wrong turn down Disaster Street.

She pulled into a park about five minutes from her neighborhood and just sat, thinking.

Her past was coming back to throw her picture-perfect world into a tailspin.

Her past. She'd tried everything to erase the past from her memories but like a jilted, obsessive ex, the past refused to go away.

And as she sat in the driver's seat in the parking lot of Memorial Park, memories of the past returned fast and furious.

· · ·

"Okay, Kayla, I need you to push."

"What do you think I'm doing?" Kayla screamed.

Usually Kayla wouldn't dare think of being disrespectful to her elders. Her mother had taught her better than that, but right now, all of her life lessons had gone out the window. Right now, all she cared about was getting this thing out.

"Okay, I see the head. I just need you to take slow breaths. You're doing good," the doctor said.

How women *wanted* to do this was beyond her and the thought that some women actually prayed for this was a concept that she couldn't understand. Who would want to endure this kind of pain? Her cousin, Nikki, had told her that the pleasure that created this position made it all worth it, but she wouldn't know anything about that. There had been no pleasure in creating the life inside her. Since it had happened, Kayla had spent every waking moment trying to erase it from her existence.

"Push, Kayla, push!" the doctor urged.

She wanted to scream that she was pushing as hard as she could. But the pain was so unbearable, she just wanted to pass out.

"Argghh!" Kayla screamed as she summoned every ounce of strength inside her and pushed.

A nurse held her hand. "Come on, sweetie, you're doing good." She stroked her hair. "You're almost there; it's almost over."

Kay couldn't wait for this nightmare to be over. For nine months she'd endured the shame, the changes in her body, the sickness, and the hatred from her parents. And she had literally done it all by herself since her parents would barely look at her.

"Arggghh!" In what was the most excruciating pain ever, as her privates felt like they were being ripped apart, Kay gave a final push. Then she felt a glimmer of relief, followed by the wail of an infant.

"It's a boy," the doctor said, taking the baby and quickly handing him to a nurse. "You've got yourself a little boy."

The nurse took the baby away and wiped him down using some kind of suction-like instrument. Kayla did what she'd been doing for months. She cried.

"Do you want to hold your baby?" the nurse asked.

Kayla had hated that thing for nine months, so why did she have a sudden urge to hold it? But before she could say anything, her mother swooped in.

"No, that will only make this more difficult. We've already discussed this. Please take it away."

Him, Kayla wanted to say. Take *him* away. But she bit her bottom lip and stayed quiet as the infant continued wailing. They'd had this discussion many times; her mother had even warned her that it might be difficult, that maternal instincts might kick in. Kayla didn't know what that feeling was inside her heart right now but it couldn't have been that maternal instinct her mother was talking about. She couldn't have been attached to that demon seed.

Demon seed. That was the name she'd given the child she'd carried. Because he was indeed created from the seed of the devil himself.

Kayla had wanted to abort the baby but heaven forbid her ultra-religious parents succumb to abortion. "A baby's life is precious," they'd told her. Not precious enough for her to keep. But precious enough to live. Not that she wanted to keep this child anyway. She didn't need a constant reminder of Pastor Elton Jones. And she didn't want to end up like her cousin, Nikki, living in this deadbeat town raising babies the rest of her life. She had every intention to leave Baton Rouge come September. Even with the pregnancy, even with being whisked away to be homeschooled, even with being ripped away from her few friends and life in general, Kayla had managed to get her high school diploma. She'd managed to stay on top of her grades and amass enough credits to get her diploma early—three weeks before her baby was born.

Soon as she healed, Kayla planned to be on the first thing

smoking. She would forget her rape. She'd forget her life, she would forget her son, and she would start a completely new life.

· · ·

A new life. That's what the past nearly seventeen years had been. So why was she being punished now?

Her cell rang and Phillip's number popped up. He was probably wondering where she was. Kay didn't answer, but she did start her car. She'd talk to Phillip at home and she'd tell him everything.

38

————
——

ast night was a bust. When she'd gotten home from the park
yesterday, Phillip had been gone, called out by the mother of
one of the boys he mentored who had gotten into trouble. Kay
had been asleep when he got back in. And then he was out the
door before she got up. It's like the devil was trying to keep her
secret buried deep.

Kay had no idea how Phillip was going to take the news, but
she did know one thing . . . tonight, she would tell him. She already
made sure he would be home, so there could be no backing down.

Kay gathered together the file on Jamal because she fully expected to turn it over to her boss and recuse herself from the case.

Her Prada shoes clicked as she made her way through the parking garage toward her car. She had just hit the button to turn off her
alarm when she heard someone come up behind her. Kay turned
around, the Mace on her keychain poised to ward off an attacker.

"Hey, hey, hey, little lady." Marty Simon, the man running
against her for mayor, held up his hands and smiled. "Calm down.

It's just me, ol' Marty," he said, his voice rich with a deep Texas twang.

"Marty," Kay said, relaxing. He looked like a walking cliché, the ten-gallon cowboy hat, oversized belt buckle, Wrangler jeans, blazer, and cowhide boots—all of which fit his Texas-sized personality. She'd known about him for roughly three years now, since he started lambasting the current mayor and laying the foundation to run. "You should know better than sneaking up on women in a deserted garage," she told him.

"Yeah, you're right. I forgot I'm dealing with a spunky little filly." He laughed.

She shifted her bag to her other arm and blew a long breath. "Yes, Marty? Is there something I can help you with? Is there a reason you're in my parking garage this late in the evening?"

"Well," he said, pulling back his jacket as he draped his fingers through his belt loop. "I just thought I would come and personally pay you a little visit."

"And why would you do that?" She opened her car door and tossed her briefcase onto the backseat of her car.

"Well, seems like to me this election is mighty close."

"It is." She folded her arms. "But I'm sure you didn't come over here to talk shop. So, what's up?"

"Are you sure you want to be mayor of Houston?"

She kept her smile. "I wouldn't run if I wasn't sure."

"Hmm . . ." He nodded his head. "You know, I'm sure you know my history." His twang continued to punctuate each word. "I don't like to lose."

"And so I've heard."

"I don't even like it to appear that I'm losing," he continued.

"And these doggone poll numbers are pointing in that direction."

"It ain't over until it's over," she said with a smile. The last thing she wanted was to appear too cocky with him and give him even more fuel to try to defeat her. He outspent her two-to-one already so she didn't need him beefing up spending in these last few weeks.

"Yep, that sure is right. But I think it's about over," Marty said.

"What does that mean?" Kay asked, losing her grin.

"How is your case going?" he asked, with a smirk across his face.

Kay stared at him. "What are you talking about?"

"Case? You know. The one you're prosecuting. Jamal Jones, that's his name, right? Jamal Jones. That thug that shot a police officer in Jasper. How's it coming?"

"If you've been watching the news, you've seen." She was getting nervous now. Men like Marty Simon didn't waste time on idle chatter.

"I have indeed been watching the news," he said, before slowing his words and looking her directly in the eyes, "but nobody is talking about the fact that you're prosecuting your own son."

All the air was sucked from her belly.

"Oh," Marty said, snapping his fingers, "maybe they're not talking about it because they don't know." He paused before adding, "Yet."

"I don't know what you think you know," Kay said. She was trying to make sure her voice didn't crack.

"I know that I know, little lady," Marty said with a grin. "I know that you got that secret bastard child that you haven't told anyone about. Not even your dear husband. Wonder how he's going to feel knowing he's defending his wife's bastard son."

Kay had to lean back on her car to keep from falling over. How in the world could he have known that? *Gloria*. She was the only one who could have said something, but why?

"I'm not even going to have you insult my intelligence by trying to deny it," Marty continued. "So, I'm just going to shoot straight, 'cause you know that's the only way to shoot." He lost his smile. "I'm thinking that you need to call a special press conference and tell the public that you're dropping out of the race."

She glared at him. "You know that's not happening."

"Mmm . . . let's see. Should I call your husband first?" He pulled out his cell phone. "Or the news media and let them know?" When Kay didn't respond, he dropped his phone back into his pocket. "If you need help preparing a statement, you know I got great people on my team. They can write you up something real good."

"I don't need your help doing anything." Kay shook as she tried to maintain her composure. His smugness was pissing her off. "I'm not stepping down," she added.

"Hmm . . . you might want to go home and think about that," Marty said.

"I'll tell my husband myself."

"Well, you do that," he replied, not the least bit fazed. "And I'm sure he'll forgive you. The people, however, won't be so forgiving. Especially from a politician who built her platform on truth and transparency."

"You don't know the circumstances."

"Oh, I know enough. Seems like the defendant's preacher man daddy forced himself on you when you were just a little girl. Now, Marty knows that may get you a sympathy vote from all the raging feminists, but that lying"—he wagged a finger—"I already have the commercial planned out, 'If she lied to the people, she can't be trusted to lead.' And not to mention all the rape cases you've prosecuted that will probably be filing appeals and looking to have their convictions overturned because an overzealous prosecutor was trying to seek revenge. Just sounds messy, don't you think?"

"Why are you doing this?" she asked.

"Li'l lady, Marty Simon plays to win." He winked at her again like they shared some big secret.

"You know what, Marty? The last thing you want to be doing is blackmailing a law enforcement officer."

"Oh, I'm not blackmailing anyone." His smile returned. "I'm just telling you what I know. And I told you I like things to go my way and if things don't go my way, I'm just gonna have to tell a few folks what I know."

She glared at him and said, "You do what you have to do," and then climbed into her car.

"I'll be waiting for that press conference, Mrs. Christiansen. And if it doesn't go how I want, let's just say you might want to bring your fire extinguisher to the debate because there's gonna be lots of sparks flying. You have a good day now, you hear?"

He patted the hood of her car as she backed away. It took everything in her power not to floor the accelerator and run him over, but she simply pulled out of the parking garage before he could see her completely break down.

39

Her husband was no saint. Gloria had known that from the day he started wooing her when she was in the ninth grade at Baton Rouge High School. He was a senior and she had been smitten. He was a man of faith, even then. And although Gloria grew to despise some of his ways, she loved him enough to overlook his flaws. She was always overlooking things in the name of love.

Gloria had believed in him, blindly believed in him. She believed in him when he said Kayla had seduced him. She believed him when he said how devastated he was and begged for her forgiveness. And she believed him, she told herself, because she didn't want to believe her husband was capable of something so horrible. But with age had come wisdom and Gloria knew better. Even if Kayla had been some type of seductress, he was the adult. He was her spiritual leader. He was supposed to say no.

They fought for weeks after the Matthewses showed up at her doorstep, breaking the news of Kayla's pregnancy. That had been the most difficult time of Gloria's life. The Matthewses hadn't pressed charges, but they had told the church board, and of course, the rumor mill took it from there. The scandal had cost Elton his church and he sank into a deep depression. That had hurt Gloria's heart and, like Elton, she found herself blaming Kayla. They moved to Lake Charles just to escape the gossip and start over. For months they lived in fear that the Matthewses would change their minds and press charges, but they never heard from Gwen or Robert again—until one day, Gwen called.

"Hello," Gloria had said, answering her ringing phone.

"First Lady?"

Gloria grimaced. Nobody called her First Lady anymore. Didn't a First Lady require a church? She and Elton had nothing.

"Yes, this is Gloria," she said.

"It's Gwen. Gwen Matthews."

Gloria had had to sit down. She wasn't sure if this was the call they had been dreading. The call to let her know the Matthewses would be pressing charges. But instead Gwen simply said, "Kayla had the baby."

"Okay," Gloria said, only because she didn't know what else to say. "What did she have?"

"A boy."

Gloria didn't know why, but she felt something in her stomach. It was almost as if her longing for a child had been reawakened.

"We are at my sister's in Arkansas. We have an agency that is going to take him. He'll be put in foster care. But we need Pastor—" Gwen paused—"we need Elton to sign away his rights. The agency won't take the baby without it."

Gloria didn't know how she was supposed to respond to that. So she was silent for a minute. Then finally, "Okay, I'll let him know."

"I need to hear back from him today."

"I'll give him the message." She took down the number to reach Gwen and then waited for Elton to come back from the store. That's what he spent his days doing now, reading the Bible, praying for redemption, as he said, trying to get back in tune with God, and going to the store. Their savings had been exhausted and both of them took odd jobs just to make ends meet while Elton searched for another church.

"Hey," Elton said as he walked up the stairs and watched her sitting on the front porch in an old wicker rocking chair. "How are you?"

"I'm fine," she said. "Got a call."

Since she'd hung up with Gwen, Gloria had been thinking and thinking. And the longing in her loins had exploded into a full-fledged fire.

"Kayla had the baby."

Elton looked away, shifting as if he didn't know how to respond. "Oh," was all he said.

"They need you to sign some paperwork, giving up your rights to the baby. To your son," she found herself adding.

"Son?" he said.

"Yes, she had a boy."

More silence, then finally, "Okay."

He came up onto the porch and passed her as he headed inside, but just when he reached the screen door, she said, "I've been thinking."

He turned to her. "About what?"

"We've lost everything," she said, rocking back and forth. "Maybe this is God's way for us to make it right, to start over. Maybe this baby is your redemption."

"I don't understand," he said.

She stood and went to face her husband, "I think we should take the baby."

"What?" he exclaimed.

"The Matthewses are giving the baby up for adoption. They don't want to have anything to do with the child. They're in Arkansas and planned to leave the child in a foster home there. I think we should take him and raise him as our own."

"Woman, are you crazy?" he said.

She folded her arms. The idea had just come to her, but now she felt it to the very core of her bones.

"I want the baby," she said with finality.

"Come on, Gloria. How will this work? Everybody knows you haven't, that you're not pregnant."

"Then we move. There is nothing keeping us here. We get the baby and we move somewhere else and start over and we raise the child as our own and we redeem ourselves. We can go to Jasper in your father's house." Elton's father had passed away last year, but Elton was too sentimental to sell his house.

"Gloria, I don't think that's a good idea."

She glared at her husband. After everything that he'd put her through, this wasn't open for discussion as far as she was concerned. "The number is on the kitchen table," she said. "Call and let them know what time we'll be by to pick up our son. I'm going to go start packing up our stuff."

And with that she went inside, leaving him on the front porch. This baby was her consolation prize. The pain that Elton had caused her, she might as well get something out of it, and that something would be the thing she most wanted in the world.

40

S hut the front door and jump off the roof." Kay couldn't help
but laugh at Camille's cornball saying. Her own laughter was
a welcome sound. She'd been so stressed this past week, laughter
hadn't dared show up on her doorstep. But that's why she loved
the woman sitting in front of her. She silently chastised herself for
not spending more time with Camille. Camille always managed
to bring laughter into her life, and right about now, Kay needed
a whole lot of that. After all, who could take in the news that
their best friend had been essentially living a lie and this be their
response?

"Hello!" Camille said, snapping her fingers in Kay's face. "You
can't drop a bombshell like that, then zone out."

"Oh, sorry," Kay replied.

"You're sorry, all right. Keeping some juicy stuff from me all
this time."

Kay leaned into the table, setting down her spicy pineapple
margarita. They were at the Cheesecake Factory, where Camille

had all but demanded Kay meet her because she said she could hear in her voice that something was wrong.

"So, let me get this straight," Camille said. "You got a baby."

"He's not a baby anymore."

"Okay, so you *had* a baby. You gave him up for adoption and now he's back as the defendant in a case you're prosecuting and your husband is the defendant's attorney?" Her hand bounced like she was dissecting a sentence.

Kay nodded. "In a nutshell."

"Chile," Camille said, taking a sip of the drink, "Lifetime ain't got nothing on you. Shoot, you need to be calling up TVOne, BET, HBO, somebody needs to make this a movie of the week."

One of the things Kay liked about sharing with Camille was that there was no judgment. Not even a hint. Of course, she was shocked because she called Kay a "Dolly Do Right" who could do no wrong, but outside of her shock, she didn't try to make Kay feel bad.

"You know I'm speechless, right? I mean, I knew something was wrong, but I was expecting you to say you were mad because Phillip left the toilet seat up or something."

"No, but that's only the beginning."

"You mean there's more?" Camille barked. "Hold on." She summoned the waiter and he scurried over. "I'm going to need another one of these, like real fast." The waiter nodded before taking off. "Okay, what more could there be?"

"Let's see. Shall I begin with the fact that I'm being blackmailed with the fact that Jamal is my son or that I'm thinking I need to step down from the case?"

"Whoa. First things first. Blackmailing? Who's blackmailing you?"

"Marty Simon. Somehow he found out about everything and now he's threatening to expose me if I don't drop out of the mayoral race."

"Wow," Camille said. "See, that's why I can't be a politician. I'd be on the news right now for cutting his throat the minute he came at me with this mess."

Kay smiled. Camille wouldn't have resorted to murder, but she was hot-tempered enough that she wouldn't have taken a blackmail threat lightly.

"Of course, it caught me off guard," Kay said.

"So, what are you going to do?"

Kay shrugged. "I'm not stepping down. I have too many people that have invested time and effort into my campaign and I really do want to make a difference for the city."

"Yeah, I get that. And I don't think you should step down. But let's back up. You have so much going on I just can't figure out where to start. How are you going to represent the state in prosecuting your son?"

"I can't," Kay said, then let out a heavy sigh. "Ethically, I have no choice but to step down. And even if Marty didn't know, I know. What do I look like trying the son I gave birth to? Can I be responsible for putting him on death row? I've already said I was going for the death penalty. How would I look taking it off the table now?"

"Because you know Texas will execute somebody in a New York minute."

"I know. I can't bear that burden."

"So, what does Phillip say about all of this?"

Kay bit down on her bottom lip. Camille stared at her, closed her eyes, and shook her head. She picked her glass up and downed the rest of her drink. She set the empty glass back down, opened her eyes back up, and looked at Kay. "Your husband doesn't know," she said. It was a fact, not a question.

"No."

"And you're sitting here with me at the Cheesecake Factory and not at home breaking the news to him?"

"I just don't know how to tell him. I mean, I was on my way to tell him about Jamal, then Marty stopped me."

Camille leaned into the table. "Tell him like you just told me. Come on, Kay. Phillip is one of the good guys. I'm sure he's going to be mad, but he'll get over it. You can't let him find out about this some other way."

"I know. I know. It just all came at me so fast."

Camille picked up her napkin, reached for her purse, then pulled out a pen.

"What are you doing?" Kay asked.

"I'm making you a to-do list." Camille scribbled away on the napkin.

"A what?"

"To-do," Camille said as she kept writing. When she was done, she slid the napkin across the table.

Kay picked it up and started reading. "Number one, tell my husband about my secret. Number two, stab Marty Simon in the neck."

Kay laughed. "I'm not stabbing anyone."

Camille took the napkin back, scratched through the word *stab* and wrote *maim*. "No?" she said, raising an eyebrow at Kay.

"No," Kay replied.

"Okay, we'll come back to that one," Camille said, sliding the napkin back toward her. "Keep reading."

"Number three," Kay continued, "find out how Marty got the information to blackmail me." Kay looked up at her friend. "Well, I think I know that. It has to be Gloria, Jamal's adopted mother. She's a desperate mother fighting for her son's freedom."

"That doesn't make any sense," Camille replied. "Why would she give Marty the info to blackmail you? Why would she even care about a mayor's race?"

"I don't know. I can't figure that part out."

"I don't know about that one. It's just not adding up. I deal with a lot of lowlifes and I don't see what she'd get by working with Marty. It's somebody else behind that."

"Well, I don't know who else would do it."

"Well, that's what number three is, find out," Camille said, tapping the napkin. "Keep reading."

Kay returned her attention to the paper napkin. "Okay, number four . . ." She was quiet for a moment, then looked at Camille. "Meet my son?"

"Yep. You can't tell me it doesn't bother you. I see it in your eyes. You may have given him up and tried to erase him from your memory. But you can't erase him from your heart."

Kay looked away. "No, what in the world would I say?"

"Okay, fine. But you will come back to number four. Read number five."

Kay read the fifth thing on the to-do list and smiled. "Really? Get my hair done?"

Camille nodded and raised an eyebrow as she looked in Kay's direction. "Yeah, girl, your weave is kind of jacked right now."

"Are you serious?" Kay said. "I can't believe you."

"You know I'm going to keep it real with you. You can't be representing black women everywhere as mayor with jacked-up hair, and while I'm at it"—she motioned to Kay's outfit, a silk blouse and slacks—"your blacks don't match." She took the paper, scribbled again. "Number six, fire the wardrobe consultant."

Kay couldn't help it. She busted out laughing. Yeah, she needed to make more time for her girlfriend because Camille had made her feel better than she'd felt in weeks. Kay was just about to tell her that when she heard someone call her name.

"Kayla?"

Both Kay and Camille turned to the pretty brown-skinned woman dressed in the waitstaff uniform. She looked very familiar, but it wasn't until Kay saw her name tag that she remembered who the woman was.

"Maxine?"

"Wow," Maxine said, shocked. "It's been, what, eighteen years since I've seen you."

"Almost," Kay said, standing and hugging her old childhood friend. After Kayla had turned up pregnant, her family moved from Baton Rouge and she never saw any of the people from her church or school again.

Camille cleared her throat, causing Kay to smile as she turned to her. "Camille, this is an old friend. Maxine Lewis. We knew each other back in Baton Rouge."

Maxine shook her head like the memories were too painful. "A lifetime ago," she muttered.

"Maxine, this is my best friend, Camille." They nodded before Kay said, "I didn't know you were in Houston."

"Been here about four years," Maxine said. "You know, trying to find something different." She motioned to her uniform. "But ended up with the same old thing."

"Maxine, they're calling for you at table four," Kay and Camille's waiter said, approaching their table.

"Well, I gotta go. I just saw you over here and came to speak. Maybe we can exchange numbers before you leave." She paused. "I really have some things I'd like to talk to you about."

Kay didn't know why, but the tone of Maxine's voice sent shivers up her spine. "Sure," she said, although she had no intention of ever talking to Maxine again. Maxine reminded her of her past. And anything in her past needed to stay there.

After she was gone and Kay had sat back down at the table, Camille said, "Why do I have the feeling that you'd rather duck out a side door than give that girl your phone number?"

"Because you know me so well," Kay replied, as she picked up her margarita and downed the rest of it in one gulp.

41

In all her years in law enforcement, Kay had never done anything like this. No one could have ever paid her to even believe that she would violate every ethical thing she believed in by using her position to get information for personal purposes. Normally, Kay was a by-the-book type of woman. She wanted to make sure that there were no improprieties when it came to handling her business. But desperate times called for desperate measures. She'd overheard Gloria on speakerphone telling Phillip that she was staying at her mother's house in Fifth Ward this week and Kay had someone at the DMV find out where Gloria's mother lived.

That's where she sat now, in front of the small rickety wood-frame house, waiting and trying to get up the courage to go knock on the front door of Gloria's mother's home.

After she'd left Camille (and snuck away without exchanging numbers with Maxine), Kay had planned on heading home and in fact had gotten about five minutes from her house. But she hadn't figured out what she was going to say to Phillip just yet and she had something else she wanted to deal with first. Her life was about to fall apart. There was no doubt Marty would make good on his promise and Kay needed to prepare for that. But first, she needed to look Gloria Jones in the eye and find out what type of game she was playing by giving Marty that information. Kay didn't exactly know why she needed to see Gloria. The damage was done, Marty knew, so what purpose would confronting Gloria serve? Kay didn't know, but she was no longer a scared, timid child. She was a woman who was not going to sit idly by and let Gloria Jones hurt her. Again.

Kay shut her car off and then walked up the sidewalk. It was almost nine o'clock at night, so she was sure her arrival would catch Gloria off guard. She had just hit the first step when the door swung open.

"Kayla?" Gloria said, looking at her surprised.

Kay pursed her lips and glared at Gloria. "I don't know how many ways to tell you or how many times I need to tell you, but my name is Kay. Just Kay."

"Sorry," Gloria said, "but ah, yeah, what's going on?"

"I need to speak with you."

"Umm, okay," she said. "My mother is inside, but I can ask her to step out so we can talk."

Kay had no desire to go into that woman's house. "No, I can say what I need to say right here."

"Okay." Gloria closed the door as she stepped outside onto the porch.

"You came to me and told me all you wanted was to save your son," Kay began.

"And that's the truth."

"And you think blackmail is the way to do it?"

Gloria looked confused. "I'm sorry. I'm not quite sure what you're talking about."

"Of course you aren't," Kay snapped. She wasn't going to be fooled by Gloria's fake act. "So what did you think you would accomplish by selling my story to the highest bidder?"

Gloria shook her head in protest. "Kay, I'm sorry. I really have no idea what you're talking about."

"My competition in the mayoral race, Marty Simon. He knows everything, all about Jamal," Kay spat. "And don't try to pretend that you aren't the one who gave the information to him. I'm just trying to figure out why."

"I'm sorry," Gloria replied, "but I don't know this Marty Simon. I don't know what you're talking about and I hadn't nor would I ever try to blackmail you. My son's fate is in your hands, so why would I make such a horrible decision to infuriate you?"

"Cut the crap," Kay said. She was conflicted. Either Gloria was a great actor or she really didn't know, because she was really looking clueless. "Let me just be very clear with you," Kay continued. "The only thing you've done is piss me off. Which is not what you want to do when you're trying to get the best possible outcome for your son."

"Kay, calm down," Gloria said. "I'm telling you the truth. I have no idea what you're talking about. I didn't have anything to do with telling anyone about you. What would I stand to gain? I don't know anything about a mayoral race. I'm not concerned about a mayoral race. The only thing I'm thinking about is my son."

Kay studied her. She really did look like she was telling the truth. But Gloria probably had learned to master the art of lying over the years.

"Kay, I know you have a bitterness toward us. I know you hate us. I know you wish this had never happened. I wish it had never happened. But it did. I promise you, though, it would serve me no purpose by selling this story. We built a good life and all we want is to return to that life. Me letting the public know you're Jamal's mother wouldn't do anything but hurt us."

"I'm not his mother," Kay countered. She'd stopped being his mother the day she gave him up for adoption.

"Okay, fine. I wouldn't let anyone know that you gave birth to him," Gloria corrected. "That wouldn't serve anyone any good."

"You're doggone right about that," she said.

Gloria took a step toward her. "I'm sorry you feel like I'm somehow responsible for this getting out, but I assure you, you need to be looking elsewhere because I didn't have anything to do with this. You've got to believe me."

Now Kay didn't know what to believe. On her way here, she had been so sure that Gloria had been the one behind this, but now she simply didn't know. But if Gloria wasn't the one who gave her story to Marty, who was? And why? She had no ties to her past. There was no way anyone could have just figured this out.

"You might want to check your circle," Gloria said. "But you can cross me off the list. I'm guilty of a lot of things, but that's not one of them.

They stood in a silent face-off before Kay said, "Forgive me, if I don't trust you. Been there, tried that. I trusted you more than my own mother and you repaid me by telling your friends I was a whore."

The grimace on Gloria's face told Kay that those words opened the door to some painful memories. But Kay didn't care. The pain couldn't be worse than what she had felt.

Gloria's eyes were downcast as she said, "I want to apologize. That day you saw me at Wal-Mart, the day you overheard me say that . . ." Her words trailed off.

Kay remembered that day well. It had been ingrained in her heart for years. She hadn't intended to address that memory, but she couldn't help it. "The day I overheard you telling your friends about the young whore that threw herself at your husband."

Gloria's eyes misted. "I-I was just trying to defuse some of the gossip."

"At my expense," Kay snapped. "It was bad enough how utterly vile my parents treated me. It was painfully disgusting how your husband forced himself on me, taking away my virginity, but I don't think anything hurt as much as hearing you say the stuff you did. You, a woman I adored and respected, who I helped at Sunday school, who I actually wished was my mother instead of my real mother. Do you have any idea what it did to me to hear you utter those words?"

"I-I was just . . . I'm so sorry, Kayla, I mean, Kay. I'm just so sorry." Gloria was in full-blown crying mode now.

"Keep your apologies, Madame First Lady," Kay spat. "I needed them then. I don't need them now. Just know that if I ever find out you had anything to do with this conspiracy with Marty, all the hate I've held on to all these years will rear its ugly head. And you will regret the day you ever met me."

Kay didn't give Gloria a chance to respond as she turned and raced back to her car. She hadn't known why she felt compelled to see Gloria but as she sped toward the freeway she decided she didn't need to understand why. All she needed to do was forget the day she'd ever met Elton and Gloria Jones.

42

Gloria had hoped the drive to Jasper would calm her nerves. She'd been a basket case when she went back inside after talking to Kayla last night. Luckily, Gloria's mother had dozed off so Gloria didn't have to answer any questions.

She'd left early this morning so that she could get home, get some more clothes, and get back to Houston in time to visit with Jamal.

Elton had called yesterday morning and agreed to come with her to visit Jamal. That was part of the reason she went ahead and came home first. If she left it up to Elton to drive up, he'd concoct some excuse, yet Jamal needed to see his father.

But Gloria was surprised to find Elton sitting at his desk, still in his pajamas.

"Why aren't you dressed?" she asked.

"Hello to you, too," he casually replied.

"Hello. But why aren't you dressed? I told you we needed to get back up to the jail by four."

"We still have time." He gave her his undivided attention. "But I need to know about Kayla." Gloria had still been upset this morning when Elton called and she'd made the mistake of telling him Kayla had come to see her. He wanted her to tell him what they talked about then, but she told him she'd talk about it when she got home. Now she really didn't want to go into it.

Watching her husband sit there, for a fleeting moment, she wondered if he had anything to do with the blackmail. But she shook away that thought. No, Elton wanted to stay as far away from Kay as possible.

"It's nothing," she said.

"Gloria, can we stop with all the lying? Please?" he said.

"She wanted to ask me if I was behind blackmailing her, or rather playing a part in providing information to her opponent in the mayoral race. He's using the information about Jamal to blackmail her."

Elton gasped. "You mean someone knows?" he asked.

"Apparently the guy she's running against for mayor approached her about it. He wanted her to step down or he was going to take it public."

Elton fell back in his seat. "Oh, my God."

"Needless to say she wasn't happy. She thought maybe I had something to do with it, which of course is crazy. I told her I didn't. Neither of us did." She narrowed her gaze at her husband. "Did we?"

"What?" he said, then it dawned on him what she was saying. "Absolutely not. Why would I want to help anyone blackmail her?"

"That's what I told her. So she caught me off guard yesterday. I wanted it to be very clear. I don't want her taking anything out on Jamal."

"Great," Elton mumbled, "this is exactly what we need. More negative publicity."

"I can't argue with you today," she huffed. "Can you just go get dressed so we can go?"

Elton busied himself with some papers on his desk. "I'm not going today."

"What? You had me come back here to get you."

"I wanted you home." He looked up at her. "You need to be home."

That she was not about to do. "Elton, get dressed."

"I'm not going," he repeated. "Besides, I have a meeting at the church."

"Hold on." She moved closer to his desk. "You are seriously talking crazy. This is our son we're talking about. He's been up there for three weeks and you haven't bothered to see him."

"You're there every day," Elton snapped. "Neglecting home to baby him."

"Are you serious?" she asked, dumbfounded. Then, determined not to fight, she added, "Just please come. He's always asking about you," she lied. Jamal had asked once where Elton was. Now he didn't bother.

"I have a meeting at the church," he said, dismissing her.

"That church needs to take a backseat."

"Why? Because our son decided to get wrapped up in some foolishness? Now I'm supposed to neglect my duties as pastor?"

"Damn your duties!" she snapped. Her outburst obviously horrified him because his eyes widened in disbelief.

She couldn't take it. The stress of Jamal, the frustrations of everything, she was simply fed up with Elton Jones. The fact that in the midst of all they were going through, all he kept talking about was negative attention pushed her over the edge.

"You know, Elton," Gloria began, "you're mad at the world behind all of this. Like no one can be forgiven. And you're the biggest transgressor of us all."

"Excuse me?" he said.

Years of pent-up emotion reached a boiling point. "I didn't stutter," she snapped. "You sit there so self-righteous and acting like you can do no wrong. But in reality you're at the root of what's wrong with this family."

"Woman, you better watch it and tread lightly," he warned.

"Or what?" She didn't back down. "I'm tired of biting my tongue. You raped that child and instead of owning up to what you did, you blame everyone but yourself."

He was so angry he was shivering. "I atoned for my sins. I was forgiven."

"By God, yeah. But I'm not sure if you've ever forgiven yourself. If you had, you wouldn't be so mean and resentful to a son that didn't ask to be brought into this world."

"I am not resentful." He didn't sound like he even believed that.

"Tell that to someone who doesn't know you," Gloria said. "Jamal ruined your picture-perfect existence. He reminded you of your great sin and you have hated him for it."

"Don't turn our son's crime around on me."

"Don't you get it, Elton?" she cried. "Your resentment of your son is why you turned him in in the first place."

"That is not true!"

"Whatever, Elton. But there is a wall between the two of you built by you and your contempt. And I'm just tired. Tired of the lies. Tired of pretending you're this perfect infallible man. Tired of being the only one on earth who has any love for that boy."

"I-I love my son."

"You tolerate your son. I don't know if you even know what love is."

"You will not make this about me!" he bellowed. "I lost one church behind that boy, I'm not about to lose another," he said with conviction.

And just like that, every piece of contempt she'd had for her husband recently returned. In that very moment, she knew it was over. Any feelings she had left for Elton Jones left with that one statement.

"So, that's what this is all about. You lost a church."

"N-no. I didn't mean it like that," he stammered.

"Whatever. I can't do this with you." She walked back into the bedroom. She had planned to just grab a few things but Gloria reached up onto the top shelf and pulled down her luggage.

She opened her drawers and just started snatching out clothes and stuffing them into the suitcase. After emptying several drawers, she repeated the process in the closet, until there was no more room in her suitcase. After grabbing a few toiletries, she wheeled her suitcase back into the living room.

"I'm leaving," she muttered. Elton had sat back down and returned to working.

"Fine." He released an exasperated sigh and looked up at her. "When are you coming back?"

She stood in silence for a moment. Then she said, "I'm not." Uttering those words, which she had never truly considered, felt freeing.

He had the nerve to chuckle. "Oh, so you're really leaving me?"

She nodded. "I'm doing what I should've done a long time ago. I'm leaving. I'm going to stop putting you and your feelings first. Right now, I'm doing what's best for my son. And once I help him get out of this situation, then me and my son will figure out what we're going to do next."

"Wait. You're serious?"

"More serious than I've ever been about anything in my life. Take care of yourself, Elton."

Gloria headed out the door, ignoring the sounds of her husband screaming her name.

43

I t was time to face her past. Marty knew and since she was not dropping out of the race, it was just a matter of time before everyone else knew as well. Phillip would be devastated if he turned on the television and got this news. She couldn't wait another day to come clean.

Kay pulled into the garage and parked next to Phillip's white Range Rover, one of the few luxuries he afforded himself, and even that had been a battle to get him to purchase. He wanted something "more efficient" but Kay told him as hard as he worked, he needed to get him something he really wanted.

She walked into the house to see her husband's head leaning back against the sofa. Files surrounded him on the coffee table, on the floor, on the sofa next to him. Like her, he had thrown himself into his work. She fought the urge to take a peek as she picked up the folders to move them to the side. She never would violate his trust like that. *He trusted you to be truthful.* Those words came out of nowhere. But Kay knew the little voice nudging her ahead was telling the truth.

"Hey, honey," she said gently, shaking Phillip's leg.

He stretched, then yawned, and slowly opened his eyes. "Oh, hey. Sorry, babe. I sat up here and dozed off."

"Where are the kids?"

"Selena got them to bed," he said. He sat up and tried to get himself together.

"Oh, okay, well, umm, I see you've been at it." She fidgeted in front of him.

He looked at his watch. "Wow, it's ten o'clock. Didn't realize it was that late. I guess you've been at it, too, since you're just getting home."

She nodded, but didn't reply.

"Sorry about all this," he said when he noticed the mess he had made. He began picking up files.

"Well, I was, um, I was wondering if I can, umm . . . talk to you a little bit?"

"Yeah," he said, frowning as he stood. "Of course. Is something wrong?"

She sighed, then swallowed the lump in her throat. They had built their relationship on honesty, and now she was about to tell him that their foundation was a lie. "Can we just go in our room and talk?"

"Are you hungry?" he asked. "I mean, it's late. But Selena left a plate for you in the refrigirator."

"Nah," she replied. "I don't have much of an appetite."

"Okay, now you're worrying me. I hadn't heard from you all evening and now you're acting real cryptic." His hand went to her forehead.

"No, I'm fine. Sorry for worrying you," she said. She led him into the bedroom and then as he eased down on the bed, she sat next to him. "I have something to tell you." She took a deep breath and willed her strength to come forward. "I haven't been completely honest about my past."

He moved his hand back, which only made this more difficult, yet she forged ahead.

"Okay, now you're really scaring me," he said.

"Let me back up." She took a deep breath. "You know that I'm from Baton Rouge?"

"Yeah." His reply was slow and drawn out. He knew she was orphaned and often talked of his desire to have met her folks. Every time he mentioned it, she wanted to come clean. But she hadn't. Now here she was.

Kay continued, "Well, when I was fifteen, something terrible happened."

Once again, Kay took a journey back to the place she'd spent all of her life trying to forget. When she was finished—when she told him all about being pregnant and giving the baby up for adoption, and how the pastor and his wife had taken that child and raised him—Phillip sat in stunned disbelief.

"I'm—I'm very confused," Phillip finally said. "So you have a child?"

She nodded. "Technically, I gave birth, gave him up, and then I just tried to block it out of my head."

"Why wouldn't you tell me something like that?"

"I don't know. Ashamed. Trying to pretend it never happened." She lowered her head in shame.

"Wow." He paced back and forth across the room. "Did you think I wouldn't accept your child? You accepted Ryan."

"No, I never thought that. The only thing I knew is that I wanted to forget it ever happened. And I think that's what I tried to do."

"So, why now? Why are you telling me now?"

This was the hard part. She inhaled. Then exhaled. "Because my past has resurfaced."

"What? You've had contact with your son?"

She didn't know quite how to word it. Finally she just said it. "I haven't had contact with him." She paused. "But you have."

"Kay, you need to stop beating around the bush and tell me what you're talking about." He was getting very irritated, so Kay knew she just needed to say it.

"Jamal Jones is my son," she blurted.

Phillip's mouth dropped open. "My client, Jamal Jones?"

She nodded as the tears she'd been fighting back finally escaped.

"Are you freaking kidding me?" he yelled.

She wanted to tell him to lower his voice so that he didn't wake the children. But she simply replied, "I wish I was."

"So when did you find this out? How could you let me represent him?" He started hurling question after question at her as he sped up his pacing.

"Wait, wait. I'll answer everything, Phillip," she said, trying to stop him before he got too worked up. "I didn't let you represent him. I didn't know you were going to represent him, remember? And then, when you told me, I didn't know he was my son. I gave him up at birth. I never named him."

"But you . . ." His words trailed off as he stopped. His mind looked as if it was racing. "So is that what your outburst in Judge Raymond's chambers was about?"

"Yes."

He shook his head in disbelief. "So, you lied to me and told me you were sick? But in reality, you were scared because the people who adopted your child showed up?"

"It's much deeper than that," she protested.

"So, there's more?"

She hesitated, then said, "The reason they adopted the child was because it was Elton Jones's son."

A still quiet filled the room. "I'm sorry, I don't understand."

"Pastor Elton Jones is Jamal's biological father. He raped me when I was fifteen years old."

Phillip had to take a seat on that revelation.

"I'm sorry I didn't say anything. I didn't know how or what to say," Kay said.

"That was two weeks ago," Phillip said. "You've been walking around here with this secret since then?"

She had no words, and could only shake her head. The reality was, she'd been walking around with that secret for seventeen years.

"I'm sorry," she finally said.

"So this man raped you? Where were your parents? Did he go to jail?"

As painful as it was, Kay filled him in on her parents' reaction, how no one believed that she'd been raped, how she'd been blamed for her own pregnancy. She didn't know why, but she expected Phillip to take her in his arms and comfort her.

"Wow, I'm feeling like I don't even know you," Phillip said when she was finished.

"You do," she replied, hurt by his reaction. "I'm the same person you married."

He stood and backed away from her. "No, because the woman I

know wouldn't walk around and hold on to this lie. And even if she was so ashamed of what happened, she wouldn't have continued the lie once it showed up on our doorstep."

"Please forgive me."

"Forgive you?" he said, looking at her sadly. "Right now I don't even know you."

He grabbed his pillow and blanket and walked out of the room.

44

I was like Kay was walking a path of chaos and destruction. Once again, she had delivered the news that she was Jamal's mother and left someone speechless. This time it was Sam Turner, her boss.

"Please tell me this is an April Fool's joke in October," he said.

She shook her head. "No, out of the two million people in the city of Houston, I would be handed the case with the son I gave up for adoption."

When she'd walked into his office, Kay was sure that Sam had no idea that this was the bombshell she was about to deliver.

He'd been excited to see her. Her interview with Ming had aired last night and everyone was talking about it. But all of his excitement was gone now. She'd told him everything, even about the rape. Sam leaned back in his leather seat, a look of disbelief still across his face.

"When did you find this out?" he asked.

Kay didn't want to tell him the truth, but she was tired of the lies. Even still, letting him know that she'd known for weeks would just create unnecessary drama, so she simply said, "I just found out."

Either that satisfied him or the issue of when didn't really matter, because he didn't respond.

"The bottom line is this all could get very ugly," she continued.

"Oh, this is not good. Not good," Sam mumbled.

"Exactly, and that's why"—she handed him the piece of paper—"I need to officially ask to be recused from this case and I think it's best I take a hiatus from the prosecutor's office while this case is going on."

He looked like he wanted to argue. But Sam didn't like bad publicity and he knew just like Kay that this had bad publicity written all over it.

"Wait, isn't your husband representing him?" Sam asked.

Kay nodded.

"Is he going to continue?"

"I don't know," she said. "Probably."

"Well, maybe nobody has to know. At least before the trial." He stood and started pacing. "We can just say you're stepping down because of the mayoral race."

"Marty Simon knows," she said before he got too comfortable with that plan.

Sam abruptly stopped. "Marty Simon knows? So what in the tarnation am I supposed to do now?" he exclaimed.

"I wish I had an answer. I wish this had never happened," Kay said. She really didn't know what to tell him. Marty's threat had been eating at her insides. The debate was in a week so she'd have to come up with a plan asap.

"Okay, fine," Sam said, shuffling papers on his desk like he was really looking for something. "I'll start briefing one of the ADAs. Do you think Harold . . . ?"

"No," Kay immediately said, "he's not ready to go at this alone."

If she were unethical, Kay would tell Sam to go ahead and let Harold prosecute because no way could Harold win this case.

"I just have to figure this out," Sam said, dismissing her.

She knew she had ruffled his feathers. But if they escaped with no negative publicity he'd quickly get over it.

. . .

Kay had just returned to her office when she stopped in her tracks at the sight of Maxine sitting in the lobby outside of her office.

What in the world did she want? Kay didn't want to be rude but she wanted no parts of her past—including reconnecting with Maxine.

Kay debated dipping out the side door but a thought that maybe, somehow, Maxine was connected to Marty's blackmail propelled her forward.

"Maxine?" Kay said.

"Kayla?" Maxine jumped to her feet.

"Umm, yes. How are you?"

"I'm okay." Maxine looked like she'd aged thirty years. At the restaurant, Kay hadn't noticed the bags under Maxine's eyes, the drooping and discolored skin, which indicated years of hard drug use. She wore tight leggings, platform boots, and a long, tattered sweater. Her stringy hair was pulled back haphazardly in a ponytail.

Maxine looked around the office, unsure of what she should say. "Sorry to just pop by, but I wanted to catch up and, ah, you left the restaurant the other day without exchanging numbers."

And you couldn't get the hint? Kay wanted to say.

"Well, I, ah, I saw you on TV and that you worked in the DA's office and so, you know, I just dropped by."

Kay glanced over at her secretary, April, who had been watching them, possibly to make sure Maxine wasn't some crazy person they needed to call security on.

Kay held up a hand to let April know that everything was fine. She had no clue what Maxine wanted, but the girl seemed harmless. She definitely didn't seem like she could be connected to Marty Simon in any way. Besides, Kay reminded herself, there was no way Maxine could've known about Jamal.

"Glad you dropped by," Kay said, "but I'm about to go into a meeting."

"Well, um." Maxine twirled her hair around her finger as she spoke. "I was just, um, wondering if maybe I could talk to you."

Normally, Kay would've tried to sugarcoat things, but she just didn't have the energy. "Maxine, I have a lot going on and really, now isn't a good time."

"It's just . . . I mean, I need to talk to someone who knows what I'm dealing with."

How in the world could Kay know anything about the hard life Maxine had obviously lived?

"I wish I could help," Kay said. "But I have this meeting that I'm already late for. Then I have to head to a luncheon to speak," she said in case Maxine offered to wait.

Maxine pursed her lips, then let out a sigh. "Okay. Cool. Sorry to bother you."

For a moment, Kay felt bad. But then she decided that she had her own personal issues and didn't need to add someone else's drama to her plate—especially someone that was a reminder of her past.

"Leave your number with my secretary and I'll get back in touch."

Maxine nodded as she slid her purse over her shoulder. "Take care of yourself, Kayla."

Kay watched her walk away. Truthfully, she hadn't expected Maxine to go so easily, but she was glad that she had. Maybe she just needed a friend. Unfortunately, that couldn't be Kay.

"Mrs. Christiansen, just a reminder, your team is waiting on you in your office," April said.

"Okay." Kay headed into her office and greeted everyone. After extending an apology for her tardiness, she slid into the seat at the head of the long table.

"Are you ready for your debate?" Valerie asked. "Only a few more days."

"As ready as I can be," Kay responded. Going head-to-head with Marty Simon was the last thing she felt like doing right now. But she got into the zone because it was evident Loni and Jeff, who were sitting across from her, were ready to work.

"Good. I'm going to review some last-minute points I want to make sure you touch on," Loni said before going down an extensive list.

Jeff then chimed in and gave the talking points he wanted her to focus on. They discussed the campaign for the next hour and finally, when they were finished, Kay closed her portfolio, crossed her hands, and prepared to break the news to her team.

"Look, you probably should hear it from me first because I'm sure it will be getting around the office soon. I'm stepping down off the Jamal Jones case."

"What?" Valerie said.

"Yes!" Loni and Jeff chimed in at the same time.

Loni shrugged. "Sorry, but you know I need your undivided attention anyway."

"I agree," Jeff added. "But why are you stepping down?"

"It's a personal matter, one that I'm sure you'll hear about soon enough. But in the meantime, I need you to transfer all the files to Sam and he'll get them to the new prosecutor."

While both Loni and Jeff looked thrilled at the announcement, Kay couldn't make out the expression on Valerie's face. She looked shocked and frightened. Maybe she was scared she'd lose her job if Kay left.

"And don't worry, your job is safe."

"Okay," Valerie said, pulling herself together. "Well, good luck on your debate. That Marty Simon can be a pushy one. But I know you can hold your own against him."

Kay weighed Valerie's words as her assistant headed back to her desk. In the past, she would have agreed with Valerie without a moment's hesitation, but now she honestly wasn't so sure.

Kay had thought that work would ease the fear of what Marty would do. He was capable of getting down and dirty and she needed to strategize. She wasn't stepping down so she needed to prepare for the worst.

She shook away thoughts of Marty. Right now, she needed to be preparing to turn all of her notes over to Sam. Kay picked up a folder marked "personal—Jamal Jones." It was the file she'd asked

Valerie to gather. She pulled out his school transcript and while his grades were below average, she was speechless at his test scores. He'd scored in the top five percent on both his SAT and the ACT. Suddenly, Kay found herself wondering if circumstances would have changed Jamal's outcome. If she had stuck around to be a mother to him, would he be facing the death penalty?

Now she needed to walk that fine line of giving her predecessor just enough information so that she couldn't be accused of doing anything improper. She would not help them put Jamal away forever. Or worse, give him the death penalty.

Kay had sat at her desk for a few minutes going over her other files when she realized she was missing a folder she'd had Valerie get together for her earlier. She'd given it back to Valerie and asked her to add some more details on supporting case law and had forgotten to get it back.

"I have too much on my plate," she mumbled. The file was probably still on Valerie's desk, so Kay would have to retrieve it herself.

Valerie's light was off and she'd obviously gone for the day so Kay did a quick glance. She didn't see the file on top of the desk so she opened a drawer and started looking where Valerie stored the current case files. It wasn't there, either.

"Okay, now I'm going to have to call her," she mumbled.

Kay hated disturbing her employees when they were off because they worked hard enough as it was. She reached for Valerie's phone and punched in her number. Valerie's voice mail picked up. "Hey, Valerie," she said after the tone, "it's Kay. Trying to find out where you put the police brutality case law files. Call me when you get this."

Kay had just placed the phone back on the hook when out of

the corner of her eye, she noticed a piece of paper on the floor next to the trash can. It looked like someone had tried to toss it in the trash and missed. It looked like a bank receipt, and since Kay didn't want the janitors getting a hold of Valerie's information, she picked it up to put it in the trash can. And that's when she noticed it was a Chase Bank deposit receipt. Normally she wouldn't have thought twice about it because she knew that's where Valerie banked. But it was the figures on the slip of paper that gave her pause: $500,000. *Where in the world did Valerie get $500,000?*

The answer came before the thought left. And Kay could only pray that she was wrong.

45

The sight on her TV was making Gloria sick. Rev. Clayborn was bellowing something about "racism and justice." The news was covering a rowdy protest held by the Black Justice Coalition last night in Jasper, which had ended with four people being taken to the hospital and eight people arrested.

All in the name of justice for Jamal.

Gloria couldn't help it. She snatched up her phone and swiped Elton's name.

"Gloria?" he said, answering on the first ring.

She wasn't even going to beat around the bush with any formalities. "Can you please get them to stop? All of this protesting and anger. This is not helping our son."

Elton paused. "I can't keep them from doing what they do."

"That Reverend Clayborn said he had our support! He's telling the news reporters that we're supporting this foolishness," Gloria exclaimed. Just watching him on TV right now made Gloria want to toss her shoe at the set.

"It actually isn't as bad as it seems."

"Four people had to go to the hospital, Elton!"

"Well, they think if you and I would just come out, it would give a calming voice," he said.

"They're selling T-shirts with my son's face on them!" she yelled. "What part of 'I want no part of that' do you not understand?" She lowered her voice, trying to regain her composure and not bring her mother out of her room. "I don't support this, Elton. You might be okay with them using you, but I'm not supporting that and you need to make them stop."

"I don't have any control over what they're doing," Elton repeated.

Gloria was seething. "Fine," she said. "I'll just go to the media and tell them we don't support these people. I'll speak out against them since you're more concerned with lining the church's coffer."

"Don't do this, Gloria."

"Elton, this should've been done a long time ago. If you won't handle it, I will." She slammed the phone down on him and turned to see her mother standing over her.

"Now, that's what I'm talking about." Erma chuckled. She was dressed in a leopard skin blouse with some skinny jeans and black low-heeled boots.

Gloria was not in the mood for her mother. She loved Erma Hurley dearly, but at a time like this, she couldn't take her mother's two cents, which her mother never failed to offer.

"What, Mama?" Gloria asked.

"Just glad to see you finally standing up to that man."

Gloria pulled the afghan up over her head. "Mama, don't . . ."

Not to be dismayed, her mother walked over to the sofa, pulled the afghan back down, and said, "I'm just trying to figure out where I went wrong with you."

Gloria sighed as she sat up. "What are you talking about?"

"You've been in here just boo-hooing, crying yourself into oblivion. You sure got your daddy's soft ways." Erma shook her head in pity.

Gloria often wondered how her parents ended up together. Her mother, a former Black Panther, had been the strong militant type, protesting any and every thing. Her father, on the other hand, had been a typical, Southern "yes" man, trying to ruffle as few feathers as possible. And while her mother had long settled down from her militant ways, she still had that rebellious spunk, and right about now Gloria guessed she was once again trying to figure out why her daughter didn't have it.

"I'm just going through a lot right now." She hadn't told her mother details of her split with Elton but decided to tell her now. "I left Elton," Gloria said.

Erma didn't seem fazed. "Good. You should've done that a long time ago!"

"Mama, this is serious," Gloria said.

"I know it is. You don't need any man that makes you lose yourself. You've made excuses for him since the day you married him. You can't help anyone face their demons, when you're helping justify their actions."

"I know, Mama." Gloria sighed. "But right now, I can't deal with it."

"Okay." Erma threw her hands up like she was leaving it alone. "I'm going out on a date."

"You're almost eighty years old. When are you gonna get somewhere and sit down?"

She grabbed her purse, a leopard skin number that matched her blouse. "When they put me in the ground."

"Okay, fine, whatever." Gloria lay back down.

"I know it's fine, because you're just going to lie here on the sofa and weep. You need to come with me. Benji got a friend he can hook you up with."

"Yeah, I have no interest in hanging out with an old man named Benji and his old buddies."

"Who said anything about him being old?"

"Ugh. Good-bye, Mother."

Erma chuckled as she left. For a fleeting moment, Gloria wished that she had her mother's spunk. Despite being total opposites, her father hadn't been able to change her mother. He'd tamed her, but he hadn't changed her. And he'd loved her just the same. Until the day he died, she was his everything.

Thinking about her parents' love had Gloria reflecting on her own marriage. She was sad about leaving Elton, but she wasn't heartbroken. Why wasn't she heartbroken? Did that mean they were really over?

Gloria's heart screamed a resounding *yes*.

46

_____

Kay didn't know exactly what a ride-or-die chick was, but if she had to guess, she would definitely say it was the woman sitting in the passenger seat of her Mercedes-Benz.

"Let's go. What are you waiting for?" Camille said as she motioned for Kay to pull out of Camille's driveway.

"I'm just trying to figure out where you're going in all black with a skullcap." Kay chuckled.

"Umm. I'm prepared," Camille said.

"We're just going to talk to Valerie, not beat her up." When Kay had called Camille to tell her about the deposit slip, Camille had gone directly to work. She put on her tracking skills and found out Valerie made a deposit the day before Marty approached Kay in the parking garage. The deposit was a check from RJS Holdings, which Camille had discovered was a manufacturing company owned by Rosalyn Simon, Marty's wife.

Of course, Camille had been ready to roll right after that.

"A good Girl Scout is always prepared." Camille pulled a gigantic tube of Vaseline from her purse and said, "Here."

"What in the world is that for?" Kay said.

"Look, we might have to revert to some old collegiate ways and stomp this chick."

Kay pushed the tube away. "First of all, I have never stomped anyone, collegiate or otherwise. Second, I'm a law enforcement official."

"Yeah, so that means you got a legal right to stomp somebody."

Kay shook her head as she backed out. "Girl, we're grown women. We're not about to go and stomp anybody. We're going to question her."

"Exactly, and if we don't get the answers that we want, we're stomping her."

Kay could only laugh at her friend. They made their way across town to Valerie's Galleria area apartment and pulled into a parking space in front of her building.

"So, you said she's normally home from the gym about this time?" Camille asked.

"Yes. She takes a Pilates class from seven to eight that she's always trying to get me to attend. I know she comes straight home after that. I probably should have gone and talked with her alone. But I want a witness," Kay said.

"No, you did the right thing," Camille said, "because we're going to get to the bottom of this. I promise you that. Now, what I can't figure out is how she found out. But Bailey's Bail Bonds ain't been around this long for nothing. We got a knack for getting information out of reluctant folks."

"Girl, will you calm down? We're just going to talk," Kay reminded her.

Camille shook her head, undeterred. "Nah, this chick is consorting with the enemy and she's supposed to be working for you? She doesn't get a pass on that."

They pulled up to Valerie's townhouse. Kay looked around and didn't see Valerie's Honda Accord.

Kay glanced at the clock on her dashboard. "Well, we're still early. It's ten minutes till eight."

Camille pulled down the rearview mirror and gave herself the once-over before popping the cap on the Vaseline. She looked over at Kay. "Do you know where this goes?"

"I don't know," Kay replied.

"Oh, well." Camille shrugged and then took a glob of the petroleum jelly and rubbed it under each eye.

"There she is," Kay said, as she noticed Valerie in her gym clothes, making her way up the stairs. She hadn't even noticed Valerie pull in.

"Valerie," Kay called after she jumped out of the car and raced over to her. "Valerie!"

Valerie looked shocked as she stopped. "Mrs. Christiansen?" she said.

She looked even more confused when she saw Camille appear on the side of Kay.

"Uhhh, is something wrong?"

"You better believe it is . . ." Camille began.

Kay held up her hand to stop her friend. "I got this."

"Hmph," Camille said, but she did step back.

"What's going on?" Valerie asked.

"Can we come and talk for a minute?" Kay was going to give her a chance to explain. She hoped that Valerie had an explanation. She hated to think that the girl had betrayed her like this.

Valerie looked around. "Uhh, uhh."

"That was a rhetorical question," Camille said, moving toward the door.

If the situation wasn't so unbelievable, it would actually be quite funny, Kay thought. Camille was acting like she was one of the Sopranos.

Valerie unlocked her front door and then led the way in.

"Where's your daughter?" Kay asked.

"W-with my mom," Valerie stuttered. She dropped her gym bag and then turned to Kay. "Are you okay?"

"Not really," Kay said as Camille locked the door, then stood in front of it as if she was guarding it. "Valerie, how long have you worked for me?"

Valerie hesitated. "A little over six years."

Kay walked around, taking in the modest apartment. It was sparsely decorated with lots of pictures of her daughter, Daisy. "Have I been good to you?"

"Oh, yes, ma'am," Valerie said. "I love working for you."

Kay spun around. "That's what I thought and that's why I'm trying to understand why you would betray me."

Valerie was quiet for a moment, then she said, "B-betray you? I d-don't understand."

"B-but is there an echo in here?" Camille snapped.

"Camille," Kay said.

"Hmph." Camille stepped back again, but Kay could tell her input was far from over.

"Valerie, do you know Marty Simon?"

Although she tried to play dumb, her expression answered for her. "Marty Simon?"

"Yeah, you know, my opponent."

"Uh, other than, you know, the stuff when you're running against him, no, I don't know him."

Kay decided she was tired of beating around the bush. "Have you ever had any contact with Marty Simon?"

Valerie opened her mouth, but Kay stopped her. "Before you say anything, let me remind you, I'm a prosecutor. It's my job to get to the truth."

Valerie let out a sigh, but didn't respond.

"It's also my job to prosecute those who break the law."

"I . . . I didn't break any laws," Valerie said, her eyes growing wide with fear.

"But you did do something, right?" Camille stepped forward.

"Who is she?" Valerie said, taking a step back as she cowered from Camille's towering presence.

"Who I am is not important," Camille hissed.

"She's a friend," Kay said. "Look, I'm not here in an official capacity. I'm here because I just want to know why."

"I don't know what you're talking about," Valerie said.

"Stop lying," Camille said, slamming her palm on the door over Valerie's head. It made Valerie jump and she started to tremble.

"So, what did Marty do? Offer you money to spy on me?"

Valerie was quiet for a minute, then looked at Camille, who glared at her. Finally, Valerie slowly nodded her head. "Yes, he approached me and he made an offer I couldn't refuse if I could just get some dirt on you," she confessed.

"Wow." Kay was hurt. Valerie never crossed her mind as the one who could've given Marty the information.

"I am so sorry," Valerie cried. "You know I adore and respect you, but the money and my daughter and I was thinking about her future and—"

"Just trifling," Camille interjected.

By this point tears had filled Valerie's eyes. It tugged Kay's heart, but Camille wasn't moved. She rolled her eyes, clicked her teeth, and mumbled, "Don't fall for that bull," before taking her post back by the door.

"How did you find out?"

Valerie just kept trembling.

"You'd better tell her because if I have to come up off this door one mo' time," Camille threatened.

Valerie lowered her eyes. "When you had the meeting with Mrs. Jones in the conference room. You were so nervous when she kept calling and I thought something was up with that. So, I-I set up a recorder. I heard everything."

"And you sold it to the highest bidder." Kay couldn't believe that she'd let herself be played so easily. Valerie had pushed for her to meet with Gloria and even arranged the meeting in the conference room. And Kay had never suspected a thing.

"I'm so sorry. Please don't hate me," Valerie pled.

Kay shook her head in disbelief. "Well, thank you for admitting it." She headed toward the door. "I suspect you won't be at work tomorrow."

"So, I'm fired?" Valerie asked.

Kay just looked at her, but it was Camille who spoke. "Really? You gotta ask that? Go work for Marty Simon. And you're lucky she's the nice one because if it were me, I'd put that cute little chickadee"—she picked up a picture of Daisy—"in a foster home because her mom would be in the morgue."

Kay was already out the door. At another time, she'd have a hearty laugh over Camille's Tony Soprano act. But right now, all Kay wanted to do was cry.

47

Even Leslie knew something was wrong.

"Mommy, why does daddy look so sad?" their little girl had asked this morning as they left the house.

Phillip was still angry. And while Kay understood why, it didn't make the situation any easier.

"Daddy just has a lot on his mind," Kay replied. That seemed to satisfy Leslie because she went back to playing with her Barbie in the backseat.

After Kay dropped Leslie off at daycare, she headed to a campaign strategy meeting. Her mind was all over the place and she was in no mood to strategize. Plus she needed to figure out how to handle Marty. She had so much on her plate, she didn't know how she could possibly focus on a campaign, especially now with Valerie gone. But since time was winding down, Kay didn't have a choice. That's why she was sitting, without complaint, with Loni and Jeff, going over some strategies. Luckily, the temp that the agency had sent over this morning was diligently taking notes.

"You're pretty good at that." Loni motioned toward the pad that the temp was writing on. "You don't miss a thing."

The temp, Morgan, gave a modest smile. "Yeah, I'm very meticulous with my notes. Hopefully, it will be good enough to take me somewhere."

They made more small talk about the campaign, then a text came in from Phillip.

Call me. It's urgent.

She'd been in the meeting for most of the morning so she hadn't even realized that she missed five calls from Phillip, and since her secretary had been instructed not to put anyone through, he probably hadn't been able to get in touch with her that way, either. Something had to be wrong because he hadn't said a word to her this morning.

"Hey, guys, if you'll excuse me. I need to make a call." All of them nodded as they made their way back to their respective offices.

Kay punched in her husband's cell phone number. "Hey. I'm sorry I missed your call. I was in a meeting. What's going on?"

"Ryan's school called," Phillip said, skipping any formalities. "I'm on my way up there now."

"What? What's wrong?" Kay said, sitting up in her seat.

"He's okay. But apparently he's gotten into some trouble."

"Trouble? Ryan? What kind of trouble?" Kay asked in disbelief. Not her straitlaced son.

"I don't know. Something about drugs."

"Drugs! Are you kidding me?"

"Apparently they found him making them or something. I don't have details. Just meet me there."

"Okay, I'm on my way," she replied, her heart racing.

"All right. I'm about ten minutes away."

"See you soon," she said hurriedly. She stood and gathered her things. This wasn't making sense. Ryan never got into trouble. Somebody was setting him up, or wrongfully accusing him of something. She'd almost have to catch him in the act to believe he was capable of doing anything that would warrant a call from the school headmaster, let alone believe he was mixed up with drugs.

Twenty minutes later, both Kay and Phillip sat in front of the headmaster, Mr. Montclair, at Whittington Academy. They spent big money to keep their son in the prestigious private school and this was their first visit to the school for disciplinary reasons.

"Thanks for joining us," Mr. Montclair said as he shifted in his seat behind his large cherrywood desk. A stout man with snow-white hair and brass-rimmed glasses, Mr. Montclair was all about business.

"Okay, Mr. Montclair. You have our undivided attention," Phillip said.

Just then the door opened and Ryan was led in by one of the school security guards. His eyes were downcast and his demeanor revealed his shame.

"Ryan, have a seat," Mr. Montclair sternly said before turning his attention back to Phillip and Kay. Ryan still didn't look at them as he slid onto a bench along the back wall.

"Mr. and Mrs. Christiansen, I'm sorry to have to inform you of this but Master Ryan has found himself in a world of trouble and Whittington Academy is faced with no other choice but to expel him."

"Expel?" both Kay and Phillip said at the same time.

"What happened?" Kay said.

"Well," the headmaster said, looking at his notes, "it appears Ryan has been manufacturing drugs on our campus and has even set up an elaborate distribution system, involving other students."

"What? That's ludicrous," Kay said. "My son isn't some drug dealer."

Mr. Montclair reached in his drawer and pulled out several Baggies of what looked like small blue pills. "These were found on another student today. He was trying to sell them. When he was caught, he fingered Ryan as the person who gave him the drugs to sell."

Ryan sat up in his chair. "He's a li—"

Phillip turned to him. "Don't you dare talk like that!" he snapped.

They rarely got angry with Ryan, so this fury was completely out of character.

"Mr. Montclair," Kay began, "I'm sure you understand due process. We are going to need more than just the word of someone who was actually *caught* selling drugs that our son is the one behind this all."

"Of course," he replied. "We believe in having all the facts as well. That's why we set up cameras in the chemistry lab." He tapped some keys on his desktop computer, then turned the screen around to face them. "Master Ryan is on camera manufacturing drugs."

That was indeed Ryan in the deserted lab, weighing, measuring, cutting, and tapping away on a computer. But it looked like he could've been doing any kind of experiment.

They must've been on the same page, because Phillip asked, "How do you know it's drugs?"

"Trust me, Mr. and Mrs. Christiansen, we wouldn't have you here unless we were absolutely sure. You son was making, then distributing, ecstasy."

"What?" Phillip exclaimed. Kay was too stunned to speak.

"As you know," Mr. Montclair continued, "we have a zero-tolerance policy here at Whittington Academy. That means any child with even a first offense involving drugs is permanently expelled."

"Ryan, do you want to explain to me what's going on?" Phillip asked, turning to glare at his son. The last time Ryan had been in any trouble was when he was nine and had sneakily eaten all of his cousin's cupcakes. He'd gotten sick and thrown up all over the birthday boy. So to go from cupcakes to drugs was unfathomable.

"Answer me, son."

Ryan shrugged. "I don't know what he's talking about . . ." Kay couldn't understand what was going on. Ryan was acting cocky and nonchalant. She'd expected that he'd be crying apologetically.

Mr. Montclair shook his head, like he was thoroughly disappointed. "Well, when you're as intelligent as Master Ryan, it's not that hard," Mr. Montclair said. "We just had hoped he would use his intelligence for good."

Kay was dumbfounded as she stared at Ryan. "So all those nights you claimed you were doing chemistry equations you were trying to figure out how to make drugs?" she asked in disbelief.

"I didn't do anything," Ryan said. "Someone's setting me up."

Mr. Montclair turned the screen back around and signaled he would no longer entertain any lies. "Again, I assure you, we have all the evidence we need to back up our claim, which we will gladly produce should you wish to pursue this legally. But let me urge you to consider that route carefully." He closed the file on his desk. "The only reason the police aren't involved now is because we don't want the stain on the legacy of Whittington Academy. But we won't hesitate to press charges and answer any questions, within the measure of the law, of course, posed to us by the media."

His veiled threat hung in the air. He knew Kay was running for mayor and this was not something they'd want getting out.

"Unfortunately, per our policy, you know that we don't refund tuition for moral expulsions," Mr. Montclair continued. "And it saddens me to say this, but effective today, Ryan is no longer a student at Whittington Academy."

Both Kay and Phillip could tell there would be no more discussion, no changing Mr. Montclair's mind.

"Thank you, sir," Phillip said, standing. "My wife and I will handle this from here and our sincerest apologies on behalf of our son."

Phillip wasn't a violent man, but as he yanked Ryan up off the bench, he looked like he wanted to drag Ryan out by his curly hair.

Kay led the way out of Mr. Montclair's office and was shocked to see Camille sitting with her husband and son in the waiting area outside.

"Camille, what's going on?" Kay asked.

"You tell me," Camille said, looking directly at Ryan, who all but retreated behind his father's back.

"Hello, Phillip, Kay," Vincent said, standing. When he saw the look of confusion on their faces, he continued. "We're here, we assume, for the same reason as you. Drugs."

"Yeah, apparently Charlie was caught selling drugs." Camille snatched him up from the bench. "He says Ryan was making ecstasy pills here at school and had him selling it."

Kay should've known it was Charlie that Ryan was working with. "Well, we don't know exactly what happened, but yes, it appears the boys were caught up in some illegal activity," Kay continued.

Charlie suddenly began crying. He looked scared out of his mind. "Mama, I didn't want to do it. But Ryan said it made us cool because everybody was coming to us to get the pills. He made it where they could still get high but it's not as dangerous. He said we were actually doing the druggies a favor."

"Shut up!" Ryan yelled. "You're lying."

"Stop it!" Mr. Montclair said, appearing in the lobby. "All of you stop it! We will not do this on the campus of our beloved institution." He turned to Phillip and Kay. "Mr. and Mrs. Christiansen, we would appreciate it if you'd get your son and leave the premises. His locker has been cleared out and the security guard is waiting out front with all of his belongings." He turned to Camille and Vincent. "Mr. and Mrs. Bailey, I will see you in my office now."

Kay was crushed at the hateful glare Camille shot her as they walked past. Neither Kay nor Phillip said a word as Phillip grabbed Ryan by the arm and pushed him out the door. As they walked to Phillip's car, Kay wanted to cry as she looked at the expression on Ryan's face. She'd seen that look one too many times. Ryan looked guilty.

48

If seeing her son go to jail was the hardest thing Gloria had ever done, going to tell him the truth was the second hardest. Gloria had tossed and turned all night trying to figure out what to do. But if that man was blackmailing Kay, that meant it was just a matter of time before Jamal got wind of the story. He had to hear it from her. His hatred for Elton was deep enough as it is. She would die if he started hating her, too.

"Sign right here," the guard at the front desk said.

She despised the degrading process of checking in to visit inmates. She was searched and treated like a common criminal herself. But unlike Elton, at no time did she blame Jamal. She really did feel like he was a victim, just like the poor officer who lost his life. And while Gloria would never justify or excuse taking anyone's life, she would go to her grave knowing her son wasn't a cold-blooded killer.

"You can wait in here," the officer said, directing her to an oversized waiting room that was filled with weeping wives, sad-faced children, and disheartened mothers. She looked around at the twenty or so visitors in the room, and none of them appeared to be fathers. Was that part of the problem? These fatherless children? Her immediate reaction was to say that Jamal wasn't fatherless. But if she was being honest with herself, essentially he was.

Gloria sat and fiddled with her purse strap. She'd brought some cookies to give to him. But that had been the first thing the guard confiscated. She offered to let him taste some, but he still wasn't having it. They weren't allowed to bring anything in from the outside. The door opened and Jamal shuffled in, metal shackles around his feet and arms.

Do not cry. Do not cry, Gloria told herself.

Jamal struggled to smile. She knew he was trying to be strong for her. So she returned his smile.

"Hey, baby. How are you?"

"I'm still here," he said, falling into his seat. "Ma, has this case really blown up?" he asked. "Folks inside are talking about there are protests. They're talking about it on CNN and Fox and all the TV stations."

Gloria nodded her head. "Yes, sweetie. Some people are using it to further their cause. Some are really upset about what happened. Those Justice Coalition got Brian and Dix out and have them doing a lot of interviews. But we're only focused on you."

"You mean *you're* only focused on me."

"Your father would be here," she said, knowing that was what he was implying, "but . . ."

"Ma, don't even make excuses. He's not here. He hasn't been here. Because the good reverend can't bear being seen going inside a jailhouse."

Gloria wasn't even going to try to cover for her husband any-more. So she just patted her son's hand. "Well, I tried to bring you some cookies. Your favorite, chocolate chip pecan."

He closed his eyes as if he were savoring the thought of the cookies. "Let me guess, the guards confiscated them?"

"Yeah. They said I couldn't bring them in." She feigned a laugh. "I guess they thought I was going to give you a knife or something to break out of here."

He lost his smile. "I wish I could break out."

She squeezed his hand. "You'll be out soon enough. I promise you."

His eyes started to glisten. "Don't make promises you can't keep."

Gloria changed the subject, filling him in on a few other hap-penings in Jasper and what it was like staying with his grandmother. But they both could tell it was empty conversation. And as Gloria saw the clock inch closer toward the end of visiting hours, she knew she couldn't delay any longer.

"Jamal, honey, I have something to tell you."

His eyebrows scrunched and he frowned. "What?"

She took a deep breath. "I have wrestled with this because I'm just going to be honest."

"Okay, Ma. You're scaring me. Didn't want me to know what? My case? You don't think I'm getting off?" He sat up as his face filled with panic. "You think they're going to kill me?"

"No, no. It's nothing like that. It's nothing about your case," she said. "It's about you and us."

"Mama, can you just spit it out? Visiting hours are almost up."

She took another deep breath. "Father, forgive me," she mum-bled. "Jamal, we love you. We always have since the day you came into our lives."

"You mean the day I was born?"

Her words felt happy as she said, "The day you were adopted."

"What?" he said, pulling his hands away.

"In my heart, you are mine," she said through tear-filled eyes. "You will always be mine."

"I'm adopted?" he asked.

"Technically," she said.

"So, you and Dad aren't my mom and dad?"

"I'm not your biological mother," she said. "But I'm your mother in every sense of the word."

He was stunned. "Who are my biological parents then?"

Gloria was too nervous to speak.

"You need to spit it out, Ma, and tell me what's going on!" He raised his voice a little too high, but she understood his frustration. A guard shot him a look and he settled down. "Ma, what are you talking about? You need to stop with the lies and tell me now."

"Well, your father," she said, swallowing the lump in her throat, "your father is your biological father."

"What!" he exclaimed.

The words suddenly just rushed out. And she told him everything. When she finished, he sat with his mouth gaping open. "So my real mother is the one trying to put me in jail?"

"I'm sorry, son. We didn't know. We just put two and two together."

He sat speechless for a moment, then finally said, "Why are you telling me this now?"

She reached for him. He scooted back away from her touch.

"We wanted you to be aware."

"Everything is a lie. *You're* a liar."

Those words tore at her soul.

Tears trickled down his cheeks and he trembled as he spoke. "I have beat myself up, wondering what I did wrong. Why I felt like a burden."

"You were never a burden."

He slammed his palm on the table. "Don't you get it? I've killed myself trying to figure out why Dad had this animosity toward me and you can keep lying and say he didn't but I felt it." He pounded his chest. "I felt it right here!"

"Jamal, w-we just wanted . . ." Gloria didn't know what to say. She expected him to be mad at Elton, but she had no idea he'd be so angry at her, not with the way she'd loved him.

"Why didn't you tell me before?"

She glanced down, trying to find the right words. But somehow, *I never wanted you to know* didn't seem like the right thing to say. "I've wanted to many times but I couldn't find the words and as far as I was concerned, you belonged to me."

"That's just it," he cried, "I don't. I belonged to a girl who was raped by my dad. And you helped him cover it up!"

Gloria trembled. She was at a loss for words.

"All my life, you and Daddy been preaching about doing the right thing and y'all are nothing but liars," he continued.

"Jamal, please," she cried.

He ignored her as he called for the guard.

"Son, your time's not up," the guard said.

"Yes, it is," Jamal said. "Get me out of here before I do something I really regret."

He looked at Gloria with a hatred that she knew would haunt her the rest of her life.

49

The sight of her husband sitting on the deck smoking a Cuban cigar tore at her insides. Kay knew that he only smoked his cigars when he was in deep thought and something was truly bothering him. Usually it was reserved for a case that he thought he would lose. She knew tonight it was because of her.

"Knock, knock." Kay tapped on the door that led out to the back deck. "You up for a little company?" she said as she stuck her head out. She didn't want to get too much in his face if he wasn't ready to talk to her. It had only been a week since she'd told him the truth, but with a love like theirs, that was a lifetime.

Phillip nodded and motioned toward the seat across from him. The last time they had been on this deck together, he had been mulling a difficult case. He told her that just her presence gave him peace. Now she wondered if he'd ever feel that way again.

"I'm so sorry," she began.

He inhaled his cigar, let the smoke linger for a moment, then released it. "I know," he finally said.

"Will you ever be able to forgive me?"

He slowly nodded. "Yeah," was all he said.

Relief filled her. If Phillip left her on top of everything else, Kay did not know what she would do.

"What I don't get," he said, tapping the ash from the cigar into an ashtray, "is why you felt like you couldn't be truthful with me. I don't understand why you would be ashamed, and I don't get why you thought you couldn't tell me."

She looked at him sideways. "Of course, I was ashamed."

"Why? You were raped. A man you knew and trusted took advantage of you. That's nothing to be ashamed of. If anything, you could have given a voice to other young women who have gone through something similar."

"No, I couldn't let the world know that happened." Kay had shut down after what she considered her family's betrayal. An already delicate family situation had completely shattered. Of course, she cried at their funeral, but it wasn't the type of cry that came with a void in your heart. She had cried because they never made peace.

"I get that part," Phillip said. "But you could have let me know." The hurt was strong in his voice.

She didn't know how to reply because her husband was absolutely right. It was wrong of her to withhold that information. It was wrong not to trust him enough to be truthful.

"So, what now?" Kay said after a few moments of silence.

"That's what I'm trying to figure out. With everything I know, I've got to figure out what to do with this case. How can I represent Jamal? How can I work for the man that violated my wife?"

Kay weighed his words. If she were solely acting on her hatred of Elton Jones, she would have been quick to tell him that he couldn't. But Gloria's words hit home to her. Was Jamal supposed to suffer because of the sins of his father?

"I've recused myself from this case," Kay said. "Sam wasn't happy, but it had to be done. For me and for the appearance of any improprieties. I don't know what to tell you to do. But I've come to realize this much: This isn't about Elton. It isn't even about me. It's about Jamal, and I don't know, a part of me feels like he deserves a shot."

That caused Phillip to do a double take. "What? Is that the hard-nosed prosecutor talking?" he said with a slight smile, a welcome sight for Kay. "Makes a difference when it's your own child, huh?" Phillip added.

Kay shrugged. She didn't know if she'd ever truly see Jamal as her child, but she remembered how despite the hate that she felt for his father, the year after she gave birth, every time she had ever thought about the baby she gave away, it was accompanied by a pang in her heart. Which is why she tried her best to push him from her memories.

"I wish I could say that I felt love or something that made me want to have a relationship with him. That I felt this bond with Jamal that was changing my perspective. But I don't and that honestly scares me. But what I do feel is everything that has happened with Ryan just caused me to see that one bad decision can truly alter the course of someone's life. Ryan is lucky that all he got was kicked out of school, but if he had been in public school, or had been caught by a police officer, he could very well be behind bars just like Jamal."

Phillip nodded as if he was proud of her analytical thinking. "Yeah, I'm probably going to continue to represent Jamal. But I'm not even going to fake the funk. His father better not get anywhere near me."

Kay wasn't about to argue with that.

"Does Jamal know?" Phillip asked.

"No, of course, I wouldn't tell him and I don't think Gloria has told him," Kay replied.

He looked at Kay. "I think you should go see him and tell him."

"What?"

"I think you should go see him. I think you should tell him that you're his mother."

"No." She shook her head. That had never been an option. "Some secrets are best left buried."

"I don't know, Kay. Even when they're buried, they have a way of shifting to the top." He looked at her one last time, then stood. "And when they catch you by surprise, they can cause irrevocable damage."

Kay had no reply for that. Seeing Jamal and having no idea that he was her child was one thing. But how could she face him now? And as much as Kay couldn't stand Elton, he was the only father Jamal knew. Was she supposed to shatter that bond? He was dealing with enough as it was. This would only turn his world upside down even more.

As if he could read her thoughts, Phillip reached over and took her hand and pulled her up out of her seat. "You can do it. It'll be hard, but you have to do it. It's time to let go of the hate."

She laid her head on his shoulder. Phillip was right. She'd told him. She'd told her boss and her friend. Now she needed to tell Jamal. She didn't know how she would find the strength, but she would go see Jamal and let him know that she was his biological mother.

50

Gloria had never in her life been inclined to watch a political debate. But right about now, she sat riveted to the television.

"How much longer is that going to be on?" her mother asked her. "I watch *Family Feud* every night at seven o'clock. You messing up my schedule. I don't like my routine messed up."

Gloria sighed. There was a reason she'd left her mother's house at eighteen.

"Okay, Mama. You know normally I leave you alone. But can you please let me watch this?" If Gloria had been thinking, she would've brought Jamal's small TV to watch while she was staying with her mother since Erma only had one TV.

Erma walked over and stood next to Gloria. She turned her nose up. "Why do you want to watch that mess anyway? Vote for the black girl," Erma said. "There, you don't need to watch a debate. Decision made."

Gloria side-eyed her mother. She didn't want to hear a lecture. Her mother knew they'd adopted Jamal and quiet as it had been kept, Gloria nonetheless suspected Erma even knew he was Elton's biological child, because she often made quips about how much alike Jamal and Elton looked.

"You know you sound crazy, right?" Gloria couldn't help but say. "I mean, in this case, the black woman is the better-qualified one. But you don't vote for people just because of the color of their skin."

Erma raised an eyebrow at her. "*You* don't vote for people because of the color of their skin. I do. I'm always putting my money on black. Look at that man. He's got beady eyes."

"Okay, Mother. Whatever you say."

"That's because whatever I say is right." Erma folded her arms in irritation. "You need to hurry up. I don't like to miss my show since Steve Harvey took over."

Gloria didn't want her mother hovering over her, nagging her while she was trying to watch the debate. "I have an idea," Gloria said. "Why don't you go take your bath and I should be done watching by the time you finish?" She just wanted her mother to go away so that she could watch the debate in peace. It had already started. Gloria had never seen Kay in her element, but she seemed like a natural fit. Like she wasn't intimidated by the big cowboy-looking man and his condescending tone.

"Fine, but when I come out, that TV is going to *Family Feud*," Erma huffed.

Gloria didn't bother responding. She just turned the TV up as her mother stomped out of the room.

The moderator asked a few questions about the state of the city and just when the debate was about to lose Gloria's interest, she heard Marty Simon say, "Well, this has been a very competitive race. But I do believe there is something Kay Christiansen would like to tell the great people of Houston." He turned to Kay and she just stood there looking like she had lost her voice.

"Isn't there, Mrs. Christiansen?" he repeated when she didn't reply. He had a big cheesy grin on his face. "Or would you rather I tell it?"

When Kay didn't say anything the moderator jumped in. "We would like to know what you two are talking about."

That stupid grin grew wider. "We're talking about being trustworthy," Marty announced. "The person you pick to lead this beautiful metropolis needs to be somebody you can trust," he said like he knew a big secret.

Gloria drew a breath as she felt the volcano about to erupt.

"Are you trying to say we can't trust Mrs. Christiansen?" the moderator asked.

Kay finally spoke up. "I think my record reflects—"

Marty let out a big laugh before interrupting her. "Please, let's not talk about something being a reflection of." He turned back to the moderator. "Because, Gail, if you want to know the truth, you're not gonna get it from this lady." He looked at Kay one last time. "You still plan on staying in the race, right?" he asked.

Gail and several other people in the room looked confused.

Kay looked like she was clenching the podium to keep her balance. But she finally spoke, although some of the confidence was gone from her voice. "I will repeat myself. I have no intentions of dropping out of the race for mayor. I think the people of Houston deserve someone fair and who has the best interest of this beautiful city at heart, not the interests of select groups."

"Awww, that's so sweet," Marty said. "And such a load of crap."

He shook his head at her. "Well, it's your funeral." This time Marty turned his attention to the camera pointed in his direction. "My opponent is right that the people of Houston deserve fairness, and commitment, and might I add honesty. And when you talk about honesty and trustworthiness, you want someone that's going to do what they say they're going to do when they say they're going to do it. You want people that know you are about your word. You want people with core family values, not people that have illegitimate children and who toss them aside."

Gloria's heart broke at the pain on Kay's face. The moderator looked at Kay, then back at Marty. "Would you care to elaborate?"

He smirked as he looked over at Kay. "Maybe Mrs. Christiansen would," he said with a chuckle.

Kay's eyes glistened as if she was trying desperately not to cry. She could see Loni off to the side about to have a stroke.

"What Mr. Simon is alluding to," Kay began, "what he has been threatening me with, is something that he learned while paying my assistant to spy on me, then using that information to blackmail me to drop out of the race."

That wiped the smile right off his face.

Kay took a deep breath and composed herself, the pain she felt resonating through the screen.

"I have never told anyone this until recently and it is something I would've rather kept to myself, as I'm sure anyone out there understands who has endured a personal tragedy. But since I am refusing to drop out of the race, Marty Simon is about to tell you in hopes that you'll turn against me and he'll win the mayoral race." The arena hall was deathly silent as she continued. "As a teenager, I was raped. That resulted in a child, which I gave up for adoption. It's a personal matter that Mr. Simon now wants to take public."

Not to be outdone, Marty added, "Well, I wanted to take it public because what Mrs. Christiansen is failing to tell the American public is that her son is the one that shot that police office in Jasper and I felt like the people had a right to know."

The room erupted in chatter. Photographers and other media personnel began scrambling. Marty seized the moment, raising his voice.

"I mean, she was going to prosecute this hoodlum, probably tricking the people into believing she was working for justice and then throwing the case so that a cop killer walked free!"

Gloria wanted to come through that TV and hurt Marty Simon. He was just another person using her son to further his own cause.

"Oh, my. Is this true?" the moderator asked.

Kay inhaled. "It is, at least the part about Jamal Jones being the son I gave up for adoption. But I didn't find out until recently, which is why I stepped down as prosecutor in the case."

"So, you're no longer the prosecutor?"

"No, I'm not."

Marty pounded his podium as if he was trying to quiet the noise in the arena. "My point is if you can't trust her to be open and honest—"

Kay cut him off. "Gail, I am here to discuss all that I can bring to the city, not rehash a painful part of my past. If the people want someone that's perfect, who has never sinned, who has no flaws, then yes, they may want to vote for Marty Simon, if Jesus isn't on the ballot." Several people chuckled at that. Marty didn't find anything funny. "I'm not perfect," Kay continued. "I never claimed to be. That was a personal tragedy that has recently reared its ugly head and I'm dealing with it as best I see fit. But it has no bearing on who I am now and what I can bring to the city of Houston."

Marty looked frazzled, like he was upset that his announcement hadn't gone quite like he planned.

Gloria leaned back in her seat as the moderator struggled to regain control of the debate. Now the world knew that her husband was a rapist. They hadn't made his name public yet, but Gloria had no doubt that soon they would. But she no longer cared what that revelation would do to Elton. She was worried about what it was going to do to her son.

Erma reappeared in the doorway, her silk kimono wrapped around her petite frame. "I hope that debate show is over, because I'm 'bout to watch *Family Feud*."

This time, Gloria was glad to see Erma snatch up the remote and change the channel.

51

When it rained, it was a freaking tsunami. Kay sat across the kitchen table from her best friend, the girl she had just proclaimed days ago as her "ride-or-die chick." But at this very moment it was like she didn't even know the woman.

After last night's stressful debate, the last thing Kay wanted to do was go at it with her best friend. Or judging from the look of contempt on Camille's face, former best friend. But Camille had called her and demanded a meeting with her and Phillip this evening.

"So, let me get this straight," Kay said, trying to process what Camille had just told her and Phillip. "You believe that my husband and I should pay for Charlie's new school?"

Camille sat like a plaintiff on one of Kay's cases. Her soon-to-be-ex-husband, who was sitting next to her, leaned in. "Look, we don't like this at all. We wish neither of the boys got in trouble," Vincent said. "But the bottom line remains this was all Ryan's idea."

"Says your son," Kay countered.

"And I believe my son," Camille replied.

On top of everything else in her life, Kay couldn't believe that she was now battling her best friend. How much could one woman take?

"Look, we don't have it like you two," Vincent continued. Kay couldn't help but wonder since when did they become such a united front.

"Yeah," Camille added. "It's no big deal to you that Ryan got kicked out of Whittington. You'll just enroll him in another ritzy school and foot the bill. Meanwhile, Charlie lost his scholarship and he can't just bounce to the next private school."

"I don't understand why you think we're liable for that," Phillip said.

"Because our son was selling drugs that your son was manufacturing. So your son is responsible for ruining his life," Vincent said.

"Wow. Really?" Kay looked at Camille. Surely, this cockamamie accusation was coming from Vincent. "You agree with this?"

Camille glared at her. "The school has proof this was all Ryan's idea. All of the chemicals, the chemical blueprints were found in Ryan's locker. Charlie doesn't know how to make drugs."

"We didn't come to debate with you," Vincent continued. "We just decided to present it to you first. We can always get the money we need for his school by selling this story to a tabloid."

Kay knew there was a reason she never really cared for Vincent. This had to be all his doing.

"Camille, you know you and I are better than this," Kay said.

"Don't go there with me, Kay. This isn't personal. This is my son."

"You're supposed to be my best friend and this is what you do?" Kay asked.

"That's. My. Son," Camille repeated, her tone unblanched. "And I'm sorry, at the end of the day, he is the most important thing to me. Not my best friend, not my job. My son. The bottom line is Ryan is the one who got him caught up in this mess and I'm not gonna let my son have his life ruined for that." She leaned back, her words pierced with finality.

"I don't believe this," Kay said.

"What do you expect us to do, Kay?" Vincent asked.

"Did our friendship mean anything to you?" Kay couldn't help but ask.

Camille seemed to be getting angrier by the second. "You know, you can try and go there with me if you want," Camille said. "But you are the one always talking about 'those thugs.' Maybe you needed to be keeping tabs on your own little thug."

Kay was appalled at the words coming out of Camille's mouth. It was like it was a totally different person sitting in her dining room.

"If this was anybody else's child," Vincent said, "you have to admit, you'd be the first one trying to throw him into jail."

"Even if it was her own child, she would be ready to crucify him." Camille rolled her eyes.

Kay didn't understand where this anger was coming from. Just days ago, she and Camille had been laughing and playing *Thelma and Louise*.

"Now, that's not even necessary," Phillip said. "This is stressful for us all."

"Tell me about it," Camille snapped. "The only reason my son got expelled was because he hooked up with Ryan."

"Camille, can I talk to you privately?" Kay said. She didn't understand what was happening and she needed to find out why the 360-degree turn.

"There's nothing for us to talk about," Camille said defiantly.

"Yeah, really, there is." They faced off, then finally Camille stood, scooted away from the table, and followed Kay outside. "What is your problem?" Kay asked.

Camille glared at her before answering. "My problem is that you are so busy trying to convict everyone else's son, so busy talking about all these, quote, trifling young men out there, and you got one living in your own house. I had a good kid and your little pride and joy has ruined his life. And now I'm doing what I have to do to make sure that my son's future isn't ruined. You can buy your son another future. Charlie has to work for his. I'm not going to let him mess it all up because your son talked him into doing something crazy."

Kay was dumbfounded. She would have never believed this if she wasn't living it.

"And Vincent was right," Camille continued. "You're always standing in judgment of some child. He must be a thug because he has a tattoo, because he wears baggy clothes, because he hangs out with his friends," she said, mocking Kay. "Even your own son, your real son Jamal, who you were ready to hang out to dry. Now, I don't even get how a mother can disconnect from her own son like you did, but that's neither here nor there. The point is, that boy's mom came to you and told you he was a good kid who had made a bad choice and you weren't trying to hear her, but now that your son is in the same boat—"

"My son isn't accused of murder," Kay said.

"I saw the video, Kay. It was an accident. Your *real* son is not some murderer. But you can't see past your self-righteousness, woe-is-me-because-I-got-knocked-up mentality to get that. But the fact remains, Jamal Jones seems to be a good kid who got caught up in a bad situation and you convicted him because he looked like a thug. For that you were ready to write him off. You're no better than some of the racist people you rail against. Your son doesn't have a tat anywhere. He wears khakis and Polos, makes straight A's, and oh, yeah, is a drug dealer."

"He isn't a drug dealer," Kay said, her voice quivering. "He did something stupid. Should he be punished for the rest of his life?"

"Exactly," Camille said. "For whatever reason, your son who has it all, who has the perfect life, the perfect grades, the perfect future, for some reason he made a dumb decision. Just like Jamal."

Kay's eyes watered up.

Camille moved toward the door. "Now, I'm sorry that this is turning out like this," she continued. "But I'm like Gloria Jones. My number-one priority is protecting my son, even if that means losing my best friend in the process."

She pushed past Kay and went back in the house, summoned her husband, and left without saying another word.

52

Gloria didn't know what Phillip wanted, but the tone of his voice left knots in her stomach. When he'd called and asked her to come by his office, she'd asked him what it was about. But he was cold and standoffish. Not the same person he'd been since she'd met him. She'd had her mother drive her here and her insides did flips the whole way over.

"Hi, Mrs. Jones," Phillip said. "Thank you so much for coming." Stress lines filled his forehead. And for the first time since she'd met him, Phillip Christiansen didn't look polished and refined.

"Are you okay?" he asked her. That touched her heart. He was carrying the weight of everything his family was enduring and yet he was still concerned about her.

She nodded because she couldn't find her voice. Phillip had requested that Elton not come with her. He didn't know that she'd left Elton, but that request alone spoke volumes.

Gloria took a seat. "Is this meeting you requested regarding the case? Is there some new evidence?"

Phillip sat down at his desk and looked at her. "Mrs. Jones, I like you a lot. And I like Jamal, too. I think he's a good kid who's getting a bad rap."

"He is."

"That's why it pains me to have to do this."

"Noooo," she muttered, because she knew what was coming next.

"I'm going to have to step down as your son's attorney."

The sob she'd been fighting back escaped. She buried her face in her hands and cried.

"I am so sorry. But now that I know everything, I just can't. I told my wife I was going to stay on, but the more I think about it, the more I know I can't do it."

"I am so sorry," she said. "I'm sorry I didn't tell you, but please don't leave us."

He held his hands up to stop her. "You know, I could even get over the fact that you weren't entirely truthful. But your husband violated my wife. The woman I love. What do I look like helping you guys out?"

"You're not helping us out. You're helping Jamal," she cried. "Please don't do this."

"I have some great people that I can recommend." He started sifting through some business cards.

"We go to trial soon."

"I'll ask for a continuance."

"That means Jamal will have to stay in jail even longer." Gloria scooted to the edge of her seat. "Please, Mr. Christiansen. You don't even have to work with Elton. I left him."

Phillip stared at her like he was trying to determine if she was telling the truth.

"I swear. I left him two weeks ago. I'm not going back."

"I'm sorry. My mind is made up," he said. "Besides, I think it's a conflict of interest anyway."

"How is it a conflict for you to fight for my son? For your wife's son?" she couldn't help but add.

She regretted that because Phillip grew tense and said, "I'm sorry. I'll pass on the name of an attorney, or if you prefer, I can speak with the attorney with the Black Justice Coalition and bring him up to speed. I know they really wanted this case."

"I don't want that attorney. I want you."

"And I don't want to bring my wife any more pain than she's already enduring," he said. "We have a lot of things going on personally and I don't want to add any more stress, especially to my wife."

Under different circumstances, Gloria might have admired his loyalty to his wife. But right now, she was feeling a pain like never before.

"Please . . ."

He stood, signaling the end of their conversation. "I'm sorry. I'll see you out."

Gloria eased the cards he'd given her into her purse. She struggled not to have a meltdown in the lobby of his law office.

Gloria didn't know how she made it back out to the car. Her mother was sitting in the front seat, nodding off. Gloria eased into the car and began sobbing.

"Hey, what's wrong?" her mother asked, groggy from her nap.

"He's dropping the case."

"What?"

"He's dropping the case," she repeated.

"Oh, Jesus," Erma replied.

"He said he just can't with everything that's going on." She'd told her mother everything last night. Erma had held her as she cried, but thankfully, hadn't said much else.

Erma was silent for a few minutes, then said, "Well, the way I see it, you have two options. You can sit here like a blubbering fool or you can do something about it."

"Do what?" Gloria sniffed.

"I don't know, find a new attorney."

"I can't find someone this fast."

"Seems like to me you sure got a lot of things you can't do," Erma said.

"We're about to go to trial, Mama, not to mention the money," she replied.

"Then you have to convince him to not give up on the case," Erma said, matter-of-factly.

"How am I supposed to do that?"

"Look, you're the same woman that can take a baby and convince the whole world that he is yours. Well, everyone except me." She smiled.

Again, Gloria was thankful her mother didn't launch into a rampage of *I told you sos*.

"Jamal is mine."

"Then act like it. All your life, I've been telling you that you have a fighter's spirit in your blood. You're more like me than you care to admit. You didn't like your daddy's sit-back-and-take-it attitude when you were little. You let your husband take you away from that. But you're a fighter." She tapped Gloria's chest. "You're a fighter in there. Are we gladiators or are we bitches?"

Gloria couldn't help but burst out laughing. "Really, Mama?"

"Okay, so you know I love some *Scandal*. The fact remains that you gotta pull it together, baby girl. All this whining and moping, working my last nerve, is just too much. Your son is in trouble and the only person who can help him is you."

"What am I supposed to do?"

"You keep telling Jamal to hang on. You gotta do the same. You have to have faith and you got to keep on fighting. The devil tests us when we're at our weakest moment."

Gloria was a little shocked. "When did you get to be so wise?"

"I always have been. My family just underestimates me. Now, come on. Let's go by the drive-thru daiquiri shop so we can get a daiquiri and strategize your next move."

Her mother slid her oversized sunglasses on, let the top down on her convertible, then sped toward the daiquiri shop.

53

Gloria had never prayed so hard. She remembered Elton preaching a sermon one time about surrendering when you had nowhere else to turn and all hope was lost. Simply surrendering to God and knowing that He would work it all out. That's where she was now. She was surrendering. She'd prayed. She'd cried. She'd turned it over to God.

And like her mother said, she was ready to fight.

Yes, Gloria had faith, but she also knew that God helped those who helped themselves. That's why she was here about to give God a little assistance.

Gloria lightly tapped on the front door. She felt like a stalker, having followed Kay home from her office. She hated to be coming to this woman's house, but Gloria didn't think she'd make it past the receptionist at her office. Gloria knew Phillip wasn't at home because she had called his office on the way over. But right now, she was at her last resort. She was just about to ring the doorbell when the front door swung open. The most adorable curly-haired teenage boy stood there.

"Hello," he said.

"Hi, is your mother home?" Gloria asked.

He looked her up and down, like he was unsure whether he should answer. "Yes, she is," he finally said.

"Well, can you tell her that Mrs. Jones is here to see her?"

The boy nodded. "Hold on, please."

She smiled. He was a mannerable boy and Gloria found herself wondering if that's how Jamal would've turned out if he'd grown up with Kay. She shook that thought off. Jamal had grown up right where he was supposed to. With her.

After a few minutes, Kay appeared in the doorway. Shock registered across her face. "What are you doing here?"

"Can I talk to you for a minute?" Gloria shifted.

Kay folded her arms and glared at Gloria. "I don't think that's a good idea. I mean, I'm not prosecuting your case anymore so I really don't know what we have to talk about."

"I know," Gloria said, "but I'm here to talk to you"—she paused—"woman to woman." She looked up at the teen, who had appeared behind Kay. "Mother to mother," Gloria added.

Kay turned around. "Ryan, go on back inside, son. I'll be in in a minute."

Ryan hesitated, glanced back and forth between the two women, then eased away. Kay stepped outside and closed the door.

Gloria wasn't going to lie. She had hoped to be able to go inside and see Kay's lavish home. But today, that wasn't her mission. So she refocused on the real reason she was here.

"I need your help," Gloria said, getting straight to the point.

"I don't know what you think I can help you with," Kay replied. "I turned the case over. I recused myself. I'm out of it."

"But your husband has stepped down as well."

Kay looked shocked, like she had no idea. Finally, she said, "I have no control over what he has done."

"I know. But we're too far in the process and Phillip is committed and we can't lose him. The trial starts in two weeks."

"Well, I understand that you have lawyers lined up to represent you."

"We have lawyers lined up to get in the spotlight that this case brings. Phillip is here because he cares about what happens to Jamal."

Kay folded her arms across her chest. "Yes, my husband is very committed to getting justice for Jamal. But I guess he was committed to his wife more. I'm sorry, I can't help you. He doesn't want to stay on the case because he knows what your husband did. *You* know what your husband did."

Gloria took a deep breath and then looked back up. "You're right. I was wrong. He was wrong. I was wrong to believe him."

Kay gave her a *tell me something I don't know* look.

"But, please, try to understand my position," Gloria continued. "You know your husband. If someone came to you and told you the worst thing ever, something no amount of money could make you think he was capable of doing, wouldn't you be inclined to believe him?"

Kay stood for a minute, thinking.

Gloria continued, "I never saw that man who," she paused, inhaled, and readied herself to utter words she'd never admitted, "who raped you. He had never shown himself to me so I couldn't believe he existed. I didn't want to believe he existed. I really did believe that you . . . that it was consensual. Or maybe I just wanted to believe it."

Gloria could tell she was getting through to Kay, so she didn't let up.

"That doesn't excuse it. It doesn't justify it. I should have listened. I should have opened my eyes. I should've let my head lead me and not my heart. I shouldn't have been so quick to judge. After you left that day with your parents, my gut told me something wasn't right. That's why it haunted me. And I asked for Jamal because I wanted to make it right. I wanted that child, who didn't ask to be brought here, to be loved. I wanted to give him a chance at life. I wanted to make up for not standing up for you. And I wanted to find joy in tragedy. That's why I insisted that we adopt him."

Kay's eyes started misting. "It was your idea to take him?"

"Yes. I mean, Elton didn't fight me on it." Gloria didn't see any sense in telling Kay how Elton had been against the idea. "And we have loved Jamal. We have tried to give him the best. He doesn't deserve to be where he is. He's a good kid."

"Most mothers say that."

Gloria stood silent for a moment. "We deserve that one," she said. "My husband did something very, very bad seventeen years ago. He should've been punished for it. But we can't change the past. All we can do is try to create a better future. And that's what I'm here to do."

"What do you want from me, Gloria?" Kay sighed.

"Jamal needs Phillip. We need you to convince him to stay on our case."

Kay rolled her eyes. "Even if I could, it's not my place to convince my husband of anything. He can't support what your husband did to me."

"I've left Elton," Gloria blurted out. "So he shouldn't even be a part of the equation."

Kay's mouth dropped open. "What? Is that some kind of trick?"

"Please understand, my son's life is on the line. I'm not playing games, doing any tricks. I'm just trying to save him," Gloria said. "This situation simply opened my eyes to my husband. I've discovered so many things about him that I can't stand. That I've excused over the years."

Kay stood for a minute. "Well, that's on you," she said.

"I just need you to try to talk to Phillip. Please, I'm begging you. Help me save my son. Help me save *our* son."

Kay didn't say anything at first, then finally said, "Fine. I'll talk to him. But he's his own man and I can't make any promises."

"That's all I can ask. Thank you. Thank you," Gloria cried.

She didn't know why she felt so confident. Maybe it was the look in Kay's eyes. It was the look of a mother. And ultimately, that trumped everything.

54

Would this nightmare ever end? Kay had barely closed the door when she heard Ryan say, "Was that his mother?"

"What?" Kay said. She was a little flustered because some of the things Gloria said were resonating with her.

"Was that his mother? Your son's mother?" he repeated.

His words caught her off guard. She had no idea that he knew. "Were you eavesdropping? You know you're in enough trouble as it is."

Ryan stood, staring at her. "Why didn't you tell us you had a son?"

For a moment, Kay wanted to take her parents' approach and tell him to stay out of grown folks' business but she'd hated it when they'd done that to her and she really didn't want to do it to Ryan.

"Have a seat," she said, motioning toward the living room sofa. "What do you know?" she asked after he was seated.

"Everything that's out. I read a lot of stuff on the Internet. I don't know what's true and what's not."

She sighed, debating how much she should share. "Well, it's true that I have a son I gave up for adoption," she said.

"But I don't understand. You're such a good mom. You seem like you like kids. Why would you give yours away?"

"I love kids," she replied. "It's just that the circumstances, they were very different."

"Was it true that you were . . ." His words trailed off as if he couldn't bear to finish the sentence.

"Raped?" she finished for him. She nodded. "Yes. By someone I knew and trusted. But my parents made the decision to give my child up."

"So if it was up to you, would you have kept him?"

Nobody had ever asked her that question before and she didn't know the answer. Until the point that she brought Jamal into this world, she would've said no. But the minute she gave birth to him, a part of her longed for him.

"I don't know the answer to that," Kay responded.

Ryan's face was blanketed with confusion. "My mom left me through death and it left a hole in me . . ." He paused. "I hope I don't make you mad by saying this."

"No, of course, you can speak freely." That was one of the things that they never talked about, Ryan's mother. Whenever Kay or Phillip tried to broach the topic, Ryan would change the subject and start talking about something else.

"It left a hole in me that no amount of love from anyone else can fill," Ryan continued. "So I can only imagine how someone feels to know that their mother just gave them up. And I know the stuff I read said he shot a cop, but from what I saw, it was an accident. I also know you don't really like bad kids, but I can't help but wonder if your son had stayed with you, would he have turned out different. I know you and Dad like to say I'm a good kid, and I am, well, except for the whole making drugs thing, but I'm good because I was raised by two good people. That can make a big difference."

Kay sat in silence for a moment. The rightness of everything Ryan and Gloria had said was weighing on her. "You've given me some food for thought. You really are an intelligent young man."

Even though he smiled, a blanket of shame covered his face and he lowered his head. "I'm sorry I let you down."

She lifted his chin. "Your father and I have never been more disappointed in you but we know that you're a good kid."

"Dad is so mad at me."

They'd taken away his computer privileges and grounded him, which was difficult because it was not like he ever wanted to do anything anyway.

"Why did you do it, Ryan?" She hoped this rare moment of openness would give her the answers she and Phillip hadn't been able to get since he got expelled.

Ryan let out a defeated sigh. "I was trying to fit in. I was just playing around with some formulas and came up with a less potent dosage of X. I knew it was wrong, but I told someone, who told someone, and next thing I know, people were asking for it and I started getting popular."

"But you are the one always talking about you're a self-proclaimed nerd."

"Yeah, that's usually what nerds say to make themselves feel better," he said. "I'm just grateful for a second chance. You don't ever have to worry about me getting in trouble again."

"I hope not, Ryan. Because you not only let us down, you let yourself down."

"I'm lucky to get a second chance, aren't I, Mom?"

She nodded. "You sure are."

"Maybe Jamal deserves one, too."

She hesitated, unsure of where that came from. "You and Jamal are different," she replied.

"We are. He's your *real* son. I'm your *step*son. If you have enough love for me, you can have enough love for him. Face your past and I bet you can learn to love him, too." He looked at her, then stood and walked off.

"He's wise beyond his years."

Kay turned around to see Phillip standing in the doorway. She hadn't even realized that he'd come in.

"He is."

Phillip walked over, kissed her on the cheek, then sat next to her on the sofa.

"I heard him talking about learning from his mistakes. You think he has?" Phillip said.

"I really think so. He feels awful about what happened."

"I just don't understand why. We gave that boy everything," Phillip said.

"Maybe that's the problem." They sat in silence for a few minutes, then Kay said, "Do you think what he said is true, that Jamal deserves a second chance as well?"

"Yes. He's a good kid who got caught up in a bad situation," Phillip said. "I hope they find a good attorney."

Kay turned to face her husband. In that moment, she decided to go against every ethical thing she'd ever done.

"Phillip, this doesn't need to go to court," Kay said. "That boy's life has been turned upside down. Get them to settle on reduced charges, with time served."

"I'm not representing them anymore," he said.

She took his hands. "I know what you're trying to do and I appreciate it, I really do. But this isn't about me, or you, or even Elton. He's going to have to pay, but his karma will be dealt with by a higher power. Jamal doesn't need to have his life ruined. Call Gloria and tell her you're back on the case."

"Are you sure?"

"I've never been more sure of anything."

She saw relief fill his eyes. "I love you, you know that?" he said.

"I love you, and you'll be happy to know this whole situation has opened my eyes to a lot of things."

"So, when you become mayor you'll remember all of this?" he asked as he pulled her into a hug.

She smiled. "You think I still I have a shot?"

"I know you do. You're Kay Christiansen, Superwoman."

She snuggled closer. "Right now, I just want to be regular old Kay." Her phone had been blowing up after the debate. Much to Marty's chagrin, his revelation hadn't had as much of a negative effect as he would've liked. Yes, she'd dropped some in the polls, but she was still leading him by three points.

Phillip grabbed the remote. "Then I have the perfect solution. No more work tonight." He picked up the remote and flipped the TV on. "Let's pop some popcorn and find a movie to watch. You know there's a Tyler Perry marathon playing on one of these channels."

Kay laid her head on Phillip's shoulder and for the first time in months, pushed everything out of her mind and just enjoyed a quiet moment with her husband.

55

S he'd survived the debate. She was handling the media scrutiny. Yet Kay still felt a pang inside her soul. And at the core of what she was feeling was the son she gave away.

Face the past.

Ryan's words rang in her head. It was funny. Her fifteen-year-old gave her the wisest words of all.

Kay needed to deal with her demons so she could pull herself together. If she had any hopes of not only winning the election but moving on with her life, she needed to face the past.

And she was facing it with Gloria at her side.

Kay knew Gloria had been shocked to get the call yesterday asking if Kay could go see Jamal. Not only had Gloria said yes, but she'd offered to come along since she said Jamal knew and might still be angry. So now the two of them sat together once again. But this time they both were nervous. They'd lived a lifetime of deception and it was time to face the consequences.

The clank of heavy metal signaled the arrival of Jamal. They turned to the door as a guard guided him in. Kay couldn't help but look at the shackles. Usually the sight didn't bother her. But today she wanted to say, "Are those really necessary?" Yet she remained silent.

"Hi, sweetie." Gloria stood to hug Jamal. Before the guard could stop her, he ducked out of her reach. The move caused her face to fill with pain and for a moment, Kay's heart went out to her.

Gloria slid back down into her seat as Jamal glared at Kay. He didn't look at Gloria as he sat down.

"So, it's true?" was all he said.

Kay didn't know how she was supposed to answer that. How did she tell her son that she'd given him up without a fight?

Gloria leaned forward. "Let us explain."

Jamal looked at her, his words hard, his tone dry. "No disrespect, Ma, or rather, Gloria, but I think you've given me enough lies to last me the rest of my life. So if you don't mind"—he turned and glared at Kay—"I'd like my *real* mother to tell me the truth. You are my real mother, right?"

Kay didn't know what to say.

Jamal choked back his words. "You *are* my real mother, right?" He pounded the table.

"Hey, hey, hey!" the guard said, causing Jamal to take a deep breath, then lean back and wait for her answer.

"Gloria is your real mother in every sense of the word," Kay said.

"Did you give birth to me?" he snarled.

Kay nodded.

"Wow." He released a pained laugh. "So, my daddy really did get another woman pregnant. The good minister got another woman pregnant," he repeated as if he was still trying to process the news.

"Where is good ol' daddy?" Jamal said, finally looking at Gloria. "He didn't have a self-righteous speech he wanted to come give me?"

"Jamal, I understand you're bitter," Gloria began.

"You don't understand anything!" he snapped. "I have spent my life wondering what I did to that man to make him hate me."

"He didn't hate you."

Kay was stunned by that revelation. Elton had had the audacity to hold a grudge against his son?

"Now I find out all I did was be born?" Jamal continued. "He despised me because I brought shame to him? He's the one who got a woman other than his wife pregnant, but *I* brought shame?"

"He loves you," Gloria said, her voice shaking.

"Kinda like he loved little teenage girls?" His words made Kay cringe. She felt like she should interject, but she would never come to the defense of Elton Jones.

"Yeah, I read the paper," Jamal continued. "Everybody's talking about it. What are the odds? The cop-killing kid was being prosecuted by the mother that gave him up for adoption after being raped by her pastor. That sounds like some jacked-up B-movie."

"Jamal . . ." Gloria said.

"No!" he yelled, eliciting another piercing glare from the guard. "Why isn't he here? Why hasn't Dad been to see me? He's a coward, that's why."

"Your father made mistakes. But he loves you," Gloria said. Kay could tell that she was now just saying words to try to ease Jamal's anger.

"That's what I was. A constant reminder of his sin." Jamal laughed. "That's why he hated me." Before Gloria could say anything else, Jamal spun in Kay's direction. "Why are *you* here?"

"I just . . . I don't know."

"Me, either. I read the newspaper. You living it up in a life of luxury, raising a stepson while pretending your real son doesn't exist." His words were soaked with hatred and each syllable dug into Kay's soul.

"Y-you don't understand what it was like . . ." Kay stammered.

"How do you know I don't know what it's like to be raped?" He sneered. "I'm fresh meat in a jail full of criminals."

Gloria let out a muffled cry and Kay felt a pang in her heart.

"Jamal, just—"

His voice quivered. "I've felt out of place for years. I didn't know why. I thought I was going crazy. If my God-fearing parents had just been honest, maybe I wouldn't have spent years torturing myself."

"Jamal, I'm so—"

"You!" His words caused Gloria to jump back. "You don't get to talk to me. I'm tired of the adults in my life lying to me. My daddy is a rapist. My biological mother is a coward. And the woman that raised me is a liar. I'm freakin' doomed."

"Jamal . . ."

He scooted back, knocking over the chair as he stood. "Matter of fact, let me up outta here!" He made his way to the door, but then stopped and turned back to face them. "Don't come back here. Either one of you. My whole existence has been a lie. I'ma tell my attorney to take a plea. I'd rather rot in here than see either one of you again."

Kay didn't realize she was trembling as he walked out. She knew he was hurt, but she never imagined the toll it would take on him. She felt horrible that all this time, as she'd thought about what having him did to *her*, she'd never considered what giving up Jamal had done to *him*.

56

Gloria felt a myriad of emotions. Relief, nervousness, fear. She looked to her left and seeing Phillip gave her strength.

The visit with Jamal had left her in a pit of despair. But the call from Phillip had lifted her spirits.

She'd been ecstatic when he'd told her that if they would have him, he'd be honored to get back on the case. He apologized to her for abandoning them.

From there he'd gone to work. He'd spent the last three days wheeling and dealing. She told him any deal that would give Jamal the least amount of jail time, she was all for. And they thought they'd found it, reaching a deal with the prosecutor for Involuntary Manslaughter.

"So, are all the parties here?" Judge Raymond asked. Harold, the former second chair, stood.

"We are, Your Honor."

Gloria sat behind Phillip and Jamal on the opposite side of the courtroom. It pained her that Jamal didn't look her way, but she knew getting over her betrayal would take him some time. But she had nothing but time. She would love him past his pain. And no matter how cold he acted, how angry he got, she'd never give up.

"Will the defendant please rise?" Judge Raymond said. "Jamal Jones, it is my understanding that you have accepted Involuntary Manslaughter charges?"

"Yes, Your Honor," he said.

Judge Raymond looked over at Harold. "And what is the state's position?"

"Your Honor, the state is willing to accept the charge," Harold replied. He seemed relieved that the case wasn't going to court.

"Fine. I will review the case and come up with an appropriate sentence. In the meantime, I will allow the defendant to be released on bail until sentencing. Bail is set at one hundred thousand dollars."

"What?" Gloria exclaimed.

"Your Honor," Phillip began. They had expected bail at no more than $20,000 and Gloria was prepared with the ten percent. But she had no idea where she'd get another $8,000.

"Yes, Counselor?" Judge Raymond said.

"I implore you to reconsider the bail amount. My client is not from a wealthy family and would be hard-pressed to come up with that bail."

"Counselor, have you forgotten that a police officer is dead? Regardless of the why, he's dead, and his family would not appreciate such a meager bail. So my order stands. If the defendant cannot make bail he shall remain in the state's custody until he can."

"He can make it."

They all turned to see Elton standing in the back of the room.

"We can post the bail," Elton said. "I will put our house up, whatever it takes."

Relief filled Gloria's body. Jamal even looked shocked. "Okay," the judge said. "Then it's settled. We'll see all parties back here in a week for sentencing."

She banged her gavel, dismissing them.

Gloria jumped up and wrapped her arms around Jamal's neck. He nodded but didn't reply. His eyes were no longer on her, though. He was looking at his father.

Gloria looked over her shoulder as a teary-eyed Elton eased out through the courtroom door. She didn't know what the future held for them, or even if they had a future. She knew the road to healing would be a long and treacherous one. But Elton needed to heal himself first. They'd never be a family again, that much she knew, but maybe they could mend some of the damage they'd caused. She shook off all thoughts of Elton and turned to Phillip.

"Okay, what do I need to do? I just want to get my baby out of here."

Phillip smiled at both of them. "Jamal, just hang on a few more hours. We're going to work on getting your bond posted, then we'll work on getting you home."

That made him lose his smile. "I'm not going back to Jasper," he said.

Gloria stepped toward him. She already knew they couldn't go back there. Between the cops out for blood, the gossiping church members, and Elton, there was nothing for Gloria or Jamal in Jasper.

"Don't worry, honey. Mama has it all taken care of. Today—as soon as you're released—you and I will begin the rest of our lives."

57

Kay was back in the courtroom. But this time, she was on the defendant's side. The media had been having a field day, with Marty leading the battle cry of how this was a "case of blatant injustice." As if he cared about this case. But he wanted to further drag her name any way he could. Loni had launched a full-scale campaign to try to boost her numbers back up since they were still down from the debate. After weeks of a solid lead, she was now neck-and-neck with Marty and the election was just a week away.

Kay had resolved that whatever was to be was to be. She still wanted to win but she decided that she'd be content in the DA's office. That's if Sam even wanted her to stay. If this thing ended too ugly with Jamal's sentencing hearing, so might her career in the DA's office. But that was another thing she couldn't worry about.

She'd also done something that she'd never done before—she'd gone to Sam on Jamal's behalf. She'd convinced him that since the charges against Dix and Brian had been dropped, the quickest way to make this case disappear was to settle for a lesser charge.

"All rise," the bailiff called out as Judge Raymond entered.

Kay stood along with everyone else in the courtroom. Everyone but Elton, that is. Gloria had asked Kay to come to the sentencing hearing, but the only way Kay would agree to that was if Elton stayed away. Gloria said he'd been upset at the request but he understood, especially when Gloria reminded him that the media would be there and would try to get an interview with him. Officer Wilkins's family along with half the Jasper police force sat on the other side of the courtroom.

"You may be seated," the judge said as she took a seat at the bench.

Jamal glanced over his shoulder at them. Or rather Gloria. Kay wanted to believe he was looking at her, but when she saw the love in Gloria's eyes, she knew better. Gloria blew him a kiss, then clutched her hands together in a prayer mode. That woman loved her son. Loved *their* son. Kay had never thought about how blessed Jamal was to have grown up with such a loving mother and she was grateful that Gloria was able to do what she had not.

Kay was glad that the judge had closed the courtroom to the media. From what she'd been told, the bail hearing had been hard enough for Jamal. Having to deal with media while he was sentenced would only make things worse.

"Counselor, I understand that you have reached a sentencing agreement?" the judge asked.

"Yes, Your Honor," Phillip said.

Judge Raymond turned to Harold, the ADA. "Are the terms agreeable to the District Attorney's Office?"

Harold stood. "Yes, Your Honor, we find the terms satisfactory," he said. Usually in nonjury cases, she issued the sentence, but she'd allowed the two sides to work this out.

"Will the defendant please rise?" the judge said.

Both Jamal and Phillip stood. Gloria instinctively took Kay's hand. Surprisingly, Kay found comfort in her touch.

"Young man, you need to consider yourself very lucky," the judge said. "There are hundreds of young men who come through my courtroom who never get this opportunity. I hope you know how blessed you are."

The judge looked over at the Wilkins family, who sat teary-eyed clutching one another. "I understand that no punishment can bring back your loved one. And it is heartfelt when I say I am sorry for your loss. However, I have to concur with the defense that this was indeed a tragic accident." She turned back to Jamal. "I can only hope that one day you will overcome the thing that had you so fearful of police to the point that your immediate reaction was panic." She turned toward the officers. "The same applies to police. It is my hope that your days of automatically stereotyping and assuming the worst when you see these young men become few and far between. I can only hope that one day that gap will be bridged so that we have no more tragic losses."

Finished with her admonishment, Judge Raymond removed her glasses and stared at Jamal. "Mr. Jones, because this is your first offense, I am going to accept the Involuntary Manslaughter recommendation. You will serve three years' probation. If you get into any kind of trouble, I promise you, I will make sure that you do time. I want you to seize your second chance." The judge looked up at Kay and smiled. "And I understand that you have someone who you need to get to know."

Her words made Kay's heart flutter.

"Do you understand and agree with these terms?" Judge Raymond continued.

Phillip looked at Jamal, who nodded and said, "Yes, ma'am."

The relief in his voice pierced Kay's heart. And for the first time she really thought about what it felt like to be in his shoes. She felt awful about the Wilkins family, especially when she recalled the promise she made the little girl.

"Okay, then, your attorney will advise you of your next move. Court is adjourned."

The courtroom erupted in chatter. Officer Wilkins's widow glared at Kay as her father led her out of the courtroom.

"So, I'm done?" Jamal asked.

Phillip nodded. Gloria leaped from her seat and raced over to Jamal. "Thank you, Jesus!" Gloria held him close as both of them sobbed.

Kay didn't realize that she was crying, too, until Phillip handed her a tissue. "We had a victory today," Phillip said.

Kay looked at him and smiled. "We did."

Part of her wanted Jamal to acknowledge her. She found herself longing to reach out and hug him as well, but she couldn't move. That would have to come in due time.

Phillip did hug him and Kay's heart flickered when Jamal flashed a small smile in her direction. Kay realized that was all that she would get but she would take that. For now. Gloria would always be his mother, but Kay would do everything that she could to become his friend.

58

This speech wasn't giving her the joy that she thought it would. Maybe that was because over the last few months, Kay had learned what really mattered in life. She had always been committed to her family, but now, she wanted that commitment to include the family that she'd forgotten.

But it did put a smile in her heart to watch Marty Simon conceding.

"You can tell it's killing him," Loni leaned in and whispered. They were standing around the big-screen TV in their hotel suite at the Hilton Americas, watching the election returns. The polls had been closed for four hours and Kay held a very strong lead, but Marty refused to concede until the very last moment.

"We did it," Jeff said, appearing on the side of them.

"Yes, we all did," Kay said with a smile. "Thank you all for holding it down while my life fell apart."

"Shoot, I need to see if I can sell your story," Jeff replied. "That needs to be my next task. I see a book, movie deal, the works in your future."

Kay laughed. "No, I'm good. I have had enough publicity to last a lifetime."

"And now, she has a job to do," Phillip said, appearing on the side of her.

Kay hugged her husband, ecstatic that he had weathered this storm with her. Leslie was in the corner asleep and Ryan was talking to Jeff's son. He'd been really depressed about losing his friendship with Charlie. Kay knew how he felt. She couldn't believe that she was celebrating a monumental win without her best friend by her side. But she'd get her friendship with Camille back. She was going to make that a priority. They were going to pay for Charlie's school because they could afford it. Then Kay would forgive Camille for all the horrible things she said, and for blaming Ryan. She'd forgive her because she didn't have any room left in her heart for hate.

"Thank you so much, Kay. I'm glad you invited me," Gloria said, walking up.

"Thank you for coming. I know this has been hard on both of us."

"I'm just glad to have my son home."

Jamal was home. Or his new home, rather, in Houston. With a little help from Kay, Gloria had gotten an apartment for her and Jamal and they were all trying to help him through this ordeal.

She'd wanted him here tonight, but he refused to come.

At first Kay was sad about that, but she hoped that in time, they'd have a breakthrough. Kay had broken her bond with her son and would stop at nothing until she got it back.

Epilogue

R egret was a powerful thing, and as he watched the streamers fall from the ceiling, the massive crowd cheering in delight and Kay Christiansen poised to deliver her acceptance speech, Elton Jones was filled with regret.

Once upon a time, he was a very bad boy. His wife knew about Kayla. She didn't know about the others. There were only a handful of them, but Elton felt the pain in his heart as he thought about what he took from them. He had tried so hard to live a righteous life. But something about the nectar of a young girl had turned him on. It wasn't as perverted as it seemed now, because he was in his early thirties the first time it happened. And that girl—Patrice, a promiscuous sixteen-year-old neighbor—had pursued him. She'd flaunted her tight little body around him, told him that in "the old days," women her age were already married, toyed with him, touched him, until he finally gave in.

A slow pain filled his heart as he recalled how that became his justification for the next girl. Elton didn't even remember her name, but she'd cried silent tears as he forced himself on her. She, too, initially wanted it and then right in the middle of the act changed her mind, but he couldn't stop. Patrice had opened an appetite he didn't know existed. The next girl had been a church member. She was sixteen also but had the body of a twenty-five-year-old. He'd justified that one by saying he wasn't that much older than her. The way she'd cried, and gone from a sweet church girl to a rebellious teen, Elton had sworn he wouldn't do it again.

Then the devil led him to Kayla in that closet. He had no intention of doing anything other than chastising her, until her innocence seemed to call out for him. He'd decided to dance with the devil, not even wondering whether the other two girls would call for help, especially since . . .

Elton's thoughts trailed off as he heard a noise outside, then what sounded like a cat screeching. He stood and looked out the window. It was pitch black, but he saw the Parkers' old cat scurrying across his yard.

Elton closed the blinds and made his way back to his recliner. Kayla was still on the TV. She was giving a speech now. But he had no idea what she was saying. Her words wouldn't register. When he saw her, how she'd excelled in spite of what he'd done, he thanked God for deliverance. Hers and his.

When Kayla had turned up pregnant, Elton had taken that as a sign from God. He had accepted his son as his punishment for his sin and had prayed feverently for forgiveness. He had fasted. He had cleansed himself. And he had been delivered from the demon that caused him to hurt those girls.

He did have an occasional desire, but when it came, he locked himself in his office with his Bible and prayed until it went away.

And Gloria had never known.

His wife had been right about one thing, God had forgiven him, but he had not forgiven himself. He was angry for what he'd done and had taken that anger and resentment out on his son. He hadn't meant to, but he had.

". . . I'd like to thank my family," Kayla said, causing Elton to turn his attention back to the TV. She was at the podium, smiling and looking happy. "My wonderful husband." Phillip stepped up and hugged her. "And my children, Leslie, Ryan . . ." Then she turned directly to the camera and added, "And Jamal."

That brought a lump to Elton's throat. Jamal wasn't onstage and if Elton knew his son, it would take some time before he accepted Kayla. But Elton was just glad that his son was getting a second chance, even if that chance was without him.

Maybe one day he could make amends with Jamal, maybe even Gloria. He'd written Jamal a letter, telling him how sorry he was for everything, begging for his forgiveness. He'd asked Gloria to give him the letter and she promised that she had but Elton had yet to hear back from his son.

Gloria, on the other hand, did still call to check on him. The first time she did it, he had a glimmer of hope. But he had soon discovered that her calls were simply her nurturing nature, checking on his well-being. The love she had for him was gone. He could feel it every time they spoke. And for him, that was the ultimate price he paid for the sins he'd committed.

Elton was just about to turn off the television when his doorbell rang. He looked out the peephole and didn't recognize the young lady standing there. She was a brown-skinned girl, with a hat covering her wavy, shoulder-length hair. She was incredibly thin and for a moment, Elton wondered if she was a drug addict begging for food.

She saw him through the peephole, waved, and smiled. "Hello. I'm your new neighbor from down the street. I was wondering if I could use your phone?"

He frowned. It was late for folks to be knocking on other folks' doors, but then he let her in. Jasper seldom got new residents.

"I'm sorry. They haven't installed my phone yet and I need to call a friend and give her directions," the woman said.

"Oh, okay. Well, I'm Elton Jones. Reverend Elton Jones," he said, stepping aside. "Come on in. The phone is in the living room."

"Thank you."

He directed her to the phone; she picked it up, dialed a number, then mumbled off directions to their street.

"So you moved into the Pearsons' house? I didn't even realize it had been leased. The sign was still up there today," Elton asked after she'd hung up.

She nodded. "Just trying to get settled in." She shifted again. "May I trouble you for some water?"

"Sure," he said, making his way out of the room. "What brings you to Jasper?" he asked from the kitchen. "This isn't exactly a thriving metropolis." He laughed as he handed her a bottled water. He gave her a hard stare. "Are you sure you're new around here?" he said. "You look familiar."

"Yep, this is my first time in Jasper." She unscrewed the cap, then took a sip of the water.

"Well, what brings you here?"

"Business," she said.

"Oh, okay. What kind of business you in?"

"Score settling." She finally seemed to relax as she set the water down on the table by the front door. It wasn't lost on Elton that she hadn't bothered to use a coaster.

"Score settling?" he asked, sliding a coaster under her bottle. "Never heard of that. By the way, I didn't get your name."

The woman took a deep breath, then slid her hand into her jacket pocket.

"You gon' tell me your name?" he asked again.

The woman didn't say a word as she slowly slid her hand out of her pocket.

Elton's eyes bucked at the .32-caliber pistol pointed at him.

"My name is Maxine," she said, "Maxine Lewis."

Elton took a step back. "Wh-what are you doing?"

"I told you, settling the score." She stepped closer to him. "Do you even know who I am?"

Elton was so scared he couldn't reply. Of course he knew. He hadn't seen her in years, but he knew. He just couldn't believe he hadn't known when he opened the front door.

She let out a maniacal laugh. "Oh, I see by the look on your face, you remember. Do you also remember how I cried when you raped me? I felt worthless. I didn't know how to bounce back. I told my mother and she blamed me, called me a whore, because she had her eyes on you. Do you know what that does to a child? Not only did you rape me, but my mother blamed me for you two not being together. So it messed our relationship up. How crazy is that?" She released another pained laugh.

Was a twenty-year-old deed really about to come back and haunt him?

"You . . . you seemed fine," he found himself stammering.

"Fine?" she screeched, jabbing the gun in his direction. "You call getting on drugs, drifting from one worthless job to another, one no-good man to another, fine? The only reason I didn't get pregnant as a teen was because I refused to let another man touch me!"

"Look, I'm sorry," Elton said, eyeing her strong hold on the gun.

"Sorry?" she cried. She had started sweating and it was making Elton nervous. "I know you are sorry!"

"No, I'm sorry I hurt you." He stepped toward her. "But you don't want to do this."

She jabbed the gun again. "Back! Get back! I knew what you were going to do to Kayla that day you caught us smoking. I even asked her when she came running out of there in tears, but she acted like I was crazy. Everyone acted like I was crazy!" She took a deep breath, like she was trying to calm herself. "You know, I used to dream of ways of getting revenge on you. I'd given up until I ran into Kayla in a restaurant. Then I read the newspaper. The whole story about your son and my old friend Kayla, and then you became my mission. And now I'm here."

"Wh-what do you want from me?" Elton stammered. "I told you I'm sorry."

"I don't want your tired-ass apology. I want revenge," she snapped.

"Maxine, God has—"

"Shut up!" she screamed, putting her other hand on the gun. "Don't you dare talk to me about God. What kind of God lets you be His spokesperson?" She raised the gun and pointed it at his chest.

"A forgiving one," he said.

The gun trembled in her hands as she said, "Then I hope He forgives me, too." And then she fired one fatal shot.

MAMA'S BOY

Introduction

When a news station runs a video of a black teenager shooting a white police officer in Jasper, Texas, Gloria Jones instantly recognizes the face of her son, Jamal—and fears for his life. As a hotbed of racial tension tracing back to the 1990s, Jasper is far from a safe haven for accused killers, and Gloria knows the dead police officer's family and colleagues will be out for blood.

Poised and determined Houston prosecutor and mayoral candidate Kay Christiansen jumps at the chance to put Jamal behind bars but discovers that a dark part of her past has resurfaced, potentially jeopardizing the case, the election, and even her marriage. In *Mama's Boy*, ReShonda Tate Billingsley shows us yet again how morally ambiguous a high-stakes situation can be—and how an individual's resolve can pave the way to redemption.

Discussion Questions

1. In chapter one of *Mama's Boy,* the author introduces us to one of the main characters, Gloria. How would you characterize the relationship she has with her husband, Elton? How is her view toward her son's predicament different from Elton's?

2. Why does Kay feel so confident that her son would never be in "the wrong place at the wrong time"? How has her life up until this point influenced her outlook on crimes among young men?

3. Do you think Elton was right to turn his son in? Was he thinking about justice, trying to protect himself, or trying to protect his son?

4. Kay and her husband, Phillip, have a seemingly perfect marriage and household. What were your initial impressions of Kay's family? What do you think it's like to have the same job as your spouse?

5. How much of an influence do parents have over their children? What kind of things were outside of Kay's and Gloria's control in *Mama's Boy?*

6. How would you have acted if you had been in Kay's position after Elton raped her? How do you think a situation like that should have been handled by the adults in Kay's life?

7. Do you think Kay's allegations against Elton would have been taken more seriously if he had not been a pastor? Why do you think Maxine's and Kay's families treated them the way they did?

8. Do you think Elton deserves forgiveness from his victims or from his family? Why or why not? Do you think he deserves forgiveness from God?

9. Do you think Camille was justified in placing blame on Kay and Ryan for her own son's choices?

10. We eventually learn the complicated reasons why Pastor Jones heavily resents his son, Jamal. Would he have been more forgiving of Jamal's act of self-defense if he himself had never committed a crime?

11. Is there any crime or act you consider unforgiveable? If so, what is it, and why?

12. In the epilogue, we see Maxine carrying out her own version of justice against Pastor Jones. Do you think it's ever acceptable to carry out vigilante justice against a person who never paid for his or her crimes? Why or why not?

13. In what ways does *Mama's Boy* explore the nuances of morality—religious, legal, political, and personal? What happens when people interpret everything in terms that are black and white, and absolute?

Enhance Your Book Club

1. Through the power of social media, racially motivated violence has been brought to the forefront of the nation's consciousness with the hashtag #BlackLivesMatter. With your book club, select a recent police shooting of a black person that's occurred within the last five years and analyze it. What legalities existed that allowed or did not allow the police officer to shoot? How did social media impact the way the case was handled? Do you think there's ever a justification for shooting someone who's unarmed?

2. Have you ever been in the wrong place at the wrong time? Take turns describing an incident where misfortune led you down a certain path. How would your life be different if it hadn't happened?

3. Have each book club member share a plan to reduce juvenile crime rates within their city as if they were mayoral candidates. Make sure they address socioeconomic and racial disparities within the community. Vote for your book club "mayor" based on the best plan.

4. Visit the author's website, http://www.reshondatatebillingsley.com, and select another Billingsley book for your reading group. Compare and contrast characters and themes with those in *Mama's Boy*.